The WordCasters

by Kevin A. Elliott

ISBN 13: 9781935986690

First print edition, September 2014

Published by Liberty Mountain Publishing. Printed in the U.S.A.

Liberty Mountain Publishing

Lynchburg, VA

www.LibertyMountainPublishing.com

A DIVISION OF
LIBERTY UNIVERSITY

To my mother – Our family's strongest WordCaster

To my grandfather – For making dreams come true

TABLE *of* CONTENTS

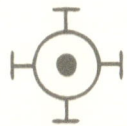

THE MISFIT

"Good Morning, class!"

A blonde-haired lady wearing black trousers, a floral shirt, and black high heels stood before her sixth-grade class, smiling.

"Good Morning, Ms. Lee," came the reply.

"Before we get started this morning, we have a new classmate to introduce! Timothy, could you stand up, please?"

A young boy with side-parted brown hair stood up nervously and stared at his blue and white sneakers. He fidgeted with the hem of his blue polo shirt.

"Everyone, please welcome Timothy Walker. His family just moved here to New Hampshire from Nebraska. Such a big move across the country can be very scary and uncomfortable, so I want you all to do your very best to make him feel warm and welcome."

A murmur of "Hello, Timothy," "Welcome, Timothy," and "Hi," floated through the classroom. Timothy slowly sank back into his seat and his gaze flicked around the room.

Two months earlier.

"His transcripts look excellent, but I worry about his distractibility. It seems that he functions well, but only when he isn't lost in another world."

The school's teachers were gathered in the break room, discussing Timothy's case and application.

"ADHD?"

"That's what's really weird. His symptoms match, but his doctor says that it's not ADHD. His distractibility is not frequent enough to be as disabling as ADHD."

"So he's just going to need extra attention and frequent interaction."

"Correct. Ms. Lee, he'll be in your classroom. Do you think you can manage him, or would you need assistance?"

Ms. Lee's gaze was focused out the window. She was staring intently at something, but no one could figure out what it was.

"Ms. Lee?"

She jumped, as if startled, and looked around the table at the other teachers, who were all staring at her, amused.

"She might need a helper to help keep *her* focused!"

"What? Oh. Sorry. I just need more coffee. I was up late last night. Yes, I can handle him."

"Ah, good."

Ms. Lee smiled, "He sounds like my younger brother when he was little."

The teacher sitting next to her reached over. "Oh! I only just heard about your brother two days ago. I'm so sorry for your loss."

Ms. Lee offered a kind smile. "Thank you."

"Alright, everyone! We're going to start off today's work by running through a vocabulary exercise. You will all find a worksheet inside your desk with today's date on it. Please write your name on the top and begin whenever you're ready."

Timothy slowly pulled the worksheet from his desk and gently laid it on the surface in front of him. He glanced around the room and lightly tapped his right-hand fingers on the center of the paper. Biting his lip, he looked nervously at Ms. Lee.

"Are you okay, Timothy?"

He paused his finger-tapping, lowered his head, and looked at the paper. He nodded his head, picked up the pencil, and prepared to write. As he set the pencil tip on the paper, he looked around at the other students. He wanted to make sure no one was looking at him. Based on his observations, he assumed that everyone else was focused on their work and that Ms. Lee was preparing the papers for the next assignment.

Slowly, he wrote his name on the top line and began reading the worksheet instructions. He felt a familiar tingle behind his ear and stopped reading. He looked up, but no one was looking at him, so he continued reading.

He has always heard that people believed him to have ADHD, but he really didn't believe it. He just felt that others wouldn't be able to handle the truth and would simply think of him as a freak or that he was possessed by a demon, as his grandparents did.

"I'm telling you, you need to take him to see a specialist."

Timothy's mother crossed her arms and looked at her father, "Dad, we've already done that. They think it's ADHD combined with some biological disorder they can't determine."

"I'm talking about another kind of specialist."

"Like what?"

"An exorcist."

"Exorcist?!"

"Cool yourself down! A pastor's good, too. Just someone who knows more about these things than we do."

"What things? *Demonic* things?"

"I was going to say *Supernatural* things, but yes. Demonic things. He's not normal."

"There's no such thing as *normal*, Dad. Everyone is unique and each person has his or her own gifts and…quirks."

Timothy's grandmother chimed in, "Well, he certainly doesn't fit into most circles."

"*Any* circles…" Timothy's grandfather shook his head and stared at his daughter.

"I can't believe you two. He functions just fine, and he's certainly not possessed. I would be able to pick up on something like that."

Her father's compassionate eyes kept staring into hers, "Are you absolutely sure about that? Wouldn't it be good just to find out? Just go and see. I assure you that it's better to know than not to know."

"If it makes you stop these accusations and attacks, then fine. We'll see a *specialist*."

Two weeks later, Timothy's grandfather answered his ringing

telephone.

"Hello?"

"Hi, Dad. We saw a pastor, like you wanted."

"Oh? Good. Well?"

"He said…"

"There's nothing wrong with me."

"No one said there was, Timothy."

Timothy shook his head and looked up to see Ms. Lee by his desk.

"You haven't written anything here. Are you sure you're okay?"

"Uh…yes, ma'am. I'm okay. Talking to myself. Thinking out loud, I guess."

"I see. Well, try to answer some of the questions before we run out of time. We need to have this worksheet finished in about two minutes."

"Yes, ma'am."

Ms. Lee smiled at Timothy and returned to her desk. Timothy sighed and stared at the first question. After the final two minutes for the worksheet, Timothy had answered all but two questions. Ms. Lee asked a volunteer to collect the worksheets and place them on her desk.

For the rest of the day, Timothy's experiences were all pretty much the same. In each classroom, he had trouble getting started, but managed to get most of the answers down before time ran out. Still, despite his successes, he just wanted the day to end. All of his teachers observed that he was carrying himself as if he was bearing a heavy burden.

At the close of the day, as children were filing from the classroom, Ms. Lee called Timothy aside.

"Timothy, I looked over your worksheet, but I have a few concerns."

"Yes, ma'am?"

"First off, I noticed you didn't provide an answer for the last two questions, but that's not really a concern. I understand you had some difficulty with getting started. Second, and most importantly, I noticed that none of your answers are correct. It was almost like you just wrote random vocabulary words."

"I did."

"Third—Wait, you did? You just wrote down random words?"

"Yes, ma'am." Timothy looked at the desk and started rapidly tapping his right hand against his right-side pocket.

"Why did you do that? Your records show that you read very well—well above your grade level, actually. Are you having trouble reading the questions?"

"No, ma'am. I…" Timothy searched for an excuse, "I just answered randomly so I could finish in time."

"I see. Well, a third thing I noticed is that you doodled a little on the edges of the paper."

"I did?"

"You didn't notice your own doodling?"

"No, ma'am. I guess I just fidget and get distracted. I'm told it's part of having ADHD."

Ms. Lee showed him the page. On the edges were random circular symbols and lines. Timothy shook his head, bit his lip, and looked back at the desk. Ms. Lee could see the tension in his expression.

"Yes, that can be part of the disorder, but when looking at the overall picture, it tells me that there's something else going on. I know you're nervous about being in a new school and having to make new friends, and even having to just jump right into the school year after it has already started."

"Yes, ma'am."

"I want you to know that you don't have to be afraid or nervous. You're safe here, you're welcome here, and we want to help you have a great educational experience. We care about you, and want you to feel comfortable here."

Timothy nodded and said, "Yes, ma'am."

"Okay, well, tomorrow I'll have you do this exercise again, but you can do it after class when you can feel more comfortable. I need to know where you stand with vocabulary so I can know how to help you in your education. Okay?"

"Okay." Timothy nodded again and walked out of the classroom.

As he walked through the front door of his home, his parents greeted him, calling out from the kitchen.

"Hi sweetie! We're in here. How was your first day at your new school?"

Timothy gently set his backpack by the door, shuffled into the kitchen, sat on a chair by the island, folded his hands in front of him on the table, and stared at his thumbs.

His father poured another cup of coffee, replaced the coffeepot, and took a seat beside him. His mother set her mug down on the island, reached over to place her hand on Timothy's, and whispered, "That bad, huh?"

Timothy shrugged.

"Would you like to talk about it?" his father offered.

Timothy shrugged again.

His mother smirked. "Okay, well, if you want to share, we're listening."

There was a long pause. Mr. and Mrs. Walker took turns taking sips of coffee from their mugs. At one point, Mrs. Walker reached over to grab a spoonful of sugar.

"It's not fair!"

Mrs. Walker paused, then asked, "I'm sorry. Did you want some sugar?"

Timothy smiled quickly, then shook his head and started, "I can't do what the other kids do! When I try, everyone thinks I'm stupid, like I have some disorder, or I need extra help!"

Mrs. Walker sighed as she poured two teaspoons of sugar into her mug. "I really wish I knew what I could do to help you. I just don't know enough about your…well…*condition*."

"I understand. I'm just frustrated. This is what happened last time. And the time before that. And the time before that! I'll find a way to make it through, I guess. Thanks, mom. Thanks, dad." Timothy slid off the chair, left the kitchen, grabbed his backpack, and went upstairs to his room.

Mr. Walker looked at his wife with a confused look on his face and asked, "What did we do, exactly?"

Mrs. Walker smiled and shrugged, "We listened."

The next day at school, Timothy was already better adjusted and more comfortable, but he still had trouble completing writing assignments or tasks that were to be read aloud. He would find something else to complete or would make up answers to the questions he did not even read. No one understood why, but when assignments involved writing or reading, Timothy would avoid them at all costs. He would listen intently and comprehend every lesson and task, but he just didn't seem to be able to complete certain assignments.

Most of the teachers attributed it to the ADHD and simply told Ms. Lee that he may need more time on task or even individual tutoring.

"That's most likely the case, but it's only his second day. I want to give him time to get fully adjusted. He's very intelligent and he's keeping up. His comprehension may even be more advanced than the other students. When he reads or writes, he can't complete the assignment, but when he is asked a question, his answers are superior to those of his peers. It's mind-boggling, really. I just want to give it more time and see."

The Principal turned to Ms. Lee, "We're not scientists. We don't experiment with these children's minds! He's not getting the assignments done. Tutoring may be necessary."

"Then he will receive it, sir." Ms. Lee was annoyed by her colleagues' lack of patience and faith, but she couldn't call the shots, so she had to arrange something.

Timothy and Ms. Lee waited until all of the other students left, and then Ms. Lee pulled a test paper out of her desk and walked it over to Timothy. He took the paper and examined it. It was the same test he intentionally failed the day before.

"When you're ready, you may begin." Ms. Lee sat down at her desk and watched quietly, but with an encouraging smile.

Timothy stared at the first question, but felt a nagging burning on his forehead. It was the tension of feeling like you're being watched, which of course, he was.

"Umm…" Timothy started.

"Yes?"

"Could you not watch me, please? Test anxiety."

"I understand, but I have to observe. I'm sorry. Just breathe normally and answer to the best of your knowledge."

Timothy winced. "Yes, ma'am."

He placed his pencil's tip above the line, exhaled, and began writing.

Only two minutes had passed when Timothy put his pencil down and returned the test to Ms. Lee's desk.

"Finished already, or did you have a question?"

"I'm finished." He put the test down and stared at the desk.

"Let's see here." She looked over each question and as her eyes scanned down the page, her gentle smile turned into a concerned frown. "Well, this is much better than before. However, there's one concern I have."

"Yes, ma'am." His words came out as a statement. It wasn't a question.

"You have the right answers to every question—some are words that are synonyms, but several grades above yours. The problem is that none of the words are finished. You have at least two letters missing off each word. Is there a reason for this?"

Timothy didn't move for a few moments, then nodded.

"What is the reason, Timothy? Remember, I'm here to *help* you, not cause you distress."

He nodded, then said, "I...I...can't."

"You can't? You can't what?"

"Finish them."

"Do you not know the last few letters?"

"I know them, yes."

"Then…?" Ms. Lee raised an eyebrow and waited for a response.

Timothy closed his eyes, clenched his fists, and exhaled slowly.

"I see this is something that causes great anxiety for you, Timothy. I know because my brother and I both had test anxiety and learning disorders when we were young. Still, this is something you need to overcome, right? Don't you want to get past this?"

Timothy nodded vigorously. "I want it to go away."

"I understand. You need to trust me, though. I can help you get through it, but you need to trust me and follow the instructions. I think it would be best if I talked to your parents about setting up tutoring for you. Does that sound okay?"

Timothy looked up quickly and stared Ms. Lee square in the eyes with a look of terror on his face. "Please don't. I'll be fine, really. I'll try harder."

Ms. Lee's gaze was stuck on Timothy's eyes and she nodded. "Okay, then." She had a sinking feeling in her stomach and a look of shock on her face. "If- if- *cough* Excuse me. If you don't pick it up, though, we're going to have to do something about it. Okay?"

Timothy looked back to the floor with an, "Okay."

As he walked out of the classroom, Ms. Lee called, "I'll see you tomorrow." As he turned the corner and left her view, she shook her head, rested her face in her hands, thought for a moment, then leaned back and said, "It couldn't be…could it?"

Ms. Lee leaned over and opened a drawer on her desk. She pulled out a small piece of paper, leaned on the desk, and stared at it. It was a picture of her recently-deceased brother. As she stared at the picture, her eyes began to tear up. She placed her head in her left hand and closed her eyes. Suddenly, she began to weep, and she buried her face in her hands, laying the picture on the desk. It had been about two-weeks since the accident, and she was finally able to mourn.

When Mr. and Mrs. Walker went to say goodnight to Timothy, they found that he was already asleep. They slowly closed the door, but left it slightly ajar. They took a few steps down the hall and started whispering.

"What can we do?" Mrs. Walker asked.

"I wish I knew. I mean, we could try to homeschool him, but neither of us has any teaching experience."

"Yeah. That wouldn't end well." Mrs. Walker shook her head and smiled briefly.

"Maybe we just need to give him time."

"And what happens when, in that time, someone sees?"

Mr. Walker shrugged, "Then they call him names, stay away from him, and we do what have been doing for several years now—we support him."

"There has got to be something else we can do…" Mrs. Walker crossed her arms and stared at an empty space on the wall.

"Our son is different, and he won't be accepted anywhere because people fear him. I mean, we moved for his sake."

"And for my job." Mr. Walker offered.

"Please! You're an electrician. Your job can be done anywhere. I'm a nurse. They need nurses all over the place. We moved because people are scared of our son."

Mrs. Walker began to cry. Mr. Walker put an arm around his wife and they went downstairs. They did not know that Timothy was not really asleep.

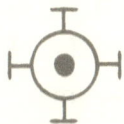

THE UNCLAIMED
SUMMONED

The next morning, Timothy left without saying a word, and his mind was full of thoughts and questions on the bus ride to school.

They moved because of me? People are scared of me? I scare people. I am scary. Well, I sort of figured that out on my own, anyway. I'm not sure what to think, now. On the one hand, I'm grateful because they're looking out for me. On the other hand, I wonder why they bother—it will never change. I will never fit in. I will never belong.

I will never belong.

"What makes you say that?"

Timothy jumped. The student next to him, a child from a different classroom, was staring at him with a concerned look on his face.

"I'm sorry. I didn't realize I was thinking out loud again."

"That's okay. I do that a lot, too. What makes you say that you don't belong?"

Timothy looked down at his shoes. "I'm…different."

"We're all different, silly. That's what makes us…wait for it… *different*." The boy smiled. "You don't look that different to me. You don't have wings, fangs, or extra limbs."

Timothy nodded. "That's true. I'm different in other ways, though."

"To me, that sounds like a good thing. If you were like everyone else, you wouldn't be you anymore. Who are you, anyway?"

"Um…" he thought about what the boy said. *I wouldn't be me anymore. Who is 'me,' and is this a good thing?* "My name is Timothy."

"I'm Brandon. You look new."

"I am. My family moved to the area last week and I just started school here two days ago."

"Well, welcome to town!" Brandon smiled and held out his hand.

Timothy glanced over without moving his head. He turned slightly, shook Brandon's hand, and said, "Thank you."

The bus slowed to a stop. "We're here. Yet another day in paradise." Brandon gave a thumbs-up and stood up to exit the bus. Timothy rose slowly, but had glanced at Brandon's face before he did. He stopped. What was that in his eye?

Timothy walked in the line toward the front of the bus as all of the children were exiting. Brandon was already going down the steps. As Timothy turned to leave the bus, the bus-driver stopped him and had a crazed look on his face. He leaned over and whispered, "You smell."

"Uh…I had a shower this morning. I shouldn't smell."

"That's…n-not what I mean. You s-smell."

"I- I- I don't understand." Timothy left the bus as quickly as he could, and then looked back at the driver. Where once sat a crazed-looking man, there now sat a pleasant looking older lady.

Timothy stared as the bus left. This day was becoming a *really weird* day…and it just started!

Timothy walked inside and sat down at his desk. He took out his required books, paper, and pencils, and then stared at his hands until class started.

"Good morning, everyone!"

"Good morning, Ms. Lee!" came the reply.

I hope we don't have to do another vocabulary exercise.

"We're going to start the day with something different, but just as fun as what we normally do."

Fun? Oh, yeah?

"In your desk, you'll find a piece of paper with the title My Park. Today, I want you to use your creative, engineering minds to design a park of any kind, but you must include scale references like we talked about last week. If you don't remember how those work, see page thirty-five in our math applications book. This park can be a nature preserve, amusement park, a living history park, or whatever you would like, but it must attract guests, so make sure you have things to keep them happy. You will have fifteen minutes to work on this. Afterwards, we'll begin the regular lessons."

Timothy sighed and smiled. *A perfect assignment for me! Thank you, Ms. Lee!* Timothy set to work immediately. He grabbed a ruler and a pencil and dove right in.

Ms. Lee watched all of the students work, but when she saw Timothy, she couldn't help but smile. His face had an ear-to-ear grin as he excitedly created buildings, rooms, decorations, roads, and vendors. This was the happiest she had seen him. She felt that they were finally breaking through something here. Maybe things would be easier for him after this.

For the next fifteen minutes, the students all had a good time while working on their park ideas. Ms. Lee would walk around the room to look at what the students were creating, occasionally, helping students with an idea or scale problem. She finally reached Timothy's desk and looked over his shoulder. He was hovering over his paper so closely that it was hard for her to see what he was drawing, but what she could see looked strangely familiar.

She whispered, "That's very nice, Timothy. What is your inspiration?"

He shrugged, "I don't really know. I just draw what feels right."

"I see. Have you ever been to a place that looks like this?"

"No, ma'am."

"Okay. Well, keep up the good work."

"Thank you, ma'am."

Ms. Lee walked back to her desk, but her mind was searching for something it couldn't seem to reach. With two minutes left, Ms. Lee said, "I would like each of you to name your park, as well, which makes it even more unique and more personal for each of you. Write your name on the top right corner, too."

Timothy was so caught up in the task that he wrote both names... and finished them! After he put his pencil down, he realized that he had written the full names and he gasped and looked around the room. No one heard him gasp and no one was looking at him.

Did nothing happen? Did it simply go unnoticed? Maybe it's gone... Oh, how great that would be!

"Okay, class. Time is up. It looks like you all finished your parks in plenty of time and you all look very pleased with your work. I'm glad to see that! You can pin your parks to the board in the back of the room and we'll get to work on the next section.

Timothy was feeling reassured and slightly more confident. He had a successful assignment, nothing weird happened, and no one was making fun of him. In fact, not only was no one making fun of him, all he received was praise and encouragement from his teacher as well as his classmates! He had not felt this good in a long time. He took his seat and prepared himself for the next assignment.

"Next we have a math worksheet to help us review what we have been covering this week."

Timothy's heart sank a little.

"Some of the questions are open-ended, so be prepared to write out your answers in at least two sentences."

His heart sank a lot.

"Also, at the end, please write a brief summary of two of the laws we covered this week—you may choose which two you would like to summarize."

There went his heart. All the way down. Bottomless pit. Bye-bye!

"If any of you need assistance, come up to my desk. I want this to be as independent for you as possible, though, so do what you can. Push yourselves a little. You may begin as soon as you get your sheet."

Timothy shook his head as he looked at the paper. He inhaled… exhaled. *I can do this. Nothing happened earlier, so I should be good, right?*

He picked up his pencil and started on the name line at the very beginning.

After writing his name, he checked to make sure nothing had happened. No tingling behind the ear. No burning sensation on his forehead. No tingling in his fingers. Nothing was on fire. No one was looking at him, so he assumed it was all clear. He read the first question.

Well, that's handy. It's just numbers.

He worked through several questions, finishing them very quickly, but he finally hit an open-ended question. He paused for a moment, inhaled…exhaled.

Just do it. If you can conquer this, maybe it'll go away and mom and dad won't have to be so sad! People won't be scared of you. We won't have to move around anymore! Focus! Get this done.

He read the first question very slowly, pausing a few times to see if anything had happened. Still no tingling. Still no fire. He smiled. *Nothing happened! Yes! It's gone! It's over! I can be normal now!* Of course, he knew the answer to the question on the test, so he placed his pencil on the paper and began writing.

He was so excited that he did not notice the gradually increasing tingling behind his ear.

Ms. Lee put her papers down and looked around the room. Every student had their head down and they were focused, except for Timothy. Oh, he was focused, of course. He was also *glowing*!

Ms. Lee shook for a second as she tried to make sense of what she was seeing. Then she saw a small spark flick off the top of Timothy's head. This spark fell a few inches and silently exploded into several other sparks. Golden sparks began flying off Timothy's head. No one seemed to notice except Ms. Lee. Even Timothy did not seem to notice—he just kept writing, question after question. Ms. Lee's mouth hung open as she tried to find a solution before the whole class would see the golden sparks. A classmate to Timothy's left began erasing an answer just as a spark landed on her paper. As she rubbed the spark into the paper, clearly not noticing it, the paper started to smoke. Then it caught fire.

A fire! This could work.

"Whoa! Everyone up and away from the fire!" She walked over, put out the fire, and checked to make sure that everyone was okay. Timothy was no longer glowing. In fact, he had stopped glowing and sparking as soon as he heard Ms. Lee shout.

The student's jaw was still on the floor as she stared at the eraser in her hand.

"I didn't mean to erase so hard. I'm sorry!"

Still shocked and slightly panicked, Ms. Lee smiled a kind smile and said, "It was a freak accident. Like spontaneous combustion, I'm sure. No one is to blame. No worries."

She got the student a new sheet, made sure everyone was settled, then asked another teacher (who was in another room, but not teaching any students at the moment, and heard the commotion, so ran over) to keep an eye on the students for a minute.

"I have to go report this to the principal, so I'll be back in just a minute. Keep working on your sheets. Also, could you please come with me, Timothy?"

There came an "Oooooo!" from the entire class. Timothy frowned and stared at his shoes. He suddenly realized what happened.

"He's not in trouble. There's just some…paperwork…that still needs to be filled out since he's a new student. We…forgot to get to it until today. Please come with me, Timothy."

Timothy stood up slowly and walked over to Ms. Lee. He followed her out the door and the other teacher took her place in the doorway. He followed Ms. Lee down the hallways, but he was practically running in order to keep up with her.

I'm in big trouble. Now we're going to have to move again. I hate this.

They raced through the halls until they reached the principal's office. Ms. Lee turned to Timothy.

"I want you to know you're not in trouble, okay? It's just that something has come to…light. Have a seat here, I'll call you in in a minute."

Timothy nodded and slowly sat down in a nearby chair. As Ms. Lee closed the principal's door, he looked around the room. It was a small office space with just a few chairs and a secretary's desk. He had to sit up a little higher to see over the desk. When he did, he could see the secretary's forehead. Either the female secretary they met when they first visited the school developed a large bald spot on the top of her head and grew very large ears, or the secretary was not the same person they met before. He sat up even higher to try to see. At that moment, the secretary turned in his direction and stood up.

It was the creepy bus-driver from earlier!

"I t-told you that you s-smell. Now you see."

Timothy gasped and sat down, hard, on the seat. He sat still for several moments. He shook his head and looked back at the desk. The man was no longer visible. He peered over the desk again, but all he saw was a head-full of curly brown hair and glasses that looked like they came right out of the fifties. The secretary was typing away at her computer. The older lady glanced over to see him peering over the desk and returned with a kind smile.

He slid back down in his seat and stared at his shoes.

What's going on? Who is that guy and what is he talking about?! I smell, but now I see something. What is it that I see, and why does he see that I see what I don't see I see before I see it?

"I've found one, sir."

"Found one *what?*" The principal looked up from his paperwork and stared at Ms. Lee.

"Another…you know."

"Ah, I see. Ms. Lee, I understand that you have not had the best experiences with this sort of thing, but there really should not be any difficulty in saying the word *Summoned*. It is not a derogatory word. It is simply what they are."

"Yes, sir. I'm trying…really."

"I appreciate that. Where is this new Summoned?"

"It's Timothy Walker, sir."

"Ah, the newest student. Really?"

"Yes, sir. Yesterday, when I looked into his eyes, I saw it. The same thing my brother had. Then, today in class, he was writing answers down and he started glowing and sparking, just like the others before him."

"Did he notice what he was doing?"

"I don't think so, sir. It sure explains his other behaviors."

"Yes, it does."

"Does he understand what he is?"

"I don't believe so."

"I see. Where is he now?"

"He's sitting in the outer office."

"Bring him in."

Ms. Lee walked over to the door, opened it and started to speak, "Timo-" She shrieked. The principal jumped out of his seat and ran around to the door. He eyes popped open wide as his jaw dropped.

Timothy was curled up in front of the desk, shaking. Lying next to him on the floor were two adult men, crumpled up on the floor, unmoving. Standing over the bodies was the secretary.

The principal started, "Wha- Wha- What hap—"

"I stepped away to do some copying, I came back to find this boy sitting in here and I noticed that my chair had been moved. Then two of 'em rushed in and tried to take him away."

"And?"

"I stopped 'em."

"We see *that*."

The secretary waved her right hand and shook her head, "Don't worry, everything's cleaned up and we just need to drop these guys off at the nearest landfill."

Ms. Lee winced. "Are they—"

"No, they're not dead. If you take the boy, I'll get rid of 'em. I hate playing babysitter. No offense, dearie." She smiled at Timothy, who was beginning to peer out of his curled up arms.

Ms. Lee and the principal nodded, helped Timothy into the office, and closed the door. Timothy curled back up, shaking. The two adults sat down in bewilderment.

Ms. Lee looked at the principal, "Has this ever—"

"Never."

"What do we—"

"No clue."

"Are you going to keep—"

"Cutting you off? Sorry. No."

Ms. Lee shook her head, then looked at Timothy. "Are you okay,

Timothy?"

Timothy did not move. He wasn't crying. He wasn't shaking anymore. He wasn't angry. He wasn't…well, anything. There were no emotions expressed, no words said, and nothing to indicate his wellness. Ms. Lee reached over and touched his elbow.

Timothy shivered, looked up slowly, then began to relax.

"Are you okay?"

Timothy nodded slowly. "What did I just see?"

"I'm not sure. We were in here and we didn't hear anything. Likely, you saw Martha kicking butt. She's good at that." The principal chuckled.

"Why did those guys try to take me?"

Neither answered him for a while.

The principal leaned forward on his desk and looked into Timothy's eyes. He could see what Ms. Lee had seen. Along the circumference of his pupils, only when the light hit them right, the principal could see a golden glitter.

"Do you know what you are?"

"A freak?"

"No. Absolutely not."

"I don't know, sir. Human?"

"Yes, but you are also something beyond a human."

Timothy stared at the principal, waiting for more information.

"You are what is referred to as a Summoned. Have you ever seen any glittering gold in your eyes when you look in the mirror?"

"No, sir, but my parents have mentioned they've seen a golden tint in my eyes."

"I see. Have any strange events occurred in your life?"

23

"Aside from almost being kidnapped? … Yes. When…When I read or write anything, I feel a tingling behind my ears and on the top of my head. Sometimes I feel a pressure on my forehead when I feel like someone's watching me. Sometimes I set things on fire, but I don't mean to. Like the test today. I really didn't mean to do that!"

Ms. Lee smiled. "I know. It's okay."

The principal said, "It may comfort you to know that that was not the first time that's happened here. It happens to almost every Summoned."

"Really?"

"Yep. It happened to me when I was young."

"You, sir?"

"Indeed." The principal removed some contacts from his eyes and opened his eyelids for Timothy to see his eyes more clearly. Now Timothy could see the gold glittering. He suddenly realized he had seen this many times before with many people throughout his life.

Timothy turned to Ms. Lee, "Are you a Summoned, too?"

"No," she smiled and shook her head, "but I was. I chose not to pursue the gift. But I knew someone else who was."

"So what this means for you, Timothy," the principal finished putting his contacts back in and looked at him, "is that you are indeed very special, very gifted, and very sought after. There is a conflict in this world you probably do not know about. There is a constant battle for Summoneds. Those two men? They were trying to take you and influence you to join their side of the war."

"War? I'm too young to be doing any fighting!"

"Not in their eyes, but they probably wouldn't have you doing any fighting until you have trained properly, anyway, which takes a few years. The reason they tried to take you is because you are what is called an "Unclaimed Summoned." You have yet to be swayed in one direction or the other, if you were to decide to go with either."

"I'm confused, and this is a lot for me to try to believe."

The principal nodded. "I know. It is a lot to digest, but rest assured that nothing we've said is a lie. There is a lot more for you to learn, but I am not qualified to teach it to you."

"So I'm an Unclaimed Summoner—"

"Summoned."

"Okay. An Unclaimed Summoned. I am special, I am gifted…and people are trying to kill me."

"Not kill you. Recruit you."

"Recruit me. For a war."

"A nasty war. A war between only two sides, fought on many different fields, with many casualties on each side."

Timothy shook his head, "I don't like this. I just want to stop setting things on fire and scaring people. I want to stop being a freak! I don't want to fight or kill! I'm not ready for that."

"You don't have to be, yet. Now that we all know who and what you are, we will protect you until you are ready."

"Who is We?"

"The WordCasters."

"Did you find him?"

"Y-Yes." The creepy, balding bus-driver-slash-secretary was wringing his hands as he stood in front of a shadowed figure in a darkened hallway.

"Well? Where is he, then?"

"Eh…School."

"You found him and just left him at school?"

"Yes."

"You try my patience. Why did you leave him there?"

"Ash and Bruce went to retrieve him. They are s-stronger than I-I-I-I am. You know I am weak."

"Yes, I do know that. Did they get him?"

"Eh…" He started nodding, then shifted to shaking his head and frowning.

"Where are they?"

"L-Landfill."

"Landfill?! *Sigh* Martha. Of course."

"But, but, but…he smelled, and now he sees."

"How is this a good thing?"

"He sees."

"I still don't understand." The figure turned and walked away, "Find him, and don't fail me again."

The creepy, balding bus driver bowed, then mumbled, "He sees. Hope." He smiled gently and walked away.

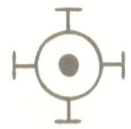

SEEING IS BELIEVING

Timothy walked up to his front door, pushed it open, and froze. The entire house was clothed in radiant white...air?! It looked as thick as water, but felt as clear as a gentle breeze. It was absolutely quiet.

"Mom? Dad? Where are you?"

He took a few steps forward, and then peeked into the kitchen. No one was there; the coffee pot was empty, and the normally dripping faucet was as still as a frightened opossum. He turned around and walked into the living room. The TV was off, the radio was silent, and all of the magazines were put away. Normally, one of these three things was being used in some capacity. He looked out into the driveway.

Yep, the car's here. Maybe they're upstairs...or downstairs?

He walked toward the cellar stairs, opened the cellar door and called down, "Mom? Dad?" No reply.

He walked to the foot of the second floor stairs, then looked up. His heart stopped. At the top of the stairs stood a man in tattered clothes, with scraggly beard and dirty hands.

"Wh- Wh- Who are you?"

"I'll tell you who I am, when you tell me who you are."

"I'm not supposed to talk to strangers."

"I'm not a stranger. You just don't know it, yet."

"What?"

"Just answer the question. I'm not going to hurt you."

"T-T-Timothy."

"That's not who you are."

Timothy paused, then said, "Yes, it is."

"Try again."

"Timothy Walker, Edward Walker's son."

The man shook his head, "Try again."

Timothy looked around and breathed heavily. "I don't know what you're asking me!"

"Dig deeper. *Who* are you?"

"Timothy is the only name I know that I have."

"I'm not looking for your name. I already know that."

"Then I don't know! I don't know! Stop asking a question I can't answer! I'm just a kid! I'm *nothing*!"

"Right there."

"What? *I'm nothing*? That's what you're looking for?"

"Yes. I wanted to hear you say what you think that you are. I wanted you to hear yourself lie to yourself. I know you as something

28

else. I will tell you who I am when you find out who you *really* are. Find my book, find yourself, find me."

Suddenly, Timothy was surrounded by the deafening noise of smashed glass, and then about a dozen masked and robed men jumped through the broken windows and into the kitchen and dining room. Timothy spun around to look at the intruders. They all held strange weapons and were moving toward him, quickly. Timothy couldn't move. He just stared at the attackers. As the nearest attacker raised his weapon, Timothy raised his arms to brace for the impact. No impact came, however. Instead, the banister reached out and punched the attacker, throwing him into the front door.

Wait...what?!

The banister reached out and punched the attacker, throwing him into the front door.

I got that, but what?!

Timothy looked at the banister, and then heard the man at the top of the stairs start laughing. He looked up and the man had his hand on the banisters and a grin on his face. The man looked at Timothy and called, "Duck!"

Timothy ducked down and watched as both banisters turned into whips and pushed away all of the closest attackers. He could hear the wooden banisters creaking and groaning as they twisted, but they weren't snapping! Timothy backed up onto the stairs, but almost jumped off when he felt them move. His stairs had turned into an escalator and they were taking him to the maniacal hobo at the top of the stairs.

"Are you doing this?"

The man nodded.

Meanwhile, at the bottom of the stairs, one banister had an intruder in a headlock while the other was fencing with three intruders who had crowbars and a baseball bat.

Timothy was almost at the top and the man asked, "Do you know who you are?"

Timothy shook his head as he reached toward the man's outstretched hand. When their hands clasped, the man said, "Find my book."

The man vanished and Timothy was filled with fear as he lost stability. As if in slow motion, Timothy began to fall backwards. Below him, the hardwood floor came closer and closer. His spine was inches away from colliding with the moving stairway.

He sat up in his bed, sweating and shaking.

A dream? ... A dream.

His ride to school was quiet, the bus driver was normal, the secretary was normal and friendly, and Ms. Lee was her usual cheery self. It was as if nothing had happened the day before. Had all of that really happened? Before he took his seat, he looked at the board in the back of the room. His park drawing was still there and the room still had a hint of smoke odor.

It really happened.

He looked up at Ms. Lee. She nodded as she wore a look of great empathy. He sighed and took his seat.

For the rest of the day, Ms. Lee did a lot more with lectures and graphical representations. The class did not have to do any reading or writing aside from what Ms. Lee provided.

At the end of the day, everything felt peaceful, nothing seemed off, and nothing was on fire, so Timothy was feeling pretty good. When class dismissed, he reached into his desk to collect his things, but pulled out a metal disc with strange etchings on it. He stared at it for a while. When the rest of the class filtered out, he walked up to Ms. Lee.

"Excuse me. I found this in my desk."

"What is it?"

"I don't know. I hoped you would know."

"It's very strange. If you'd like, I can ask the principal about it. He might know."

"May I go along, please? I have a few other questions for him."

"Certainly."

"Very interesting." The principal turned the disc around in his hands, "Tell me, when you were working on that math worksheet, you *did* or did *not* feel the tingling?"

"I did *not*, sir. I don't remember any tingling sensation."

"Mm-hmm. Very interesting, indeed."

"Why is that so interesting, sir?"

The principal held out the disc, "I have seen this kind of thing only once before and it has been many, many years. This disc is a device infused with a special aromatic herb, which numbs a person's external senses for a time. It's like an anesthetic, but only for the outside of your body. One whiff and you're numb as a woodpecker digging a hole in a boulder."

"Whiff? Wait… *Smell!*"

"Right…that's what that means. Whiff."

"I'm sorry. No, the creepy, balding bus driver told me that I *smell.*"

"Did you take a shower?"

"Yes, but that's not the point. I couldn't figure out what he meant.

Maybe he knew this was in my desk!"

"Creepy, balding bus driver? Doesn't sound like anyone we've hired. Wait…Did this man wear a flannel shirt and have a large mole on the left side of his face?"

"Uh…yes!"

The principal looked over at Ms. Lee, "Ralph."

Ms. Lee nodded.

"Who is Ralph, sir?"

"Ralph used to be a WordCaster. He and I trained together, actually. He was rather funny, too. He was a master of disguises and would play tricks on the instructors all the time. At one point, he wanted more in his life, so he bought the lies and switched sides on us. He became an enemy. I told him it's never too late to turn back, but he didn't want to hear it. So it's likely that he was the one who put the disc there in the first place. His English was never very good, either. We were lucky to get a full sentence out of him."

"He also told me that *I smelled, now I will see.*"

Ms. Lee and the principal thought for a while, but shrugged.

"I have no idea what that would mean. Try not to think about him too much, though. He can be creepy sometimes, but he's really quite harmless," the principal explained.

"Okay. You've mentioned WordCasters twice now and I still don't understand."

"Again, that's something I can't teach you effectively, so you'll need to go to an instructor to learn more. However, before you can go to an instructor, you will have to make a decision. Unclaimed Summoneds are not permitted to go into the Guild. I don't know the rules for the other place, but I assume it's the same."

"What is the Guild?"

"It's where Summoneds go to learn and train to become WordCasters."

Ms. Lee nodded, "Do you recall the park you drew?"

"Yes…?"

"From how the Guild was described to me many years ago, it appears that you have drawn an almost exact representation of the Guild. Remove the vendors and rides and you've got it. I showed it to the principal here and he confirmed it. I was confused because you knew so much about it, but you had never been there."

"I've had dreams about that type of drawing when I was really, really young. I don't remember when, exactly."

"Dreams?"

"Yeah. I dream quite a bit, apparently. I had another dream last night. I still can't make sense of it."

The principal raised a brow. "I'd like to hear about it, if you're willing to share."

Timothy described the dream to both of them and watched as their facial expressions changed from smiles to frowns, to looks of awe, then shock.

"Then I fell and woke up just before I was hurt. That was it."

"That's quite a vision."

"What does it mean?"

Ms. Lee shrugged. The principal thought for a moment.

"Well, from where I'm sitting, there are a few possible interpretations." He leaned back in his chair, "First, it could simply be something you ate. Second, it could be a dream just because of what we talked about yesterday. Your mind may have created a possible scenario to help you make sense of what you heard. Third, and this is my favorite, you could have received a message."

"A message?"

"Yep. Happens all the time, but people don't realize it until later. Some people get messages from angels, some from demons, some from deceased loved ones, and some from historical figures. That kind of thing. Whether or not it really means anything is entirely up to you."

"How would it be up to me?"

"What happens when you read Aesop's Fables?"

Timothy stared, "I set my room on fire."

The adults laughed; then the principal said, "When you read or hear the story, you are given a choice. You can interpret it literally; you can wait for the moral of the story; or you can come to your own conclusions. Likewise, when you receive a message, how you interpret it is entirely up to you. Your vision could have been simply a dream and it won't bug you again. It could have been a repressed memory, but I sincerely doubt that one. It could have also been a message from someone."

"Okay. I see that. It still doesn't help me understand what he meant."

"Well, the most intriguing part to me is that he mentions a book. WordCasters all learn from a single book, written by a man we call The Author. I don't know if that's the book that's mentioned or not. There have been attempts to make copies of that book, and our enemies use a copy for their training. Still, there will really only ever be one."

"What's in that book?"

The principal leaned forward with a smile. "Everything."

Timothy just stared at him.

"History, prophecies, names, dates, ideas…truth."

"So WordCasters learn truth, and that's it."

"Not just any truth. This is not like updated-textbook-here's-my-opinion truth. This is like here are hard facts, "read 'em and weep" truth. It's all in there; Truths about our world, truths about who we are in the world, and truths about where our world is headed. And they don't just learn truth, they learn how to *apply* it."

"Apply it how?"

"Remember the banisters?"

"Yeah? Wait…Really?"

"Really."

"Wow."

The principal smiled and nodded.

"It goes beyond the comprehension of most men and women, which is why WordCasters stay so secretive. Also, they stay secretive so the enemies, called Twisters, don't find them. Our enemies more than out-number us, and the rest of the world is not ready to understand, so all of this must be kept secret. However, it can all go away for you, depending on your choice."

Timothy sat up straighter, "It can all go away? What choice?"

"You can choose to join the Casters, you can choose to join the Twisters, or you can choose to go your own way and leave this gift behind. No one can or will judge you. It is your choice and yours alone."

"What about my parents?"

"You can tell them if you trust them, but it should not go beyond that. If it spreads too far, you may become a target. You don't have to choose right now. Give it time. Sleep on it. Think about. However, you have the gift, so at some point, you *will* have to choose. While you are an Unclaimed Summoned, you are at greater risk because both sides will try to win you over."

"You're trying to win me over?"

"Well, to be honest, my hope is that we will, but I know what we don't really have any say in the matter. The choice is yours. We cannot tell you which choice to make."

"I understand, sir. Thank you."

"You're welcome. Is there anything else you had questions about?"

"Yes, actually. Who were the men in my dream? The intruders, that is."

The principal sighed, pursed his lips, and raised an eyebrow as he spoke, "My best interpretation is that those men were you."

"Me?"

"Yes. I believe that those men are versions of you trying to stop yourself from making a choice. These are your doubts, your fears, and your self-created obstacles which make it hard for you to find your true identity and make a choice. My guess is that this is what the man in your dream was talking about."

"And the man is trying to prevent me...from preventing me...from making a choice?"

"I think that's more like him buying you time so you can make your own choice. He isn't telling you how to choose. He's telling you to do your homework so you can make an informed choice. Does that make sense?"

"Yes, sir."

"Good. Well, I will give you a ride home since the buses have already left. Ms. Lee, thank you."

The principal pulled up the driveway and parked the car.

"Mom and Dad must be out. The car's not here."

"Do you need me to stick around until they're home?"

"No. Thank you, sir. I've been home alone before."

"A responsible young man. I'll wait here until you're settled in, just to make sure."

"Okay. Thank you." Timothy closed the car door and walked to the front door. He reached in his pocket to find the key, but he noticed that the door wasn't completely closed. Slowly, he put the key back in his pocket and gently pushed the door open.

Maybe they left it open for me because they thought I didn't have a key.

"Mom? Dad? Either of you home?" Shivers went down Timothy's spine. At least the air wasn't water and the walls were all the right colors. There was coffee in the pot and magazines were out.

That's promising.

He closed the front door behind him and he walked into the living room.

"Mom? Dad? I need to talk t—" He stopped in his tracks and stared across the room.

"You smelled. You s-seen. Now you choice or die."

"Ralph! Choice or die? I'll call the police!"

"Please. Choice or die."

Timothy began to back up toward the front door. Ralph walked toward him, matching speed. Ralph placed his hand on a nearby wall and twitched his head slightly. Timothy heard the door behind him click. Timothy reached for the doorknob, but pulled his hand back quickly.

"Ow!" The knob was so hot, it was nearing the melting point. Obviously, that door wasn't going to open, now. Timothy held his hand to his chest and stared, terrified, at Ralph.

"Understand. Please? Choice or die."

"I-I-I think I understand perfectly, and I'm n-not ready to make a choice, yet! I need more time to think about it."

Ralph had a very pained expression on his face. "N-No time. Choice or die!"

Timothy started trembling and shouted, "I can't!"

"Must!" Ralph started walking toward Timothy at a faster pace. Timothy backed up against the front door and started to close his eyes.

POW!

Ralph had walked past a cabinet and its door flew open and slammed into his face. Ralph knelt down with his face in his hands.

"Stay down, Ralph."

Timothy looked up to see the principal standing at the other end of the living room, his hand planted on the wall.

Ralph turned slowly and looked at the source of the voice.

"Eric! No!" He pointed at Timothy. "Choice or die!"

"You won't be hurting him."

Ralph had a puzzled look on his face and asked, "Hurt?"

"You can leave on your own, or I can help you out."

"No go. Choice or die!" Ralph began to tear up, but kept holding his face. Apparently, he had a broken nose; blood was dripping onto the floor.

"Under normal circumstances, I would be willing to help you and try to understand you, but you chose to be my enemy. You turned from all of us. You fight against us! Do you understand?"

Ralph nodded vigorously, tears streaming.

"You have one more chance. Leave on your own feet or I make them move you."

Ralph swallowed hard, stood up, and ran past the principal out the back door.

Timothy breathed heavily and tried to relax, "Thank you."

The principal nodded, "I had a strange feeling that something wasn't right, so I checked things out around back and I saw Ralph through the window."

"What do I do now?"

"I will ask some of my colleagues to keep an eye on your house for a while to make sure this doesn't happen again. That's all we can do."

Timothy stared at the cabinet door, and then at the blood-stained carpet. He tried to stand still and stop himself from shaking. He stared at his shoes for a moment.

"Sir?"

"Yes, Timothy?"

Timothy looked the principal right in the eye and said, "I've made my choice."

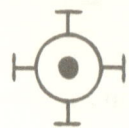

BELIEVING IS SEEING

Timothy watched out the kitchen window as he finished his breakfast on Saturday morning.

"Well, we hope you have fun with your new friends today. We're so proud of you, you know." Mrs. Walker sat across from him at the kitchen island.

Timothy half-smiled. He hadn't told his parents the whole truth. He was going out with new friends, but he wasn't going out to have fun, per se.

"If you need us, you know we're just a phone call away." Mr. Walker gently placed his mug on the counter and waited for a response.

Timothy nodded. He glanced over at the carpet where Ralph's nose had dropped blood. The blood stain was gone and there was no evidence of a break-in. Timothy didn't even know how the principal took care of it so quickly. He went to get paper towels, as the principal had asked, but everything was clean when he came back.

"Are you okay, Timothy?" Mrs. Walker asked.

"Just nervous, I guess."

Mr. Walker nodded, "That's okay. I was always a nervous child. You get over it after a while. It just takes frequent exposure to what makes you nervous. It's like when I was afraid of dogs. My parents took me to a dog park and helped me to gradually get used to dogs. Now, I am no longer afraid of dogs! Likewise, after you go out a few times with your friends, you'll feel just fine about it."

Oh, how I wish you could understand. What am I saying? I wish I could understand!

The thoughts of Ralph's surprise visit and menacing threats were still spinning around in his mind. Timothy couldn't stop thinking about it. Ralph had found him, found Timothy's house, knew when his parents would be out, and knew when he would return from school. He had been waiting for him. His parents knew nothing about it. They did not know that their son was almost kidnapped at school. They did not know that he was about two seconds away from possibly being killed at the hands of man who had been stalking him to force him to make a choice Timothy did not even know how to make.

Finally, the principal pulled up to the curb outside their house.

"Your principal?" Ms. Walker stepped to look out the window. She waved, and the principal waved back as he climbed out of his car.

"He's…supervising the group." Timothy grabbed his jacket and put his breakfast plate and glass in the sink.

He walked over and hugged his mom, "I love you. I'll be back before dinner, I promise."

He walked over to his father, hugged him and said, "I love you, dad. And don't worry, I'll be careful. I'll be in good hands."

"We know," His dad smiled. "We're proud of you. Have a great afternoon."

Timothy smiled and waved as he closed the front door. His parents watched from the window as the principal held open the passenger-side door for Timothy. The principal got into the driver's seat, they both buckled, and they were off.

It was a quiet drive. Neither of them spoke, except for their initial greetings. The principal's face showed signs of worry and concern. Timothy didn't know his principal's forehead had so many creases. Timothy also did not know his shoes had a microscopic tear on the top-right side of the right instep, right next to that small drop of blue paint from last summer's volunteer project. He brushed some sugar from breakfast off his blue jeans and continued staring at his shoes. He pulled his patchwork jacket's hood over his head, exhaled, and crossed his arms, leaning against the door.

The principal inhaled, paused, then said, "I can imagine how difficult this is for you, and how difficult it will be in a few minutes, but you are very brave for doing what you're about to do, however it turns out."

Timothy nodded, but didn't take much comfort in those words.

After this, the silence resumed. Neither knew what to say or how to be any more prepared for what would come. Eventually, they slowed down and turned. They were pulling into one of the mall's parking lots.

The principal pulled the car up to the curb, put it in park and turned to Timothy.

"Do you remember what I told you?"

Timothy nodded, "Yes, sir. Find the southern water fountain and look for Bernard."

42

"Barney."

"Sorry. Barney."

"That's okay. Barney will be able to help you get to your next step, where you make your declaration."

Neither moved for several seconds.

The principal grabbed Timothy's shoulder gently and said, "No one will judge you. It's your choice. Own it. I'm going to go and talk to your parents about everything, as you requested, and I'll be back here later this afternoon to pick you up. Okay?"

Timothy didn't move.

The principal's voice got softer, "Timothy?"

Timothy shivered a little, and then nodded. He thanked the principal, climbed out of the car, and stared at the mall entrance.

"Here, Timothy, let's read a book together."

An excited four-year-old Timothy climbed up beside his mother on their couch back in Wisconsin, his first home. Crossing his legs, he leaned against his mother's side.

"What does this say?"

"The c- ca- cat wan f- fa- fast."

"Very good!"

Timothy grinned and looked at his mom's face.

"You know, Timothy, you've got a cute little sparkle in your eye when you're smiling. It's like a ray of sunshine. Okay, what's the next line?"

Timothy stared at it for a few seconds, and then began, "The c- cat ju- jumped on the couch." Timothy reached up and scratched his ear.

"Very good, Timothy! You're getting these words very quickly now!

I'm so proud of you!" She paused. "Edward? Honey?"

"Yes?"

"Are you cooking something?"

"No, I'm doing dishes. Why?"

"I don't know. It just smells like something's burning."

"You're making fun of my cooking? Gee, thanks!"

"No," she chuckled, "You don't smell it, then?"

"Nope." Mr. Walker entered the room and walked over to the couch. "I smell it over here, though."

They looked around and Mr. Walker pointed at the couch behind Timothy. There was a small black spot, no bigger than a pin head, that wasn't there when they bought the couch a few days before.

As the fire alarm continued to blare, students filed out of a Kansas elementary school. Timothy's teacher held him by the wrist and his class all walked over to the evacuation point for their school.

Timothy sniffed back tears once again as he overheard a classmate mutter to another classmate, "What kind of a freak sets their own paper on fire to get out of doing homework?"

His teacher leaned over and asked him, "Why did you do that, Timothy?"

Timothy didn't know how to answer.

"Timothy?...Timothy?!"

"Timothy?"

He blinked several times and turned around to face the principal in the car.

"Are you okay?"

Timothy looked down at his hands, which he had unknowingly clenched into fists, and nodded.

"Okay. Well, the sooner you get it over with, the sooner you'll feel better about it. Trust me." The principal gave a nod of encouragement.

Timothy turned back around and began walking toward the mall entrance. As he walked through the doors, he made sure not to make eye contact with anyone. He had never been to this mall, and he had never gone to any mall alone. The principal assured him that he wouldn't actually be alone, but he sure felt alone. He had no idea where he was going. He didn't know if he was on the southern side, northern side, or even if the mall was laid out like that.

He looked for a map of any kind, but couldn't find one anywhere. He would have to ask someone. He approached a man on a nearby bench who wore a baseball cap and had a beard.

"Excuse, me, sir..."

The man looked up and said, "Choice or die."

Timothy jumped backwards. "Why do you keep following me? What do you want from me?"

Ralph pulled off the fake beard, wrung his hands, twisted his shoulders, grimaced and said, "H-Hope. You."

"What do you mean?"

Ralph seemed to struggle to find the words, "H-Hope. You! Choice or die! You!"

"It's about me. Okay. What is it about me?"

Ralph's face twisted and contorted, but he couldn't find anything else to say. He stood up and moved toward Timothy.

Timothy bolted into the mall. It was fairly empty, and there weren't many places to hide, so he just kept running. He looked back to see if Ralph was following. He was, but was limping along and grabbing at his left knee. Timothy quickly put distance between them and turned the next corner. He ran past many store fronts and finally stopped as he ducked into a vacant children's ride area. He crouched behind the helicopter ride and watched for Ralph. He couldn't see Ralph, but he noticed two men who were looking right in his direction.

One man pointed at the helicopter and they started walking briskly toward it. Timothy started shaking.

What happened to not being alone? I could use some help right now.

When the men got too close for comfort, Timothy jumped up and charged down the hall. He didn't know where he was going, but as long as it wasn't a dead end, that was his route.

His path led him straight into a women's clothing and cosmetics store. He looked over his shoulder and saw that the men were still chasing him. He ducked into a makeup aisle, but tripped on a carpet edge, landing on his stomach. He looked up and saw a surprised, blonde-haired woman standing there.

"Are you okay? You look terrified!"

"Please help me!" Timothy ran over to the lady and hid behind her. At that moment, the two men turned into the aisle and smirked.

"Are either of you his father?"

The two men shook their heads and started walking toward Timothy.

"You will not harm this poor innocent boy!"

The lady reached into her purse and pulled out a can of mace.

"Step aside, lady. We don't have time—"

Psssshhhhh!

46

The man grabbed his face and fell backwards, screaming. The second man started to lunge toward the lady, but she whacked him across the face with her purse.

The man shook his head and felt his jaw, "Ow! What you got in there?"

"How rude! You should know better than to ask such a question!" She turned slightly and said, "Run, Timothy!"

How does she know my name? Wait. So I'm not alone here.

He took off running and headed back down the way he came in. He stopped briefly when he saw a sign that read, *North Wing Exit.* Aha! Direction! He looked down the mall. He could not even see the shop at the end of the South Wing, so he knew it was quite a distance and quite a run. There was no place to hide and only one way to run.

So he ran.

And he ran.

No sign of the two men behind him and no sign of Ralph.

Several people looked at him funny and a security guard even called out, "Slow down, kid!"

No chance of that happening!

He reached the opposite end of the North Wing, but just as he was crossing the West Wing entrance, he heard the sound of more people running. A dark-haired lady in a red blouse and a man wearing a grey hoodie dashed out of a store front and started chasing him!

They weren't wearing uniforms of any kind, just regular street clothes, but the fact that they were chasing him was enough proof for Timothy that they weren't there to help him.

His heart was beating out of his chest, his head was throbbing, his legs were turning into jelly, and his hands were shaking, but there was no way he was going to slow down or stop. Sweat was starting to drip into his eyes, which caused his vision to get blurry and his eyes to start burning. He was half-way down the South Wing and he could almost make out the shape of a fountain in the distance, but the nervous sweat and lack of oxygen were making it hard to see clearly.

"Timothy!"

At first, he thought the people chasing him were calling him, but then he realized that there was a person in front of him, calling out his name.

"Timothy! Here!"

He didn't know if he could trust this man or not, but he didn't really have a choice at this point. He could see the fountain now, and three people stood in front of it. The man who called to him had red hair and wore a tie-less blue suit with dressy, brown loafers. A brown-haired lady in green exercise clothes and a bald man in a t-shirt and plaid shorts stood beside the first man.

Timothy did not stop running until the man caught him and placed Timothy safely behind himself. The man faced the man and woman who were chasing Timothy. They had just reached that area and stopped to challenge the man.

The man in the hoodie called out, "Give us the boy and no one gets hurt!"

The man guarding Timothy looked at his companions and smiled. "Do you really expect us to believe that? Besides, are you really willing to allow so many people to be exposed?"

The woman and man pulled out knives and started walking toward him.

The man and his two companions knelt down at the same time, and each placed a hand on the floor, and then looked at the would-be-attackers.

The man spoke again, "The ground on which you stand is Living."

The two stopped, but did not put their knives away.

He continued, "And it is ours."

The two looked at each other, grimaced, and then put their knives away. They backed up slowly, and then turned and walked away, muttering things under their breath.

The man turned to Timothy and said, "You are safe. For now. They will try again. And again. Eric told us you are an Unclaimed Summoned. That means that they will hunt you until either you make a choice, they catch you, or you are dead. Do you understand?"

"Y-Yes, sir. Thank you. I have come to declare my choice."

"So Eric has told us."

"He told me to talk to Barney."

The man put a hand on Timothy's shoulder and said, "Come."

"I gave you more Runners and you failed to capture him again?!" The shadowy figure crossed his arms.

Ralph bowed low, shaking and mumbling, "No die! No hurt!"

"What? I'm not going to kill you, Ralph. That's not how I operate."

"N-Not me. Hope."

"You don't have hope?"

"No…Hope. Boy."

The man nodded, "Cheer up, Ralph. The tides are turning as we speak."

Ralph shook his head, but looked up and asked, "W-What now?"

"Your failure is of no consequence. Before you came to me, I received word that we are no longer in need of the Unclaimed Summoned. We have located what we really seek. Soon, you and I will join the ranks of the greatest warriors our side has ever known. We will all share in the great reward our Lady is offering. Call everyone back. We're going on a little…field trip."

Timothy walked with the three Casters. At least, this is what Timothy assumed they were. They walked around to the other side of the fountain. There were several benches in the area with a few small patio tables and chairs in the center. The man pointed to an old man seated on a nearby bench and then whispered, "We have to leave now, Timothy. Don't worry, we'll be around. When you're with Barney, though, you won't need any other protectors." He winked, then smiled, and then turned and left.

Timothy looked at the old, bent-over figure on the bench.

He *is a protector?*

The man with silver-white hair was leaning his head on his right hand and grasped a cane in his left hand. The old man's shoulders rose and fell with his slow, steady breathing. With his left leg crossed over his right knee, his left foot occasionally kicked or turned slightly. Every once in a while, Timothy could hear the man snore.

Mighty defender…?

"In case you're wondering…" the man sat up slowly and turned toward Timothy, "Yes, I can protect you, if you need protection."

"I- I- I'm sorry. Did I say it out loud?" Timothy's gaze dropped to a random spot on the floor.

"No, dear boy. You are not the first Unclaimed Summoned to meet with me. I dare say you won't be the last. I just had a feeling that that's what you were thinking. That's usually what people are thinking." He chuckled.

"So, you're Barney?"

"You're a quick one, aren't ya?"

Timothy looked down at the floor again.

"Ah, I'm sorry. It was only in jest. Yes, I'm Barney. You have come to make a declaration and be claimed?"

Timothy nodded.

"Do you fully understand your options?"

"No, sir. Not completely. I mean, I understand that I either choose the side of the Casters, the side of the Casters' enemies, or my own path away from this gift. Is that right?"

"Very good. I will add a few details to your understanding, then. If you join the Casters *or* the other side, you will be agreeing to use your gift in mysterious but wonderful ways. You will join the others on your side in training. Even though there is a war, you will not be asked to fight. The whole purpose at this point is to educate people about their gift and help them to use it effectively. Casters follow the text written by the man they call The Author. The other side, called Twisters, follow the guidelines set out by the man who is called The Twister. They have a different name for him, but only they know it. If you choose to follow your own path, you will lead a normal human life, you will reject your gift, and neither Casters nor Twisters will hurt you. The war Casters and Twisters fight is only between their soldiers. We have strict rules of conduct and it is shameful for anyone on either side of the war to break any of those rules. Do you understand the things I have said?"

Timothy thought for a moment, and then nodded. "Now I am sure of my choice."

Barney nodded back.

"Timothy," his mother squeezed his shoulder, "as an American citizen, and simply as a human being, you are allowed to make your own choices. Whether or not you make the good choices is entirely up to you. Your dad and I hope you will always try to make good choices. Sometimes you'll make bad choices, but you'll know when it's a good choice or a bad choice. Sometimes bad things happen when people make good choices, so it can be confusing, but what is most important is that you always try to do what is right, good, and pure."

"How will I know?" Six-year-old Timothy put down his action figure and looked at his mom.

"There's a little voice inside all of us that will tell us when we're doing something good or when we're doing something bad. The problem is that some people don't listen to that voice. So it's important for you to always listen to that little voice and do what is good."

"Yes, mom." Timothy smiled and went back to playing with his action figure.

Yes, mom…

He looked into Barney's eyes and saw the same golden glittering he had seen in the eyes of the others. He kept eye contact with Barney for several seconds, which was quite an accomplishment for him. He inhaled…exhaled.

"I want to be a WordCaster."

THE GUILD

"This is fantastic!" Mrs. Walker turned to her husband and folded her hands against her chin.

Mr. Walker was beaming as he reflected, "Less than a week in a new school and he's making such improvements! What have you guys been doing at that school that has helped him so much?"

The principal smiled and said, "Well, we believe that every student comes to the school with their own likes and dislikes, handicaps and skills, curses and blessings. Each student has a gift and so *is* a gift. We like to allow students the time and opportunity they need in order to discover themselves and express that. It seems that Timothy is finding that sooner than many students do. We're not sure what it is, yet, but something's working."

"Clearly! A writer's guild membership within the first week of attending a new school in a new town?" Mrs. Walker's mouth was open with amazement and disbelief.

"Yes, ma'am."

"This kind of thing has *never* happened for Timothy! He's always been picked on and so he's always kept himself inside his shell and never tried anything new except for things he did with us. Family field trips were always his favorite things when we had time for them."

Mr. Walker added, "We knew his vocabulary and writing skills were beyond his age and grade level, but we didn't know they would qualify him for a group like this."

The principal nodded, "Yes, we were all impressed when we saw his…skills…exhibited. So, he's looking at the facility right now to see if he likes it, but he still needs the permission of his parents. What do you say?"

Barney and Timothy were sitting across from each other at a patio table near the fountain. At this time, only two people were still seated in the area and were on the opposite end, so Barney felt that it was safe enough to talk comfortably here.

"Repeat after me, Timothy."

Timothy nodded. He had declared his intention and so must now recite an oath of commitment in order to officially join the WordCasters. He still had so many questions.

What do WordCasters do? I hope I don't have to fight. Why do they fight, anyway? What role would I play?

So many more questions flew around in his mind, but this is how he saw it: *If I join the Casters, I join a group I don't know much about, but a lot of people have already joined. If I join the other side, I give myself to having to fight against these people I've met. If I do not join, I lose my gift and I have a normal life. The third option sounds the safest…but when I'm older, am I going to look back and regret not picking a side and doing something with the supposed gift I've been given? I'm only eleven, but I don't want to miss something I may have been called to do. Besides, if Casters can do what I saw in my dream and what I saw Martha and the principal do, that would be so cool! It's like a super power! You'd have to be crazy not to want that!*

He thought of Ms. Lee. *Why did she decide to reject her gift? Was her job more important? Did something happen to her that scared her away? Did she see something like I did when Martha completely clobbered those two guys? Did she see a cabinet door fly open and bash a guy in the face? Did she just want to be normal? Normal would be nice…no one would pick on me for sparking or glowing anymore. Then again, they'd probably pick on me for something else. As a Caster, I'd still be different, but at least I'd know why. I may even be able to help people! I would like to help people…*

"Timothy? Did you hear me?" Barney leaned in close to look Timothy in the eyes.

"Huh? Sorry, sir." Timothy shook his head.

"Perfectly understandable. You're about to commit to this, then your mind is overwhelmed with questions and concerns. It's normal."

"Yes, sir."

"Are you ready?"

Timothy nodded again.

"Okay. Upon my birth, a gift was given to me. A gift that I could choose to acknowledge or ignore at any point in my life."

Timothy repeated the words after each pause.

"This gift flows within me and it is my choice when I use it, if I use it…This gift was created and provided many ages ago by the man we call The Author, whose teachings I can choose to follow, fight, or ignore…Through his works, my gift is given purpose and I am given a new calling…I hereby acknowledge my gift and commit to pursuing the teachings provided by The Author and by my mentors. I hereby commit myself as…" Barney left a blank for Timothy to fill in.

"I hereby commit myself as a WordCaster!"

Timothy sat still for several seconds and looked around. "Is that it?"

Barney smiled, "What were you expecting? Fireworks, floating up in the air, feeling a cool breeze swirl around you and tousle your hair?"

"Well…yeah!"

"Sometimes new Casters and Twisters do feel something, but most people don't, and that's perfectly acceptable. The important thing is that you believe what you've said."

Timothy paused, then said, "I do."

"Then there you go. That is it."

Timothy felt disappointed and a little unsatisfied, but nodded. "What now?"

"Now…the fun begins!" Barney grinned, tapped Timothy's shoulder and stood up. The two walked over to the fountain and Barney handed Timothy three pennies.

"What are these for?"

Barney put a hand on Timothy's shoulder, "They are for your trip."

"Where am I going?"

"To the Guild, of course!"

"I don't—I don't know where it is."

"Oh, I see what you're thinking!" Barney chuckled, "You'd need more than that for a taxi ride, bub. Don't worry, you don't have to travel far."

"Oh…" Timothy looked at the pennies, then back to Barney, "Where is it?"

"Right in front of you."

All Timothy could see in front of him was the fountain. He leaned left and right to look around the fountain, but stopped when Barney laughed.

"I'm about to show you, Timothy. Don't worry."

Timothy felt completely embarrassed and foolish. *Well, how was I supposed to know?*

Barney took one of the pennies from Timothy and held it in his open palm, in front of himself. "Since you've never been to the Guild, I will get you there this time. In the future, once you have seen it, you will be able to open the door. All you have to do is visualize the Guild and toss the coin in the water. You just have to make sure no one is watching when you do it. We won't want to scare anyone who doesn't understand."

Timothy put one penny in his pocket, then held out his hand and tossed the other penny into the water.

"Wait! I'll do it this time because it won't work for—" Barney was cut short and his mouth slid open as the water from the fountain began to part. The fountain's water was falling everywhere in the base except directly in front of them. There was a trapezoidal space in the fountain base where no water was sitting. It was as if glass walls were holding the water back. A small section of the center of the fountain's marble structure slid open slowly, revealing a railing and the top of a spiral staircase.

Neither Timothy nor Barney knew what to say. Finally, Barney began nodding, but neither took their eyes off the fountain.

"So…I guess you were one of the lucky ones who received a vision of the Guild when you were just a baby?"

"Y-Yes, sir." Timothy nodded slowly.

Barney lowered his arm and turned to Timothy.

"Well, that explains that, then. Congratulations, Timothy, you did it!"

"Wha- Wha- Wha-…*What* did I just do?"

"You've opened the door that leads to the staircase that leads to the passageway that leads to the Guild, and on your own on the first try! That's quite rare. Not completely uncommon, but rare."

"What, am I special or something?"

"Well, everyone is special. That's one of the most important things to remember as a Caster: No Caster is more important, significant, or special than anyone else. Just because we have this gift, it doesn't mean that we are greater than anyone. Never use your gift with pride or for selfish purposes. Only use it with humility. Understood?"

"Yes, sir."

"Good. I've known too many good Casters fall into trouble simply because of pride. Whenever you are ready, you may descend the stairs and begin your new journey. I will clean up when you have gone."

"Clean up?"

"Yes. Whenever something has been done via Casting, it must be undone. That's something you'll learn about later. Just remember that you should always clean up after yourself."

"Yes, sir. My mother taught me that." Timothy smiled.

Barney returned the smile.

Timothy inhaled…exhaled, then slowly stepped into the fountain base.

This is so strange…

He bent over and touched the sides of the water in the base. He stuck his hand into the water, and then pulled it out. His hand was wet, but no water spilled from the pool into the space where he stood.

…but so cool!

Barney crossed his arms and smiled, "Pretty neat, huh?"

Timothy looked at Barney with a huge grin on his face and said…

"Yes!"

Mr. and Mrs. Walker looked at each other for only a moment before they turned to the principal and spoke at the same time.

"Great! I'll head back and finish the paperwork, then. He will need to meet with his group at the mall every weekday after school for about two hours."

Mr. Walker cocked his head and lifted a brow, "The mall?"

He principal chuckled, "Yes, it sounds a little suspicious, but they have a little space there that they use for meetings. It's more affordable that way. Don't worry—they're not allowed to wander the mall. It's heavily supervised and only cleared teachers and members are allowed access."

"So, only Casters can come through here?"

Barney nodded, "But anyone can see the change happen, so you have be completely sure that you're alone or only with a group of Casters when you open this door."

"What if I had chosen to be a Twister?"

"I would have given you money for a cab."

Timothy laughed, but realized he was being serious.

Barney said, "Twisters have another location. I am a Caster, but I was given the task of guiding members of either side to their new lives."

"Well, how did you know what I was going to choose?"

"I didn't. Eric had a feeling about it, though."

"He's good with feelings and hunches, isn't he?"

"The best. He has never been wrong."

"Never?"

"Never."

Timothy's brow furrowed as he asked, "What about my…

"Parents? Uhhh…" the principal paused for dramatic effect since he already knew what he was going to say, "The directors and teachers don't like that because it's a big distraction for the members. You can walk him to the entrance, but he has to enter on his own."

Mr. Walker shook the principal's hand as they all stood up. "This sounds good. We're so excited for Timothy."

The principal nodded and smiled as he turned to leave, "So are we, Mr. and Mrs. Walker…So are we."

As Timothy stood on the top step of the spiral staircase, he looked down and saw a nausea-inducing never-ending path of dizziness.

"How far down does this go?" Timothy held the railing and leaned over to see other angles.

"Quite a ways down, but it ends more quickly than you might think. People are coming this way, so I need to close this up. I'll be here when you get back."

Timothy nodded and turned to Barney, "Thank you." He took

two steps down, but stopped when he heard the sliding of the door and splashing of the water. When the door slid closed, it became pitch black on the stairway, but soon after, small round gems on the railing and the stairs lit up.

Oh. That's handy.

Slowly at first, then more rapidly, Timothy walked down the spiral staircase. Suddenly, out of the corner of his eye, he saw a glimmering spot on the wall to his left. He looked over and almost had to do a double-take. Upon the walls of this stairway were etched symbols of various shapes and sizes. The one that he was looking at seemed very familiar to him.

My doodles!

He recalled the worksheet and park plan from class. The symbols he drew around the borders were very similar to those etched into the walls.

It has to be a coincidence.

He shook his shoulders and continued down the stairs. He looked up through the steps to look back at the door.

Wait! There's no way I can be this far down the staircase! I didn't take that many steps!

Surely, he was about half-way down the staircase now. He stepped down once more, but cut his step short. The staircase had moved! He stepped down again and saw the same thing. The etchings on the wall were traveling backwards and up twice as fast as he was traveling forwards and down. He took a leap down the staircase and watched as the etchings flew by in a blur. He stepped up three steps and watched as the etchings flew by in the opposite direction.

"I guess that explains what Barney meant about it not taking as long as it may seem."

Timothy smiled as he walked slowly down the stairs, watching all of the strange etchings slide by—definitely man-made, but wonderfully beautiful in their own way. There was no telling how long these had been here or who had carved them. Timothy just wished he knew what they meant.

Suddenly, he stopped. There was a symbol he recognized. He knew he had seen it many times before. It was a circle with four arms protruding from it in the directions of the cardinal directions (North, South, East, and West). These arms consisted of a straight line and then a straight bar across the top, going the other direction. So, the arms looked like the letter 'T' (especially the one pointing North) but rotated around to point in each of the main directions. In the very center of the circle was a solid dot.

I know I've seen this one in particular.

As he continued his descent, he stared at the symbol until it slipped into darkness behind him. He watched hundreds of other symbols pass him by until he reached the final step. The ground before him was pitch-black, as the whole area had been at the top of the staircase when the door closed. Was there even a floor? Timothy wasn't sure he wanted to try it, but he dipped one foot down, feeling for the floor. He found it and stepped down. His new problem was that he couldn't see anything in front of him. Where was he supposed to go now?

He stuck his arms out in front of him and felt around as he walked forward. When he felt to his right, he could feel a cold stone wall. To his left it was the same. He continued walking forward until his fingers detected the cold moisture of soil. He assumed he had reached a wall of dirt and it felt like that was as far as he could go.

Great! Either I'm at a dead end, or I have to dig my way to the Guild!

He felt around the wall area and on the floor. There was nothing to indicate where he should go now. A sudden fear hit him. Was this a trap? Was this the end for him? Had he been tricked by the Twisters all along just so that they could trap him and kill him? His stomach doubled over and he began to breathe heavily.

"Hello? Is anyone there? Help me! Help!"

He started toward the staircase, thinking that he would just go back the way he came. He stopped. Barney never told him how to open the door from this side. He stepped back against the wall of soil and sat down. He crossed his arms in front of him on top of his knees and buried his face in the space created there. He hoped with all his might that the principal would suddenly appear and help him out of here.

"Hey, kid."

Timothy shot up and looked around. Not that he could really see anything, but he tried. He stood up and felt around the walls. His night vision was now operational, so he was able to vaguely see the wall nearest to him. It was in fact a stone wall with moss and everything. He realized that he didn't even know the principal's last name, and he didn't want to be rude by calling an elder by his first name, so he just stood there and waited instead of calling out.

"Hey! Up here!"

From up above, a flashlight was turned on and was pointed down by Timothy's feet. Timothy looked straight up and saw part of a figure behind the light beam.

"Stand back, kid. I'm sending a rope ladder down to you and I don't want you to get hurt."

Timothy was confused, but obeyed anyway.

As he stepped back, he heard a clattering of sorts, like wood upon stone. Then he watched as the wooden base of a rope ladder slammed into the soil wall and settled. He assumed the wooden piece was for weight and stability.

The voice called, "Come on up!"

Slowly, hesitantly, Timothy grabbed the rope ladder and began to step up. The fibers of the rope felt ancient. He wasn't sure if he should trust its strength. He wasn't sure if he should trust this mysterious voice, either!

Yet, he climbed.

When he reached the top, a strong hand grabbed the spot behind his left elbow and a second strong hand grabbed underneath his right arm. The mysterious figure pulled him up and stood him up next to him.

This area was well-lit. How could he not see this light from down below? Before him lay a long, well-lit tunnel. It reminded him of the old pictures of mining tunnels, but this had modern lights, cobble-stone floors, and stone walls. It appeared that someone must have tunneled through solid rock, then laid a cobble-stone road and added brilliant lights.

Timothy turned to face the mysterious figure. The figure was kneeling and had his hand on the top of the rope. Timothy heard the clattering noise again and watched as the rope ladder rolled itself up and over the edge, resting just beside the man's hand.

"How…how do you do that?"

The man turned to him and smiled, "That's what you're about to find out." He had a kind face, a gentle smile, and a strong jaw, but he also looked like he had been in a war or two and barely made it out alive. He appeared to have been in his mid-thirties, wore a thick, but short beard, and was wearing blue jeans and a solid black t-shirt.

"Timothy. Right?"

Timothy nodded as he glanced around the area.

"My name is Brian." He held out his hand, which Timothy shook. "It always amazes me how few people actually consider looking up." He chuckled as he stood up.

Timothy stared, but didn't realize he was doing so.

Brian glanced over, then nodded, "Yes, I'm short. I get that a lot. It's okay."

Truth be told, Brian was actually 5' 10", but with his scoliosis (a curvature of the spine), he appeared to be much shorter. He was bent over so much that he was only a little taller than Timothy. If he did not have the condition, he may have even been allowed to grow to be over six feet tall. His family was full of tall people, but he was the shortest because of his spinal condition.

Brian placed a hand on Timothy's shoulder and coaxed him to walk down the tunnel section. "My role is to maintain the tunnels of the Guild and improve them as necessary. When we reach the end of the tunnel, you'll meet Jude. He'll help you get oriented to the Guild and give you a tour of the facilities."

Timothy nodded to indicate that he understood.

"When the Author first built the Guild, it was just a small cave in the mountain side, but when the wars started, he had to find another location, so he dug deeper. Unfortunately, his enemies found his entrances, so he had to close all of them down and leave one super-secret entrance. That's this tunnel. A few years ago, the thick forests that once stood here were cut down to make room for this mall. Fortunately, the foreman in charge of the build was a Caster, so when he saw the entrance, you can imagine how excited he was. At the same time, he knew it had to remain a secret, so he and a few other Casters built the secret entrance in the fountain to cover it up and make it less suspicious. People who see the fountain, especially Twisters, think that the water source is directly below the fountain, but it's actually in a completely different part of the mall and re-routed to this point."

Timothy simply nodded as he stared straight ahead while they walked.

Brian smiled, "You're nervous. That's okay. Everyone is when they come here, but I think you're going to like it. You'll be amazed by how quickly strangers become family here. When I first came, I felt like a social outcast, but I found that my peers respected me…because they felt the same way I did. When we worked through our anxieties and accepted ourselves as we accepted each other, we grew together and we are like brothers and sisters. I don't know where I'd be without my second family!"

Timothy looked at Brian. He really *did* understand. One thing kept nagging Timothy, though. Since he was now a Caster, would he be less of a burden to his parents? Will they be able to stay in New Hampshire and actually find peace, or will this decision just make things worse and force them to move again? He could see their faces. He could hear their voices.

"You're what?!" His father yelled and started pacing across the living room floor.

"We're going to have to move again…" Mrs. Walker sat on the sofa with her cup of coffee and she stared into the mug. Her complexion turned gray and his father's turned red.

He watched his father run his fingers through his hair and clench his fists, then turn back to him. "What are we supposed to do with this, Timothy? You run off and join some…cult, just because someone told you that you've got some special gift that sets things on fire! How will this affect your schoolwork? How will this affect your friendships? Have you even thought this through?"

Timothy stared at his shoes, holding back tears.

"Well, Timothy? Are you going to answer me? Timothy?...
Timothy?...

"Timothy?" Brian turned and faced him. Timothy snapped out of
his vision and looked into Brian's eyes.

Brian stared back, then said, "I see pain in your eyes. You fear
what people might think and say? You fear what happens next? You're
worried about your...parents?"

Timothy nodded as a tear formed in the corner of his right eye.
"How did you know?"

Brian smiled, "I walked the same path many years ago. I can't tell
you everything will be okay. I can't tell you that you'll never have to
deal with such problems or worse. I can't tell you that becoming a
Caster makes things better. What I can tell you with great certainty,
however, is that when you become a Caster, you never walk alone."

"What does that mean? Never walking alone?"

"Well, there's an element of solidarity as a Caster. Other Casters
know your struggle, they know your concerns, and they also know
your joys and successes. Casters look after one another and help each
other whenever they can. You may find that Casters come from all
corners of the Earth to help other Casters. You will quite literally never
have to walk alone."

"That's nice to know. Thank you, sir."

"You're welcome. Are you ready to enter the Guild?"

"Yes, sir."

Brian nodded his head toward two large wooden doors, "We're here."

Upon the doors, more symbols were etched. Crimson paint and

gold-leaf details gave the etchings life. At least, he thought it was gold leaf. He looked at Brian and pointed at the gold details.

"Ah. The author made these doors by hand, and yes, that's real gold."

"They're beautiful!"

"The third pride of the Guild!"

"What are the second and first?"

"The second pride of the Guild is the community of Casters. The greatest pride of the Guild is The Text."

"What's The Text?"

"You'll see in a few minutes." With that, Brian pushed open the doors.

"So he's on his way?" Ms. Lee sat down in front of the principal's desk.

The principal glanced up briefly from his paperwork and nodded, "Yes, indeed."

"Do you know what he ended up choosing?"

"Not officially, but I have a hunch that he joined the Casters."

"That would be great. I could see that he has a pure heart and good motives."

"I saw the same. I just hope he keeps his commitment. Some drift away within the first two days of their declaration and commitment."

"That quickly?"

"I know a man whose sister converted to the Twisters three hours after she became a Caster."

Ms. Lee shook her head in disbelief. "Why would anyone choose to join the Twisters?"

The principal looked at her squarely and said, "Power. It's all about power for the Twisters. And they do have power. I've seen it. They like to feel like super heroes, but they use their power only for themselves. It makes them feel better, I guess."

Ms. Lee nodded and folded her arms in front of her. She paused for a few moments, and then asked, "What do you think he's doing right now?"

A young male teacher knocked on the door and opened the door. "Excuse me. It's meeting time." He closed the door and headed to the meeting.

Ms. Lee and the principal stood up together. The principal gathered his papers and said, "I imagine that right about now he's walking through the doors and saying...

"Whoa...!"

Timothy entered the Guild and his mouth fell open. His drawing really did look almost exactly like the real place! Vaulted ceilings, majestic archways, long hallways, and even a few gargoyles! Candelabras, chandeliers, fireplaces, and various carpets and paintings filled in the spaces. It was like an underground castle. The buildings in his drawing ended up being separate rooms in this enormous underground educational facility.

"And it's all carved out of the same enormous rock. Incredible, isn't it?"

Timothy jumped and looked to his right.

Brian walked over, "Timothy, this is Jude. Jude, Timothy."

Jude was a tall man and about twenty-eight years of age. He had short, but wavy, tousled black hair and a trimmed goatee. His sweater-vest and red loafers definitely made him stand out from the rest of the people he had met so far.

He shook Timothy's hand and said, "It's a pleasure to meet you, Timothy. I've heard a lot about you. You've had quite an adventure today, haven't you?"

Timothy nodded, "Yes, sir."

"Well, welcome to the Guild! I'm going to give you a tour of the facility and get you introduced to everyone you'll need to know."

Brian said goodbye, and Timothy and Jude went on their way. Jude took Timothy into each room as they passed. They first entered two smaller rooms, which served as classrooms, practice-rooms, and storage rooms as needed. Next, they stepped into the Dining Hall. In the wall to the left sat an enormous fireplace with a roaring fire. Since almost the entire Guild was made of stone, it could get quite cold. Tables, benches, and chairs of various shapes and sizes filled the room. There was no real order to the placement of the furniture, but there were enough seats and tables present to allow an entire army to eat. In front of the far wall was a buffet and behind that were two doors that led to the kitchen. Only paintings were present on the wall to the right.

Finally, they came to what they called the Sanctuary. It was the largest, safest and most-used room in the structure. About half-a-dozen people were in this room, studying books, preparing lessons, or sitting deep in meditation.

One guy was even sleeping in one corner of the room.

The Sanctuary was massive! But it didn't take much to be heard from across the room. A gentle word could sound like a trumpet's blast if you were standing in the right spot. The walls were undecorated and the lights came from small orbs like those found in the stairwell. Candelabras, a fireplace, and sconces around the room were also used to help illuminate. In fact, it was the best-lit room in the Guild.

Jude leaned over and whispered, "This is the core of the Guild. It's everyone's favorite room and this is where most of the instruction is provided. When you come in for meetings, you'll meet here first."

Timothy nodded.

"Come. I want you to meet the Guild Master." Jude pointed to the center of the back of the room where there was a cloaked figure leaning over a stone pedestal. They walked over and Jude was about to speak when the figure raised its left hand in a request for silence. Timothy could see its head moving back and forth slightly, as if reading.

After a few moments, the figure said, "Okay." The figure turned and faced them, asking, "How can I help you, Jude?"

Jude bowed slightly and said, "Madam, this is Timothy Walker, our newest member."

Timothy looked at this lady and was slightly concerned.

She must be about three-hundred years old! She's the Guild Master? How is she still standing up?

"Timothy Walker. Such a nice name. Welcome, Timothy!" She held out her hand.

Her frame was small and hunched over. Much like Brian, she was only a few inches taller than Timothy. She had a cane hooked over her left arm, so Timothy assumed she had some trouble walking. Her skin was like a raisin, only even more wrinkled. Her nails were long and sharp, like talons. She seemed to be extremely emaciated. She was practically skin and bones. He shook her hand, but he was afraid it might fall off.

He was surprised, though. For such an appearance, she had a *really* strong grip. He undercompensated, so his soft grip was met with the grip you would expect from a soldier. He was now worried, though only in jest, that *his* hand might fall off.

"When you come to meetings, I will do announcements and opening comments, and then one or two of the other teachers will conduct the lessons for the day. My role is more like a supervisor. I make sure that the instructors are teaching you the right things. Do you have any questions for me, Timothy?"

Timothy thought for a moment, then said, "No, ma'am. None that I can think of. Oh! Actually, I was wondering what you were reading."

She smiled, "But of course. This is the pride of the Guild. It is what got us here. You see, when The Author wrote his lessons and guidelines, he recorded them in this book. We call it The Text. Since it was written by his hand, there is great power in this book. There are copies we have so that others can learn. You will receive one on Monday. However, the version of The Text that sits on the pedestal holds greater power than any copy could hold. Would you like to look at it?"

Jude spoke up, "Madam, are you sure that's a good idea?"

The Guild Master simply stared at him.

Jude bowed his head and nodded, "Yes, of course you are. My apologies, Madam."

She smiled, and then slowly shuffled aside to allow Timothy to look at the book.

"Go ahead. Touch it. Look through it. You won't do any harm."

Timothy slowly approached the book and leaned over it. He scanned the pages, but all he saw were long series of those strange symbols. He half-closed the book so he could look at the cover. On the front of the ancient leather-bound book was stamped the same symbol that caught his eye earlier. A dot within a circle with four arms.

"What is this symbol, ma'am?"

"That symbol means Caster of Words. It's where we get our name. It's actually the name of the gift. WordCasting. Inside the book, you saw many other symbols. These are the words The Author wrote. He encoded them so only those with the gift would be able to read them."

"But I can't read them…And I'm afraid to try. What if I set it on fire?"

The Guild Master smiled and took Timothy's right hand. She held his pointer finger out as she opened the book to a random page. She placed his finger on the first symbol and slowly slid it across to the second symbol.

Timothy braced himself and clenched his teeth as the spot behind his ear started tingling. This was a different kind of tingling, though. It didn't feel like a burning kind of tingling. It was more like a cooling tingling. It was like a nice breeze of fresh air upon his skin.

"Now do it freely. Let it flow."

She released his hand and he placed his finger on the first symbol. Jude peered over Timothy's shoulder to watch.

Timothy inhaled…exhaled. He slid his finger over.

For he

"Whoa!" Timothy jumped back and looked at The Guild Master. She was smiling kindly. As he slid his finger across the symbols, his mind filled with colors, sounds, and a strange energy. He saw and heard the words in his mind, even though he had no idea what the symbols represented.

Timothy whispered, "It's like a translator app in your brain! I feel tingly all over…and nothing's on fire!"

"Pretty *spiffy*, huh?"

That was strange to hear that come from *her* mouth, but she was right. Spiffy, indeed.

"Try again."

Timothy stepped up to the book again and re-executed his actions. As his finger slid across each symbol, visions of the translation of the text entered his mind.

For he does not willingly bring affliction or grief to anyone.

Sounded like good advice. He smiled, but as he looked down, he saw that his hand was decreasing in brightness…as if it had just been glowing!

"Was my hand just—"

The Guild Master smiled again.

"Glowing. Yes, it was. That's normal. You see, when an Unclaimed Summoned becomes a Claimed Summoned and they make their decision, the gift fully activates, and you no longer release weak energy. The energy is fully developed when you read, now, and this means that good things will actually happen. This also means that you have to be more careful when and how you use your gift. We'll discuss this more on Monday. You should notice some significant changes in the meantime, though."

Timothy started to step down, but tripped. Jude was right there in a second and caught Timothy before he could fall. Timothy's right hand landed on Jude's chest. When this happened, Jude jumped backwards slightly.

Timothy stood up and looked at Jude. He was catching his breath and had a hand to his chest where Timothy had touched him. To Timothy, it felt like a small static electricity shock. By his appearance, it must have felt much worse to Jude. His eyes were wide and he kept shaking his head as he tried to catch his breath.

Timothy wrung his hands, "I'm so sorry. Are you okay?"

Jude nodded and stood up straight, "I'm fine, yes. It's…It's okay. Just a freak accident, I guess. Maybe some static electricity from The Text."

The Guild Master stared at Jude, pondering, and then turned back to Timothy.

"I had another question, ma'am." He waited for her approval and then asked, "Why me? Why do I have this gift? I'm a *nobody*."

The Guild Master thought for a moment, then asked, "May I have your coin, please?"

"How did you—" Timothy didn't finish as he reached into his pocket and pulled out the third penny and handed it to her.

"Barney has this *tradition* of always giving three. Most new Casters always have two pennies in their pocket when they get to this point, so I was banking on that. Alright, so what I'm hearing from you is that you see yourself like this penny. Insignificant. Worthless. No one really uses a penny anymore. Why do we still use it? That's a rhetorical question, of course."

"Yes, ma'am."

She held out the penny in her hand, palm up.

"Listen closely, Timothy. A penny can change the entire world as we know it."

He stared at the penny, then said, "It's just a penny."

She grinned and repeated, "Just a penny. Just…a penny?"

With that, the penny shot out of her hand, straight up into the air. Timothy looked up and just as he did, a large explosion filled the room with color, light, and a thunderous snap. The penny continued to travel around the room, and as it went, firework-type explosions burst in its trail. Everyone looked up and smiled—especially the man who had just been sleeping.

The penny traveled around the room twice more and left a sparkling trail of silver dust behind it on the final trip. The penny flew back into The Guild Master's hand in the same place it had been sitting before—and with the same side facing up.

"Just a penny…Timothy, in the right hands, used for the right purpose, and when treated with dignity and respect, a penny can change the entire world as we know it. You may be a penny, and that makes you different from other coins, but that doesn't mean that you are any less valuable than they are. All coins do different things, but all have their place and purpose. *You* have a place. *You* have purpose. Never forget that."

She handed Timothy the coin and he nodded, blinking away the chance of tearing up. He stared at the penny for several moments, then dropped it in his pocket.

The Guild Master smiled, and then said, "Okay, I think it's time for you to get going and get back to your parents. It's almost supper time. Remember, you must not tell your parents about what you've seen. They have been told that you are part of a Writer's Guild, as we tell all parents and guardians until they need to know the truth. They were told that you will be working on your writing skills and projects." She continued by giving him more details about how to respond to certain questions and what to do in certain situations.

"Jude, please escort Timothy…and please try not to get shocked again. We don't want anyone getting *hurt*."

Jude nodded and walked Timothy back to the entrance.

"Well, what do you think?"

"It's…like a dream! It's…surreal and impossible…but it's apparently *quite* possible. It's wonderful and terrible. It's like the ending of a really good movie!"

Jude laughed and declared, "Well said! Through these doors and at the end of the tunnel, you should find Brian. He'll let you down. You'll go up the staircase and find Barney. He'll help you get home."

"Okay. Oh! How do I open the door?"

"Oh, yes. Draw the WordCasting symbol on the wall and it should open up. If it doesn't, knock three times and Barney should be able to help you out."

"Okay. I'm just curious now, but is that the only way in?"

Jude nodded, "It is for *you*. There is another way, but that takes *years* of training."

Timothy said his thanks and goodbyes, and then departed. Back through the beautiful double doors, back through the tunnel, down the rope ladder (saying goodbye to Brian, of course), and up the spiral stairs. At the top of the stairs, he stared at the wall in front of him. He had seen the symbol dozens of times in his life, so he had no trouble recalling its shape. He just wasn't sure that his actions would do anything.

Why would drawing this shape on the door open it? It doesn't make sense.

Of course, very little of what he had been seeing today made any sense. He reached out and began drawing. When he finished, he waited about sixty seconds, just to be sure.

Just when he was about to knock three times, the door started shifting. When the door opened, he could see the amazing water wall effect and a smiling Barney waiting for him. He stepped out through the door and then out of the fountain.

"I see they already taught you how to open the door! Most people just knock."

Timothy smiled, "I was about to. Why did it take so long to work?"

"There were people walking around. That door doesn't open from

77

that side unless the coast is clear."

"How can it tell?"

Barney shrugged, "No one knows. Something The Author designed was imbued into the fountain when it was built, I guess."

Barney gave Timothy instructions on how to leave the mall to find the principal. On the ride home, Timothy shared his experience with the principal, who was very excited for Timothy and very pleased with his choice. Timothy didn't sleep well that night…but he didn't mind. It was a pleasant sleepless night.

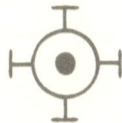

BASIC TRAINING

Sunday passed without incident. Monday morning was the same. Even though Timothy still had trouble making full eye contact and he still pretty much kept to himself, his self-confidence was more evident.

Today was the real test. If the sparking Timothy was accustomed to was to go away after he stepped away from being an Unclaimed Summoned, as the principal had mentioned, this would be the day to prove it. As he looked at the worksheet in front of him on his desk, his anxiety grew. After writing his name and the date, he placed the tip of his pencil on the first line and looked over at the question.

Write a sentence using the following word: Collide

He looked around the room. No tingling. No one was looking at him except Ms. Lee. Apparently, she also wanted to see if anything would happen.

So far, so good.

He thought for a second, and then wrote: *The boy was awestruck as he watched his two worlds collide.*

He looked back up to see if anything happened. Nothing. He smiled. He looked at Ms. Lee and saw that she was smiling, too. She nodded and his smile transformed into a grin.

He looked at the next word: Relief

Perfect.

Leaning further over his paper, he got to work, writing like a madman. He finished his worksheet in record time, leaned back in his seat, and exhaled.

Relief. I can finally be normal!

He placed his pencil on the desk and planted his hand down on top of it. The pencil flew out from under his hand and silently stuck to the back of the chair of the student in front of him. He cringed as he glanced around the room. No one saw.

Well…almost normal.

"Sir!"

The shadowy figure turned from a large oak table to face the man who called out to him. The man was wearing camouflage cargo pants, a sleeveless gray shirt, and a red, white, and blue bandana, which was used to hold back the man's long, greasy, black hair.

"The apocalypse called. It wants its wardrobe back. What news?"

The man with the bandana paused as he tried to make sense of the figure's comment, then shook his head and reported, "We're just waiting for the last few Runners to return and we'll be ready to leave on your orders."

"Good. Make sure that everyone has a weapon."

"Are we going in lethal or non-lethal, sir?"

The tall, slender figure stood still for a moment, then turned back toward the table and whispered, "Lethal."

"Yes, sir."

"Oh, and make sure everyone has eaten and carries a canteen. It's a long hike."

"Hike, sir?"

The figure turned back to the man and asked, "Did you think we were just going to fly there or something? We have to be undetected. On foot is the best way to ensure that we reach the goal."

The man bowed slightly and said, "Yes, sir. As you order." The man departed and the slender shadowy figure turned once more to the table and turned a page of a large, old book with a golden tint to the pages.

"We just want to see what the place looks like and make sure there is adequate supervision," Mr. Walker explained as he held the mall door open for his family.

Timothy tried to remember The Guild Master's instructions and turned to go down the North Wing. He and his parents approached a small bookstore and peered inside.

Aside from the shelves and shelves of books, there was little here. Several tables were set up in the back of the store. Around these tables sat several adults, teenagers, and children. One or two paintings hung on the dull wallpapered walls.

Timothy turned to his parents, "There it is."

Someone in the group rolled a handful of dice onto the table.

Mr. and Mrs. Walker looked at each other, then at Timothy, skepticism clearly drawn upon their faces.

Timothy just shrugged and said, "It's probably a brainstorming exercise."

His parents nodded, said goodbye, told him they'd pick him up in two hours, and turned to leave. Timothy walked into the shop and watched his parents walk back the way they came in.

"Can I help you?" One of the adults at the table looked up. A pimple-covered face stared at Timothy, emotionless and…well… kind of creepy. Timothy guessed he was an employee who found it more fulfilling to play this game than tend to the store and make money.

"I- Uh- No, I'm just looking."

The employee nodded and went back to their game. Timothy pretended to look through various books, and then, making sure his parents were gone, left the store.

He sped through the mall and slowed down when he reached the fountain. There was a small group gathered there. Several people were sitting still, staring at nothing in particular. Some were making jokes and laughing, and some were talking to Barney. All were approximately Timothy's age. Some appeared to be in high school, but most were definitely in late elementary to late middle school.

Barney looked up, "Timothy! Come on over. Great timing! We like to let everyone in at the same time if we can orchestrate it that way."

Barney looked around the area. Since he didn't see anyone within an uncomfortable distance, he lobbed a penny into the well. Timothy watched with awe once more as the water parted and the door slid open.

He stepped over next to Barney and whispered, "I don't think I'll ever get used to that."

Barney chuckled and said, "I've been doing this for I don't know how long. *I'm* still not completely used to it."

The young Casters entered the stairwell in single file and began their descent. They followed the path Timothy learned just two days before, greeting Brian and pushing open the large, wooden double doors to take in the amazing views. Timothy was so nervous his first time through, that he failed to notice the sensational aroma of incense burning in the distance and the deep warmth provided by the fires.

The Casters entered the hallway and were greeted by four of the instructors and subsequently escorted into the Sanctuary and asked to find comfortable seats. Since most of the seats were like unpadded church pews they weren't very comfortable, so they just had to find a seat in which they could handle the discomfort.

It's only two hours…it can't be that bad. Right?

"Timothy?"

He looked to his right and saw a slightly familiar face.

"Brandon!"

Timothy let two people slide past him so he could talk to Brandon.

"I knew it. I just knew it. I had a feeling there was something different about you, Timothy!"

"Really? How? Glittering eyes?"

"Oh, hey! You *do* have the glittering eyes! I didn't see that before. No, it was just something about how you carried yourself. It seemed very familiar."

"How I carried myself?"

"Yeah, you know. Depressed, mopey, self-hating. All that good stuff."

"Gee, thanks…"

"No, no. It's okay. I'm sure almost every Summoned goes through that."

"So you went through it, too?"

"Actually, no, I didn't."

Timothy raised a brow.

"My parents were both Casters, so I knew what was going on pretty early on. I made my commitment before I was six years old. I haven't done much with training until now because I've been too busy with school, but I think it's a good time to get into it."

The boys sat down and looked around the room. People were still finding seats.

Timothy whispered, "So, what's going to happen?"

"Well, we're going to learn some things, practice some things, maybe eat some things, and then go home. Pretty simple."

"What kinds of things?"

"Sometimes we get things like baked ham, roasted pheasant, or stuffed hoagies, but usually it's just drinks and snacks."

Timothy shook his head, "No, I meant the learning and practicing."

"Oh!" Brandon chuckled, "Sorry, I'm usually focused more on food than anything else. I have a very high metabolism, so I'm usually pretty hungry. We'll learn something different about Casting each time we're here."

Brandon looked around the room.

"However, I see several new faces, so I suspect we're going to go over the basics again. We may even have break-out groups if certain people are learning something specific."

"It sounds a lot like school."

"It does. It's a lot more interesting, though!" Brandon laughed.

"Alright! We're ready to begin!" A man wearing a gray suit and blue tie was standing up front by the pedestal with his arms extended. He folded his hands in front of his chest and continued, "Welcome, everyone! I'm seeing several new faces here tonight. If you're brand new, please stand up so we can embarrass you."

There was a wave of chuckling from the group.

The man smiled, "I'm just kidding! Please stand so we can know who you are and so we know how to be of greatest help to you."

Timothy looked around and, when he saw others standing up, he stood up as well. Five young Casters stood up—three boys and two girls.

"Welcome! Welcome! Welcome! What we'll do today is split up into break-out groups, so we ask that the five of you remain in this room when groups form. Just come up here and sit in the front row when we say. For now, have a seat and we'll hear from The Guild Master."

The group erupted into a loud round of applause as The Guild Master slowly stood up from her seat and shuffled to the front. It seemed like it took a lifetime and a half for her to get there, but she finally made it. The man in the suit provided a chair for her and she sat.

"Children of all ages, thank you and welcome! I want to begin by sharing a few announcements."

Timothy listened intently as The Guild Master shared news of other Caster groups, news about humanitarian efforts conducted by the Casters in their area, and information about the refreshments that would follow that meeting. None of it was really too interesting to Timothy, and The Guild Master took a really long time to get through it all, but he didn't want to be disrespectful or rude, so he listened to every word she spoke.

When she had finished she said, "With the announcements shared, let's get into our groups. Newcomers, please meet up here with Roger. Apprentices, please meet with Andy. Elders, please meet in the other corner with Marissa and Steve. When everyone has reached their group, you may depart."

It wasn't a very large group present, so none of the groups had very many people in them. Timothy didn't know if this was common, but he was more focused on the task at hand. Brandon waved at him as he went off to join the Apprentices. Timothy waved back and walked to the front of the room.

He and the other four newcomers took seats in the front row and waited for all of the groups to be on their way. Roger watched the groups leave and The Guild Master...

Where'd she go? How'd she do that?

She was nowhere to be found. She must have already left, but based on how she was moving before, Timothy reasoned, she should still be visible.

Strange...

When the other groups left, Roger began.

"Hello everyone. You're probably a little confused, nervous, and, hopefully, excited. Today, you won't have to worry about actually doing anything except answering questions. We're just going to go over the history, basics, and rules. You must understand these things before you can Cast effectively. Okay?"

The students nodded.

"Okay. First things first, and this is crucial. What is WordCasting? Anyone know?"

A girl with curly red hair raised her hand.

"Yes?"

"It's making things come alive and telling them what to do."

"You're close. Anyone else?"

A round boy with black hair raised his hand and answered, "It's when you read from a book and make the words do things."

"Also close, but not quite complete. Okay. WordCasting is the gift created by The Author that allows us to breathe life into otherwise dead areas and use that life to cause change. Sometimes this involves manipulating objects, sometimes this involves reading from The Text, and sometimes it just comes down to the telling the truth. What do I mean by dead areas and living areas? Well, the first task of a WordCaster is to speak life energy from The Text into an area that has not yet received it. It's like preparing an area of ground to hold the foundation of a building, and then following up by building that building. It's also like gardening. Prep work is the first step. Some areas have never been Cast into. Some already contain the life energy, and that allows us to go on to the next step. Thus, Dead areas are environments where Casting has not taken place or that energy I mentioned has been cleared out. Living areas are those environments into which that energy has been Cast…they are no longer Dead and we are able to start working."

The third boy, a blonde-haired boy with large glasses, raised his hand and asked, "Sir, why is it called *Word* Casting?"

"That's a good question! We call it *Word* Casting because the life energy comes from the words written by The Author. When we are reading The Text in order to spread the life energy, we are essentially *casting* those *words* into the area. Hence WordCasting."

The red-haired girl raised her hand, "How does it work, exactly?"

"Unfortunately, no one really knows. It was a system developed by The Author many, many years ago. It is said that he studied the 'language' of the earth, meaning ground, and created these symbols that correspond to how the ground communicates with plants, animals, and humans. When we cast these symbols, we are communicating with the ground and it *listens*. Now, this is all very mystical and confusing, but all we really know for sure is that however The Author designed it, it works."

The second girl, a black-haired, pale-skinned girl, raised her hand, "Is the ground alive, then?"

"Nice catch. It isn't alive in the same sense that you and I are alive. It doesn't have lungs, a heart, a brain, or anything like that. However, it does respond to electromagnetic pulses, heat, water, and human interactions. It holds the nutrients that allow things to grow and is strong enough to support the weight of all organic and inorganic things. The symbols somehow speak a language that the ground, and anything that touches the ground, understands. This leads me to a word of caution. WordCasting cannot be done to other humans or animals. Nothing with a will of its own should be Cast into. As far as we know, it is not possible to affect anything with a will of its own. Our function is to give life where life does not exist, then to use that life to help the living."

Timothy raised his hand, "How do we help the living, exactly?"

"In any way that you can possibly imagine. Let's say that a village is in desperate need of water and the nearest water source is miles away. This is actually a pretty common situation. We can speak life into the ground and manipulate it so that water comes to them. The Nile used to run from North to South, but in times of drought, the people in the North had nothing. So ancient WordCasters changed that to help people out. As another example, let's say a mountain climber is stuck on a cliff side. We can actually go there and tell the cliff to help him back up. You all remember the rope ladder?"

Everyone nodded and smiled.

"It works just like that. WordCasting allows us to tell things to move, grow, shrink, or anything else we need it to do. Brian tells the ladder to expand its fibers using this language and it does so. When he wants the ladder to come up, he tells it to tighten its fibers in a certain way. This causes the coiling action and forces the ladder back up. Again, I must stress that you cannot use this on people. Though we haven't tested it, we assume it can be dangerous for anyone involved and it's just an unethical use of the gift. Hopefully you won't have to use this application any time soon, but you can also use WordCasting for defensive purposes."

Timothy recalled the cabinet door slamming into Ralph's face.

"If you ever have to use it for defense, make sure you only use it for non-lethal purposes. Remember that we're trying to *help* people, not hurt people, so if you can disarm an opponent and get away, that is the best way to go. As I said, hopefully you won't have to use it for that any time soon, if ever. Any questions?"

No one raised their hands, so he continued, "Okay. That should just about do it for the basic stuff for today. Now I'm going to tell you a little story. It's going to sound fictitious and outrageous, but according to all of our records, this is exactly what happened, almost ten thousand years ago.

"No one knows his real name, but everyone calls him The Author. They call him The Author simply because he wrote The Text. Interestingly, we also don't have a better name for the book, so we endearingly refer to it as The Text. Further information was not left for us to know. With that aside, The Author was a good man, but also a strange man in the eyes of others. He preferred to be off by himself and he was often seen talking to plants and rocks. Occasionally, he would even approach animals and try speaking to them. He tried every language he knew. Bear in mind that there really weren't that many languages present at that time. Nothing was having any effect on either the earth or its inhabitants. So instead of talking, he listened. He would sit still for days at a time and listen. Just listen! People would approach him and he would interact, of course. He wasn't anti-social or anything. He could communicate very well with other humans, but he sought an understanding deeper than most humans could comprehend. He wanted to learn how to give life and maintain it, not destroy it as so many others did.

"He was a very friendly man and even had house guests and many close friends. He just wanted to learn that special language and the only way to do that was apart from other humans. Well, one day he found it. Rather, he felt it. It wasn't something to be seen, touched, smelled, tasted, or heard. He listened, of course, but it wasn't a sound that he experienced. It was an inner feeling. In his mind, he saw symbols created by these feelings. He recorded them on a stone tablet, since he didn't have a book available at that time, and waited in that same spot where he received those symbols until he had recorded every symbol he experienced. Then, he memorized them.

"It was when he went back over the symbols to memorize them that a stranger thing occurred. When he ran his fingers over the symbols or repeated the symbols in his mind, things started to happen. The ground on which he sat moved. He repeated the process and it moved again. And so began his efforts to learn what each symbol meant and what it did. Thus, WordCasting was born. Then, using these symbols, he assembled a book and recorded everything he had learned. After a period of just six days, his book was finished. He didn't eat, he didn't sleep, and he didn't talk to anyone until it was all done.

"He went and showed this book to his closest friends and showed them what the language could do. It was a bit like what it would be to teach someone a computer programming language today. It took time and a lot of trial and error, but eventually, his friends learned the skills and began spreading the teachings.

"Unfortunately, one of his friends, another name we are not told, figured out other uses of this discovery. He approached The Author and said, 'Why are we not using this for our own gain? We are all poor and own so little. Let us use this skill to grow our wealth.' The author responded, 'No! We must only use this for the good of others. Don't you see? The ground gives life, and when something does die, it provides so that something else can grow in its place! Should we not do the same?'

"The Twister, as we call him, disregarded The Author's words and went out and did what earned him his name. He twisted the purpose and he twisted the language. He used the skills to help only himself. He conned people out of their belongings and lands. He made himself wealthy beyond his needs. The Author saw the treachery and confronted The Twister again.

"The Twister responded, 'I don't need you anymore. You are only holding us back!' He sent The Author away, but before he left, The Author Cast into The Twister's ground and allowed everything to die. This angered The Twister beyond reconciliation. He spoke with their mutual friends and attempted to turn them against The Author. He spoke of killing The Author so that they would be free to do as they please. 'What kind of a friend would destroy another's property just so that he could prove a point? What kind of a friend would take away everything that you have worked so hard to obtain?' Of course, the Twister left out the parts about him conning people and stealing their belongings.

"The Twister won almost all of their mutual friends over. One remained faithful to The Author and ran ahead of the others when they all departed so as to warn The Author. 'Thank you, my friend, but I was already aware. I felt it in his heart when we last spoke. I knew this was to come. Go now, keep yourself safe.'

"The next day, The Twister and his new minions came to kill The

Author. They actually came here, to the place where The Author built his home. The place where he had trained them all. However, The Author knew the symbols and skill better than any of them, so he managed to escape. They tracked him for days and finally found him in a well-populated city we refer to as Atlantis. Scattering people in all directions, their battle destroyed the city and sent it to the ocean depths. The Twister and his friends had managed to pin The Author behind some large lumber and he sank to the depths with the city ruins. Some believe he managed to escape, but that's the legend as we know it. The Twister and his friends looked for The Text, but never found it. Before he sent his friend away, The Author gave The Text to him to protect and share with those who would listen. That's how we have it today.

"His friend took The Text and essentially built an army of WordCasters. The Twister shared his knowledge and did the same, creating an army of WordTwisters. They met on the field of battle. Most of the WordCasters, on both sides, lost their lives, but a few managed to slip through the lines and get to The Twister. They defeated him and buried him alive beneath the rocks and did what no Caster should ever do again. They stripped the life from the earth before them. By this time, The Twister had forgotten how to cast life into the earth, so the legend holds that he died in his earthy grave.

"Despite the victory, the two sides fight on. Some believe both The Author and The Twister lived. Some claim to see their spirits wandering the earth. All we know is that Twisters still fight us and we must do all we can to prevent them from winning their terrible war with Casters and humanity.

"You see, all they want is control. Control over everything. They want power. They want money. They want absolute freedom, but this freedom does not extend to Casters or the rest of humanity. It will be a dictatorship if The Twister finally wins his war. We want people to have life and to be able to enjoy it. We want everyone to be free, but to have such a freedom that allows them to do good things, unselfish things, life-giving things. This is why we do what we do."

The children all nodded slowly, taking in the story and its lessons.

The rounder boy raised his hand, "If there are all these battles everywhere, why don't we see any signs of them?"

"Excellent question. This is another lesson you must always remember. Always put things back the way you found them. You see, when a battle occurs, practically the entire area is disrupted and disfigured. If you don't put it back, you may have whole blocks that no one can use without a lot of extra work. It's best to clean up after a battle. There is also an important note. Twisters typically don't clean up. They like leaving messes and landmarks so that people know where they've won a battle. It's like a trophy to them. We don't see it that way. You know the Grand Canyon?"

They all nodded.

"That's a battle we lost." He let that sink in. "Many believe that it was formed from years of erosion, but that's not the case. That was a Twister trophy. No one knows how many lives were lost there that day."

The black-haired girl raised her hand, "Will we have to fight like that someday?"

Roger knelt down and looked them each in the eyes and said, "I sincerely hope you will never have to fight. As long as you are here, you will not be asked to do so. We have Elder and Graduate volunteers all over the place who stay in touch and respond when they are needed. Someday, some of you may take such positions, but all of us hope that you will never have to bear that burden. Our hope is that you will all be able change lives, and even save lives…not have to take them."

He stood up again, paused, then proceeded to run through the many rules of WordCasting. He had the children take notes so that they had a list they could refer to as needed. The rules included:

Do not use WordCasting to take the easy route—only use your gift when it is relevant to do so.

Do not use WordCasting to take revenge or hurt someone to spite them.

Do not use WordCasting in public unless absolutely necessary.

And:

Do not use WordCasting to attract people of the opposite sex.

Roger smiled, "Yes, some people have actually done that last one before. It never ends well. Either they end up scaring the person away because they're not ready to understand it, or they end up slapping them in the face with the sidewalk. So don't do it."

When they had finished with the rules, Roger pointed out, "These rules are provided to do three things. First, it keeps you safe. It's very tempting to experiment and mess around, but until you are properly trained, this is very dangerous. Please do not attempt any WordCasting beyond these walls until you are properly trained and know how to control your gift and clean up afterwards.

"Second, these rules keep others safe. This is one of our top priorities. If we do this and an innocent person gets hurt, we have failed our primary mission.

"Finally, these rules keep everything in the right perspective. If we are loose with how we go about WordCasting, will our mission stay intact? Will we stay focused on what we're supposed to be doing? No. So stay focused at all times. Don't get me wrong. Curiosity can be a great thing, but if we let curiosity get the better of us, bad things… irreparable things…will happen. Understood?"

All nodded.

The remainder of their time was spent going over the rules again and answering any final questions they may have had for that day.

"Okay. Excellent job, children! Wonderful discussions and questions! Great interactions with each other! Tomorrow we will finally dig into The Text and begin learning the teachings of The Author."

The children all smiled. They stood up and left the Sanctuary, joining the rest of the Casters as they walked toward the magnificent double doors. Brandon quickly found Timothy and walked next to him.

"How did it go?"

"It went very well. It was a fantastic experience. I learned a lot."

"Great! What are you doing tomorrow?"

"He said we're going to start getting into The Text."

"What?! I didn't get to start that until day *three*! I had a different instructor then, though."

"Who was it?"

"Some really crabby lady named Martha something. I haven't seen her here in a while. You know, it's funny. The secretary at school kind of looks like her. I doubt she'd be able to do any Casting, though. The secretary, I mean. She has no heart whatsoever. *No* heart!"

Timothy could only chuckle.

If he only knew.

If he only knew.

Ralph was sitting alone on the sofa in his apartment. The lights were off and he had the television on, but he wasn't really watching. As he wiped powdered cheese from his hands onto his sweatpants,

95

his mind wandered.

Need hope.

Must find hope.

Find hope.

His brows furrowed and he clenched his fists.

Tomorrow. Find hope.

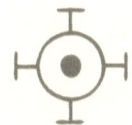

TRIALS AND TRAITORS

The next day, Timothy sat up straight at his desk, eagerly awaiting the start of the school day.

I feel great! I just have to be careful about what I think and read.

Last night, before bed, Timothy had been experimenting. He remembered the cautions from everyone at the Guild about not messing around with Casting outside the Guild, but he had to know. Were the symptoms really gone? Were things really different? He grabbed every book on his shelf and read through them on his bed. He checked his hands and smelled for smoke. For the most part, nothing happened. Occasionally, however, some lines caused strange things to happen.

After reading about a gust of wind, Timothy's right hand started glowing, slightly. He stared at it and smiled, then placed his hand back on the book. As soon as his palm touched the edge of the book, the book flew out of his hand and slammed into the wall across his room.

He also read a line about a horse running in circles. He was careful this time and was strategic about what he touched. He saw a Tyrannosaurus Rex figure on his desk.

That'll work. Let's see if anything happens.

He touched the figure and jumped back, afraid that it might start ricocheting around the room. To his surprise, nothing happened. He leaned in closer and examined the figure. Suddenly, the T-Rex started stretching its legs. Then it just took off! Well, it wasn't really going very fast, but it was moving!

Like an alcoholic duck with a gimpy leg, the T-Rex figure started racing around Timothy's desk in a circle. Timothy laughed loudly and clapped his hands.

"This is so cool!"

Suddenly, the T-Rex opened its mouth and whinnied like a horse! And it was loud!

Mrs. Walker came down the hall and knocked on Timothy's door, asking, "Uh…Timothy…What was that?"

"I'm just playing, Mom." He tried to imitate the horse whinny, but it wasn't anything near what the T-Rex produced. It worked, though.

"Okay, but get to sleep soon. You'll need energy for school tomorrow."

"Yes, mom."

Timothy smiled and stared at the T-Rex, which was still running in circles. Well, limping in circles.

"Now how do I get you to stop?"

Then there was the thing with the bed. After reading a line about a tree growing tall, he watched his right hand. Nothing happened, and he was getting tired, so he closed the book and placed his hands on the bed. He should have looked at his left hand, instead. As soon as he touched the bed, the four legs of his bed creaked and groaned. Timothy felt the bed shake and suddenly start flying upwards. He fell flat on his back and closed his eyes as the bed approached the ceiling. Everything stopped as suddenly as it started. Timothy blinked and slowly opened his squinting eyes. His nose was just barely touching the ceiling. Timothy slowly slid off his bed and down to the floor. He worked hard to figure out how to fix this one.

As he was falling asleep on his very crooked, but shorter, bed, he thought it strange that it would work for other books besides The Text.

I guess I need to ask about this tomorrow. What if I get in trouble for experimenting, though?

He tried not to think about it, but the occasional muffled whinny of a T-Rex-Horse-Thing made it tricky to fall asleep.

At school, Timothy was racing through the worksheets and even a pop quiz. He had learned enough last night to be able to avoid accidentally flinging pencils or making his desk slam into the ceiling.

A few more hours, then dinner, and then I get to go to the Guild! I can't wait. I haven't been this excited about anything for a long time! I'm still really nervous, though. I don't want to get in trouble, but I think I learned some valuable lessons on my own. It's such a wonderful feeling, though! That sensation from reading from The Text was unlike anything I've ever experienced.

Timothy laid his pencil down and sighed.

Maybe this was a good decision, after all. So cool.

"What's so cool?" The girl next to him whispered while papers were collected.

"Oh, sorry. I was talking to myself. The…The worksheet. It was a good one."

"Okay…Weirdo."

At least I didn't set your paper on fire today!

Timothy was ecstatic. For the first time in a long time, he could actually enjoy school! Also for the first time, Timothy was the first one out of the classroom when the bell rang.

At the dinner table, he scarfed down his food as his parents watched, each resting their forks on their plates as they considered the state of their son.

Mr. Walker asked, "Hungry?"

Timothy paused suddenly, put down his fork, and shook his head, "Just excited. I really like this Guild. I've already learned a lot."

"That's great, honey!" Mrs. Walker smiled, "Just don't choke on your food."

Timothy nodded and grunted "Mm-hmm" as he shoveled another fork-load into his mouth. He finished, put his dishes in the sink, then ran upstairs to do his homework before he had to leave.

Mrs. Walker looked over at Mr. Walker.

"It's amazing. Really."

He nodded, "I know. Quite a transformation. This move has been the best for him so far. And *we're* making more friends here than we have in any previous city. It's a real win-win here."

"You haven't said *win-win* for over ten years."

He dabbed his mouth with his napkin, smirked, and then said, "I'm sorry…?"

"No, it's cute." She smiled, but it quickly turned to a grin.

He pointed to her grin and said, "No, *that's* cute." He leaned over and kissed her on the cheek, then stood up to put his dishes in the sink.

In another part of town, Ralph dragged himself along the sidewalk of a small suburban neighborhood, muttering inaudible things to himself. The few people who passed by him looked away and did their best to avoid contact. He walked several blocks further and finally stopped outside house number 317. He sat down on the front step and looked across the street. He looked through the dining room window and saw a small girl with her mother at the dining table, working on homework. The little girl was about six-years-old. He sat there and watched for several minutes, eyes growing darker and his teeth gritting back and forth.

"Can't. N-Not yet."

"Hey, buddy! Get off my steps!"

Ralph scooted around to look up at the top of the stairs. A young man wearing black athletic pants, white sneakers, and a red and white hoodie stood in the doorway.

"Yeah, you! Clear out of here."

Ralph scooted back around and continued to watch the girl and her mother work. He gently placed his right palm down on the step where he was sitting.

"Creeper! I mean it. I'll call the—"

POW!

Somehow, the man's mailbox by his door managed to reach out and punch him in the nose.

The man grabbed his face and fell to his knees. Then he got up and yelled, "You got it, freak! I'm callin' the cops!" He slammed the door and Ralph heard three locks click. He smirked, then got up to leave.

"Soon. T-Timothy. Hope." Ralph twitched his shoulders briefly, took a final glance at 316, then walked away.

When the officers searched the area, there was no sign of any balding creeper wearing a red flannel shirt and blue jeans…and the mailbox certainly wasn't breaking any noses. In fact, it wasn't moving at all. It was a mailbox.

"I'm not crazy!"

As the group of young Casters began their walk down the spiral staircase, Barney smiled, nodded, and said, "Have a great evening everyone!"

Timothy turned slightly and smiled, waving. He could hardly contain his excitement. His usual behaviors of avoiding eye contact, shuffling his feet, and mumbling under his breath were hardly even evident today. They were still present, of course, but much less so than usual.

They all greeted Brian as they walked down the tunnel to the great, embellished doors. They marched into the Sanctuary and took their seats. Well, for some, it was more like skipping than marching. Some of the older Casters in the group even seemed to be doing more shuffling than marching. Still, they got there and sat down.

This evening's opening and announcements were just like yesterday's, including reminders of the efforts of Casters around the world. When the time came to break into groups, the Guild Master said, "Today, we will all stay in this room. We are going to give each of you a chance to read directly from The Text instead of from your copies. Speaking of copies, after today's meeting, anyone without a copy will receive one."

Brandon leaned over and whispered, "That's so unfair! I didn't get a copy until about a week after I started here. I wonder what changed.

Something's not right."

Timothy looked at the Guild Master's face as she spoke. As gentle, caring, and elderly as she appeared yesterday, she seemed completely different today. Her brows were furrowed, her eyes darkened as if in shadow, no smile graced her face, and her figure seemed even more bent and fragile than before. She kept glancing at Jude, too.

"I think you're right," Timothy whispered back, "Something's not right." He couldn't place it, but he just had a feeling, not a hunch like the principal gets, but just a down-in-the-gut feeling that something was up and they were not privy to the information. Perhaps she lost someone in her family? Perhaps she's retiring from her position soon? Perhaps...

Is she dying?

Timothy knew he couldn't just assume anything, so he pushed his thoughts on the issue to the back of his mind and just listened to her speak.

"Sir? Should we have gone to get Ralph before we left?"

The shadowy figure stopped climbing when he stood on top of a large boulder, and turned to face the red-haired woman who spoke.

"No, he would only get in the way. He can be useful, especially with his disguises, but lately he's been very distracted. It is best that we let him sit this one out. He's technically not a Runner, either. He does some errands, but he can't fight."

The woman nodded and continued climbing.

A bald man with a goatee and a skull tattoo on his neck asked, "Sir, how are we going to get in?"

"Through the back door, Tony." The figure began climbing up the next ledge.

"Sir? Back door?"

"Don't you worry. As long as our man keeps his promise, we'll have no trouble at all."

"What if he doesn't keep his promise?"

"Then he's dead."

"And what if he's already been found out?"

"Then he's really dead. But we shouldn't have any trouble. He's a good man to have on our side."

"Yes, sir." The bald man grabbed the next ledge and pulled himself up.

"With all of that being said, let us begin!" The Guild Master folded her hands together and managed a smile. She slowly took her seat next to an instructor, leaned over, and began whispering.

Jude stood up and began speaking, "Most of you already know this, so this is really only for the newest members. Bear with me for just a moment and we'll get going.

"The Author wrote The Text as a record of how the world and all of its members communicate. He wrote it so that anyone who read it would be able to do two things. First, understand how the world works. Second, to cast life into the world by speaking its language. You see, the symbols in this book represent hypothetical syllables, sounds, and meanings that The Author extracted from his experiences. When you read from this book, you are seeing what he saw, hearing what he heard, and speaking the language of the world around us.

"This is not a gift to be abused. This is not something to take for granted, either. There is very real power in this gift. There are very real consequences. When you cast life into an area, you save it, but at the same time, you open it up for destruction if someone were to use the gift for the wrong reason. This happens frequently. Understanding these things, you must read carefully, read slowly, and avoid getting distracted. If you misread The Text, bad things can happen. If you skip sections, bad things can happen. If you read it only for your...uh... your own purposes...bad things...uh...happen."

Jude shook his head and coughed slightly, and then said, "Excuse me. A bit of a dry throat."

He paused for a few seconds, then continued, "Today, each of you will come up and take turns reading the same passage so you gain a snippet of insight. You'll notice immediately that reading from The Text is quite a different experience than reading from your copies. That's because the symbols written in The Text were written by the hand of The Author, the first person to have the gift and the person with the most powerful thread of it in his veins. It is said that he even spoke life into The Text itself, giving the reader stronger insight, greater clarity, and greater results. The Text was needed by so many readers and was getting so worn that copies had to be made. The same effects come from reading your copy, but it's just not as strong. This is why it's such a privilege to be able to read from The Text itself.

"Okay! So let's get into it, then. Let's have everyone stand up and form a single-file line. Each of you will step up to the podium, read the line I point to, and return to your seat. It's quick and simple, but we wanted to give you all a little treat today."

The Casters all stood up and got into a line. The older Casters went first and it went back from there, ending with the newest members. Timothy found himself as second-to-last, Brandon standing right behind him. He looked back and saw that Brian had left the tunnel and was sitting at the back of the room to watch the proceedings.

The first Caster stepped up to the book and glanced at Jude. Jude pointed his finger at a certain line on the page. Of course, Timothy couldn't see where, since he was so far back. The Caster ran his finger across the line of symbols and lifted his hand as it glowed. He smiled and returned to his seat as the next Caster stepped up. She ran her finger across the symbol, but did not see her hand glow. Instead everyone else saw the top of her head glowing.

"Brandon, why did her crown glow instead of her hand?"

Brandon nodded, "Sometimes that happens. It depends on the Caster. She probably read more for the underlying meaning than what it literally said. The guy before her probably just read the line as it was written. My understanding is that when you read The Text literally, the Casting goes out. When you read for deeper meanings, the Casting goes *in* and benefits the Caster."

"Wow! That's awesome!"

Brandon smiled and nodded, "I know!"

The line moved forward as each Caster read the line and returned to their seat. Timothy's nervousness and excitement increased with each step he took toward The Text. As he walked forward, he looked around the room again. The Sanctuary seemed brighter than it did when they walked in earlier. He could see the ceiling now, which was impossible before. Gargoyles were all around the room, all appearing to be looking right at The Text.

A little creepy…

At last, it was Timothy's turn! As he stepped forward, however, he tripped on his shoelace, which had come undone. He caught himself, but knelt down to re-tie his shoe. He waved Brandon ahead of him. He was okay with waiting for one more person. There was something cool about being the last reader, too.

He stood up again and waited just a moment before Brandon

smiled and turned to go back to his seat.

Timothy's palms were sweating as he stepped up to the podium. He looked at Jude. Jude glanced at his watch, nodded, and smiled at Timothy.

"Ready?"

Timothy nodded his head vigorously, "Yes, sir!"

Jude pointed at a line on the page.

Wait. I thought he was pointing to a line further up the page. Is it different for each person? I thought he said we were reading the same line. Oh, well. Maybe I'm mistaken. This is still so cool.

He looked at the beginning of the line and placed his finger on it. He began to slide his finger across the page, but as he did so, the Guild Master stood up and exclaimed, "Jude! What are you doing?!"

Then there came flashes of lightning, rumblings, peals of thunder and a severe earthquake. No earthquake like it has ever occurred since mankind has been on earth, so tremendous was the quake.

It seemed to all be in slow-motion. By the time he finished reading the line, he finally heard the last syllable of the Guild Master's exclamation.

Jude sneered at the Guild Master.

Timothy's mouth fell open as he looked around as instructors jumped up and raced to the front, then he looked at his glowing hand.

Jude stepped quickly and kicked Timothy behind the knee with his left heel. Timothy felt his whole left side jolt and drop. He fell onto his back, and hard. Time dragged its knuckles as Timothy watched his hand float to the floor. With a dull thud, his arm and hand slapped the stone floor.

His hand was no longer glowing…and everyone stopped.

The principal sat in his recliner at home, reading a book and sipping on a cup of jasmine green tea with honey. He was an antique collector and an old record-player sat behind him against the wall. As he read his book and sipped his tea, he listened to the sweet sounds of violins, backed up with cellos and oboes. As the orchestra played his favorite classical pieces, his right foot tapped inside of its lined deer-hide slipper. He placed his mug down on the oak side table and into the subtle lighting of his amber-colored lamp. The principal tapped his fingers on his tongue to moisten them and then slowly turned the page.

Then the book fell out of his hand and slammed onto the floor.

The principal gripped the arms of his recliner and began breathing deeply. Grabbing his stomach with his right hand, he exhaled slowly and heavily. Looking around the room, his eyes landed on the empty fireplace before him.

Catching his breath, he clenched his hands into fists and forced himself to stand up.

"Honey," he called out, "I have to step out for a bit. I'll be back before too late."

Everything was quiet as the young Casters looked around to see what would happen.

Finally, the Guild Master moved toward Jude.

"What do you think you're doing?"

Jude looked around nervously. Apparently, he was hoping something else would happen. He let out an apprehensive giggle, then stepped up two steps, grabbing The Text, holding it close to his body.

He shook his head, then said, "You've been holding me back for too long! You've been holding *all of us* back for too long. I had an opportunity to realize my full potential and be something more than just a puppet that breathes life into rocks. I want to *command* the rocks! I want to have control of *something* for once!"

"So you're turning against us."

"Uh…yeah, I think that's pretty much what I just said."

"What about the lives of all the children here?"

"They've got the gift. Let them figure it out. They'll be fine. I honestly don't care what happens to them. I made a deal and I intend to see it through!"

Roger stepped forward and helped Timothy up. He said, "We can't let you take The Text."

Suddenly, they all heard a rumbling noise.

Jude grinned, "You have no say in the matter, anymore. I'm leaving. I'm taking this with me."

Roger said again, very calmly, "We can't let you do that."

The ground began to shake and everyone tried to find something to hold on to. Roger steadied himself and held Timothy by his shoulders. The ground shook more violently and stones from above began to fall. Still, no one ran.

Why aren't we getting out of here?

Timothy looked up just as a very large stone broke loose and began to fall, directly above him. His eyes grew wide and he tried to pull away, but Roger held him still and raised a hand. Roger met the boulder just above his head with his hand and a loud slap.

Immediately, the boulder broke into hundreds of small pieces, and instead of the boulder crushing them, the pieces scattered in all directions like nothing more than a light hail.

Oh. That's why.

Roger squeezed Timothy's shoulder slightly and stared at Jude.

"Put it back and end this nonsense!"

Jude thought for a moment and said, "Okay."

Roger paused, "Really?"

Jude laughed, "No, you moron! As soon as my new friends arrive, I'm out of here."

Another instructor stood up, "We could just crush you right now and it'll all be over."

Jude smirked, "Two problems with that. First, your boy there just cast into the mountain, and it's too big and too late for you to do anything to stop that, so you would all die, anyway. Second, I've got your precious book, so if you hurt me, you'll hurt the book! The only move you have is to run away…which I would really suggest you do before my friends get here…if you want to live."

The ground was still shaking and now loud crashes of thunder echoed throughout the Guild.

Roger asked, "Who are your friends?"

Jude turned as the wall behind him began to break open and into the room.

"See for yourself." Laughing, he ran over to the opening wall and waited.

Seconds later, a doorway burst open and light streamed into the room. Eight figures stepped into the room. The shadowy figure was the last one to enter, following the red-haired woman and the bald man with the skull tattoo.

As the ground continued to shake, the figures stepped toward the crowd of on-lookers.

The shadowy figure, who wore a black cloak and had a dark

bandana over his face, put his hands on his waist and exclaimed, "It's good to be back!"

Jude ran over and knelt in front of the figure. He held out The Text.

"Well done, Jude. You will be rewarded for you diligence and your patience. Our Lady will be very pleased, indeed."

Timothy looked up at Roger, but Roger looked even more confused than he did.

The Guild Master spoke, "You are not welcome here! Return The Text and leave!"

The figure turned to her, "Or what, old lady?"

The Guild Master tilted her head slightly, raised her brows, and said very calmly, "Or you will die."

"Ah, excellent. Then we will die together!" The figure pointed at The Guild Master and three of the group ran over to grab her. All of the instructors placed their hands on the walls, columns, or floor, but when they did, all of the intruders, except the main figure, pulled out automatic weapons. The instructors backed off and kept their hands up and off of things.

"Yes, we came prepared." The figure laughed. He reached over to take The Text.

Suddenly, a large object crashed into the figure's shoulder, throwing both Jude and the figure to the ground. The object flew past and was gone from everyone's sight within a split second. The Text was gone.

Timothy looked around the room, but couldn't see anything. The three Runners who went to grab The Guild Master stopped when they heard the loud crash of bodies. They spun around to see what happened. They pointed their weapons at the crowd as they looked to see if their leader was okay.

The figure slowly sat up and grabbed his right shoulder with his left hand.

"Argh! What was that?!"

Jude was laying against a column, stunned, but mostly conscious.

A gentle chuckle rose from the back of the Sanctuary. Timothy looked back.

Brian stood against the back wall. Beside him sat a wingless gargoyle. In its mouth was The Text. Brian took the book from the gargoyle, petted it on its head, and then looked back at the intruders.

"Like Roger said, we can't let you do that, Jude."

As the room continued to shake, and parts of the floor began to split apart, the intruders raised their weapons and pointed at Brian. He pointed at his right hand, which was already on the wall, and said, "Uh uh uhhh! Shouldn't do that!"

He paused, then yelled, "Sick 'em!"

Timothy watched in awe as, with a loud rumble, all of the gargoyles leapt from their positions, ran down the walls, and began charging the intruders.

Roger pulled Timothy back and pushed him down the main aisle as the Guild Master called out, "Get the children out of here!"

As Timothy charged down the aisle, he heard the automatic guns begin to fire. The intruders were attempting to shoot down the gargoyles. Pieces of rock flew off the gargoyles as they were hit, but they did not stop their assault.

Roger and several other instructors hurried to escort the children out the back of the Sanctuary to the tunnel doors. Brian met them there and began helping them through the doors. Timothy hung back to watch and make sure everyone was getting out. In the front of the

Sanctuary, the black-haired girl was immobile. In the chaos, a bench had fallen on her leg, pinned down by a large boulder that fell from the ceiling. He couldn't see for sure, but there seemed to be blood on her forehead, as if she had been hit on the head by a falling object.

The intruders had cut down two of the gargoyles, but several were left. As a tall man tried to reload his weapon, he was slammed by a gargoyle. He did not survive the collision.

Right before they could be hit, an intruder slammed his hand to the ground and a section of the floor grew straight up. The gargoyle had been right above this, so was lifted up and was split in half. As its halves hit the ground, it smashed into thousands of pieces.

Jude shook his head and looked up. He was staring right into the face of a growling gargoyle. Jude pushed himself back against the stone column behind him, wrapping his arms around the column as he slid further back.

"N- n- n- nice gargoyle!" Jude closed his eyes as he prepared to die.

Across the room, the bald man with the skull tattoo faced off with a gargoyle. He fired his last two bullets from his pistol into the gargoyles mouth. The gargoyle paused, choked, and spat the bullets out, leaping into the air toward the bald man. The man snarled, threw his pistol to the ground, and then reached his glowing hand underneath the incoming gargoyle's chin. With the strength of Samson, the bald man met the gargoyle's leap, twisted, and threw it over his head and into the column where Jude was sitting.

Jude cried out as the pieces of the thrown gargoyle and chunks of the column came crashing down around him. A large chunk of the column fell down on top of the gargoyle right in front of him, crushing it into several pieces.

Jude panted, looked around, then laughed as he stood up slowly.

The shadowy figure punched a glowing fist into an incoming gargoyles face, slamming it into the ground and breaking it apart. As he did so, he heard the crunch of another intruder's spine as she was hit by a gargoyle from behind.

He yelled, "Get the book, grab the old lady, and let's get out here!"

Timothy was waiting for a clear shot to get to the girl in the front, but he was simply running out of time, so he went for it. He raced toward the front, dodging falling rocks, stepping out of the way of gargoyles, and keeping his eyes focused on the injured girl. He slid in beside her, looked at her face, and checked her leg. She was still alive. There was a lot of blood on her head, but it was from being hit by a rock. Her leg appeared to be disfigured, so it was likely broken. He tried to move the rocks and free her foot, but everything was too heavy and he had no idea how to do the rock-flinging things that everyone else was doing.

"Timothy!"

He looked over to see the Guild Master.

She yelled, "Move over!" She slammed the end of her cane onto the ground as Timothy slid over. The stone floor beneath her cane appeared to bubble and then a shot like a torpedo sped across the ground and into the pile of rubble and bench trapping the girl's leg. As the bubble-torpedo-thing made contact with the mess, it kicked upward and launched everything up and into the far wall.

Roger arrived, picked up the girl, and ran with Timothy back to the exit. As they ran, he turned back to look at the Guild Master. Three of the intruders were upon her now, grabbed her, and started pulling her up the stairs.

Why isn't she fighting them? Why isn't anyone helping her?

They rounded the corner and Brian stopped them.

"Hold on. I've got an idea. Step back."

He lovingly caressed the doors and whispered, "I'm sorry, you beautiful things, you. The time has come, however, and I'm sure your craftsman would do the same thing in my place."

He tucked the book under his arm, placed his hands on the doors for a few seconds, and then stepped back.

As the walls around them continued to shake and split, the doors began to move. It was as if they were stretching, bending, and twisting. When Timothy next looked, the doors had become like wooden soldiers. Off their hinges, standing tall, the enormous wooden doors appeared to be even bigger than before. Though they did not have faces, arms, legs, and a torso were clear. The gold trimmings had become golden armor!

The two wooden soldiers in golden armor took large, heavy steps toward the Sanctuary and turned their stride into a run.

The four remaining intruders, who had just destroyed the last gargoyle, turned to see the charging soldiers.

Jude ran over and hid behind the bald man with the skull tattoo and said, "I hate splinters."

The shadowy figure, the red-haired woman, the bald man, a dark-haired bodybuilder, and Jude walked backwards toward the opening with the Guild Master, who looked angry, but was not fighting.

The shadowy figure leaned over to Jude and said, "Get the book or the deal is off."

Jude looked at him like he had just said the worst possible set of words a human could say. He sighed, then nodded and ran to the far wall and toward to the back of the room.

As the wooden soldiers continued their charge, the dark-haired man stepped forward and said, "I've got this."

Lunging forward, the man placed his hand on the ground and sneered at the soldiers.

As the soldiers ran, large spikes and walls of rock shot up from the ground in front of them. One soldier slammed into a rock wall, breaking the obstacle apart. The other spun around a spike as if it was playing football, and then pressed on. Leaping, twisting, smashing, and crashing, the soldiers broke through everything the man presented. Unfortunately, they did not go through without taking a few blows. Large chunks of wood and armor flew off as they blasted through the obstacles.

Timothy watched in amazement as they destroyed or easily avoided whatever came up. Then his eyes caught Jude, who was running along the side wall toward them. He stopped a few yards away, panted, then said, "Please just give me the book."

Brian smirked, "Ah, we're using manners now, are we?"

Jude shook his head as he leaned on the wall, "You have always had such a good heart, Brian. It'd be a shame to lose it."

Brian glared as he tried to determine the meaning of this statement, then his eyes shot open and his body slammed onto the floor. As soon as he hit the floor, a stone spike protruded from the wall where he was just standing.

Jude taunted, "Oh, good, you get to keep it for a little longer."

Brian slammed his hand on the floor and a large pillar shot up from the ground right in front of Jude, slamming into his jaw.

Jude fell backwards and held his jaw, "Fine, let's play that way, then!"

Roger pulled Timothy back out of the way and toward the exit.

Jude slammed his hand on the ground in front of him and a large slab of stone lifted Brian up and held him up against the wall behind him, right next to the protruding spike. Several spikes flew up in many directions and blocked Brian into a sort of thin, stone cage. Brian could have broken through it, but his hands were pinned in the wrong direction against his chest.

Back in the Sanctuary, the dark-haired man yelled, "Alright, try this!" He placed both hands on the ground and spread them apart. The ground in front of the soldiers split open, leaving a large, seemingly-bottomless pit. The first soldier did not have time to react and fell in. The second soldier leapt over the pit and landed on the other side. As the floor slid closed and swallowed the first soldier, the second soldier lifted its arms to prepare to attack the man. The man caused a large slab of stone to slide up over him like a shield, but the second soldier slammed down on top of the stone slab, breaking through and crushing the man underneath.

Roger laid the girl against the doorway and told Timothy to stay with her. He ran over to try to help Brian, but Jude sent up a wall that collided with Roger's chest, knocking him back and leaving him breathless. Timothy knelt by Roger as he watched Jude move the rock cage in such a way that the spike pried the book from Brian's arms, but so that Brian's hands were still pinned.

Jude walked over slowly and picked up the book, and with a sneer said, "Thanks for your…*cooperation*."

Feeling a renewed sense of urgency from seeing the others pinned or brushed aside, Timothy clenched his fists and yelled at the top of his lungs. He leaned forward and charged, throwing himself against Jude, who didn't have time to respond. Either Timothy was stronger than he realized or Jude was just weak, but they both went down and the book flew from Jude's hand. Timothy sat up and found that he was now between Jude and the book. As Jude stood up and walked toward him with a wicked grimace on his face, Timothy scooted back toward the book.

He didn't realize the book was open.

He didn't realize his finger was right on the symbols.

He didn't even realize that his hand slid across the page.

Jude was right on him and leaned over and grabbed the collar of Timothy's shirt to pull him up. Timothy tried to squirm away, but couldn't, so he raised his hands up and tried to push Jude's face away.

He didn't realize his hand was glowing. Neither did Jude.

As soon as Timothy's hand touched Jude's face, what felt like a bolt of lightning coursed through Jude's temples, down his throat, and into his chest. Jude threw himself backwards, curled up on the floor, and grabbed his chest.

Timothy sat still when he landed back on the floor.

What just happened?

He looked back and then realized what he had done. He tried to recall what his hand had just slid over. As rubble continued to slide around and fall from the walls and ceiling, the words came back to him.

All my enemies will be overwhelmed with shame and anguish; they will turn back and suddenly be put to shame.

Jude stood up slowly, steadied himself, still clutching his chest, and limped over to Timothy and the book.

"Enough of these games, boy. Move or be moved!"

Timothy could only sit there, waiting to see what Jude would do. Timothy didn't know how to control the gift, yet. He didn't know what to look for in the book. He didn't know how to make things move. He couldn't defend himself against Jude, so he sat there, bracing for anything, and slid the book closer to himself.

The shadowy figure had stepped forward and was dueling with the second soldier. He matched each of the soldier's steps with an obstacle or shift in the ground. The soldier matched each move with a counterbalanced step. Neither could advance and neither was willing to retreat.

"Jude! Grab the book and let's go!" Behind the figure, the Runners were taking the Guild Master through the opening and around the corner.

Jude leaned over and said, "I will not be thwarted by some slab of meat who is trying to call himself a Caster. You will not take this opportunity away from me!"

With that, Jude's fist connected with the side of Timothy's head. As Timothy's vision blurred and the room started to go black, he watched Jude grab the book and run to the front of the Sanctuary. He watched as the shadowy figure sent a stone spike through the soldier's wooden chest and split him in half, sending splinters and golden armor in all directions. He watched as the intruders escaped through the back opening. He watched as Jude placed his hand on the wall and caused the rest of the wall to collapse on top of the opening. He watched them get away. He watched them get away with everything.

Suddenly, a very violent shake caused a bench to fall on top of Timothy. As he heard and felt a loud crack in his chest, his head, torso, and right arm were trapped. He cried out in pain, closing his eyes, thinking of his parents. He didn't want it to end like this.

What about not having to fight? What about having time to learn?

This was a mistake. This was a huge mistake.

As the room continued to collapse around him, Timothy did all he could to not pass out.

Could it really be over just like that?

He heard a very large crash behind him as more of the walls collapsed.

I hope the others got out safely.

Poor Brian.

Poor Roger.

Poor…girl.

He never even caught her name. He even felt sorry for the fallen intruders. Such a dark fate. Such a meaningless fight.

Why?

As his mind drifted away to a dark, quiet, and peaceful place, he began to hear music. At least, he thought it was music. It was strange music…but nice. The lyrics were even more strange. He tried to make sense of them as he drifted out of consciousness.

Jubilee! Aye a' get jubilee.

That wasn't right. That couldn't be right.

Ah, it was a song about him. How pleasant!

Timothy!

I'll get Timothy. You help Roger. I'll get the children.

Such a beautiful composition! What elegant harmonies! Timothy felt like he was floating. Then he felt nothing.

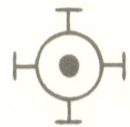

THE NEXT LEG

Timothy.

There was that music again.

The ground wasn't shaking anymore. The darkness he saw had now become a deep, reddish glow.

Slowly and carefully, he fluttered his eyes open. Blinking repeatedly, he allowed his eyes to adjust to the sunlight.

Sunlight!

"Wha- Where am I?"

Timothy slowly moved his head around to see his environment.

"What happened?"

"You're waking up. Good! You've got a nasty bruise, Timothy, but otherwise, you appear to be in good health."

Timothy squinted as he looked up and saw the principal's face staring back at him.

"Don't try to get up, yet. I suspect this is the first time you've been knocked out."

Timothy winced and sighed, "Yes, sir." He laid his left hand against his face. Yes, it was all starting to come back to him…feeling, that is.

"Ah! Ow!" Timothy grabbed his face and started to roll around. He had never been hit like that before. As far as he could remember, he had never been hit before in any capacity except falling or in sports.

The principal handed Timothy a bag of ice wrapped in a few sheets of paper towels. Timothy gently pressed it on his face and looked around again.

"Welcome to my humble abode. We've been watching over you three all night. You're the second to wake up."

Timothy reached out with his right hand and felt the back of a soft, cushioned sofa. He saw the sunlight streaming through the window. The wind was blowing, but gently. Trees swayed back and forth and the subtle ringing of wind chimes was carried past the window. He looked to his left, past the principal, and saw Roger in a recliner, hugging pads against his chest and staring into the fireplace where a small fire had been built.

Jackets, blankets, and their shoes were set on or by the loveseat across the area rug.

"Are you thirsty?"

Timothy stared at the ceiling and nodded slowly. The principal left for a moment and returned with a glass of water.

"Sir…"

"Yes?"

"What happened to the girl?"

"We took Mindy to the hospital. Her wounds were beyond any of our skills and experience. She'll be okay, though." What he didn't tell Timothy was that she was in a coma and the doctors didn't know if she would come out of it. It was too soon to tell him that, though.

Timothy nodded and then asked, "Brian?"

The principal's face suddenly appeared to age and darken. It was as if he had stepped under a thickly covered tree on a sunny day while aging by thirty years in a matter of seconds. He shook his head.

"When we found you all, he was already...gone." He struggled to keep back tears, and then he sighed heavily and continued, "The stones around him had cracked and fallen, but trapped him, and the weight was too much for him. We tried to go back for him after we got you three safe, but as we started re-entering, everything just collapsed. Even parts of the mall caved in. Brian was the only one of us who... perished. Several instructors and students were injured in the mall collapse. Most of them are hospitalized right now. Casters are working to clean up the mess and make it look like a sinkhole collapsed while emergency responders search for survivors."

"What about my parents?"

"I...already spoke with them."

"Missing?!"

The principal folded his hands together and nodded as he stood in the Walker family's living room, "Yes, ma'am. Unforeseeable event. We're all so sorry. There was a sinkhole and it took most of the mall with it, including the Writer's Guild meeting room. They're searching for survivors. Most people got out. Timothy was not among them."

Mr. and Mrs. Walker cried into each other's shoulders.

"Keep your hopes up. Timothy is a strong boy. I'm sure he'll be okay."

"Why can't I go to them?"

"It's too dangerous. If they know, the enemy will find out. Your parents must not find out the truth or they will become targets. Besides that, you injured Jude, or so I'm told. He probably thinks you were crushed. If he finds out you're alive, he will hunt you."

Timothy grimaced at the thought of letting his parents believe such a lie, but he understood that it had to be this way. This was overwhelming.

I wish this would all go away. I didn't want any of this. I wanted things to change. I wanted things to be better! I wanted to help people! I didn't want this!

"Timothy, I'm so sorry this happened this way. Know that however you're feeling, you're not alone. We all wish this could have been avoided."

Timothy remembered something, "Those were Twisters, right?"

"Yes. Runners, specifically. Runners do the real dirty work."

"I thought the Guild was supposed to be protected. Twisters weren't supposed to be able to get in."

"That's true. On their own, they can't get in there. They have to be let in. That's how it always has been. One Twister succeeded many years ago, but he didn't have to destroy anything. He snuck in when a Caster opened the door. He didn't take anything, either. It was odd. They discovered him as he was leaving and kicked him out, but since he hadn't done anything to them, they didn't do anything to him. Those were the days when honor meant something to both sides."

Timothy lay there for a few moments, and then asked, "What now? Where do we go from here?"

The principal smiled and said, "*You* rest. You're not going anywhere until you're all better. As for the rest of us, we have to regroup and discuss what needs to happen."

The doorbell chimed.

The principal left the room and Timothy listened as the door swung open and the principal spoke with someone with a younger-sounding voice. The door closed and the principal called out, "Timothy, you have a visitor."

Timothy fought the headache and sat up. Brandon walked through the doorway with a grin on his face.

"Dude! How are you feeling?"

Timothy winced, "Like a billy goat that's had too many challengers. Like a Sherpa that climbed Mount Everest, then slipped and bounced all the way back down. Like…Ow, my head!…I've been better. How are you?"

Brandon showed Timothy a bandaged arm, "From what I hear, I was one of the lucky ones. But dude! You're a hero!"

"What? No. I didn't do anything."

Brandon chuckled and looked at the principal, "Didn't do anything, he says! Didn't do anything! Pah! In the eyes of all the young Casters, you went all Hercules all up in Jude's face! They have you doing a backflip and karate kicking him in the eye and through the nose."

"I didn't do any of that."

"Doesn't matter! Whatever you did, everyone's impressed. Dude!"

Timothy tried to smile, but his face hurt too much, so he lowered his head and pressed the ice pack against his cheek again.

Brandon sat down on the floor next to the sofa and looked up at the principal, then asked, "So, what's our next move?"

The principal smirked. "*Our* next move?"

"Yeah. Timothy got to be a hero. My turn! Let's go. I'm ready to fight some Twisters and save the day!"

The principal laughed and said, "I appreciate your enthusiasm, but I'm afraid you're both too inexperienced to go after them. You're safer here. We're having a meeting later today to discuss what we need to do. You don't have to worry about it, though. Please…choose the safe path."

Brandon frowned and slowly shook his head back and forth, "Alriiiiight…"

"Eric…" Roger slowly turned his head toward the principal.

The principal walked over.

Roger pointed at himself and shook his head, "I'll keep an eye on them. There's no way I can venture out tonight. I need another day or two before I can be ready to even drive."

"Okay. Thank you, Roger. Tanya was going to come in and keep watch, but this would free her up, which we both know would be of great benefit." He turned to the boys and said, "She's the kind of person who could win a game of dodge ball against a team of fifty people…by herself."

"Whoa…" came the voices of both boys, together.

"Yeah, Whoa."

The shadowy figure sat back in his leather recliner and stared at the new book on his pedestal. The room was dark, but drips of water could be heard in the corner, splashing against the stone floor of this dimly-lit chamber. A fire crackled behind the figure, keeping his face in shadow.

A large wooden door swung open across the large expanse of room. The ominous echo indicated that the room was mostly void of furnishings.

A man wearing a black baseball cap, brown leather vest, and blue jeans stepped into the room and said, "Team two reporting in, sir."

"How did it go?"

"It is done."

"And?"

"Not a trace remains."

"Very good. Debrief and feast. We have done all we need to do, so now we play defense and see what happens."

The man nodded and closed the door behind him as he left.

Roger limped backed into the room with a tray of sandwiches and drinks and said, "Alright boys, dinner time."

He placed the tray on a small card table they had set up earlier to play games. The boys each grabbed a sandwich and bottle of water from the tray and began to eat. Roger sat back down in the recliner with his food and paused.

Timothy looked over and asked, "Are you okay?"

Roger didn't answer for a few seconds, then lifted his head and said, "Yes, I'm fine. Just an upset stomach, I guess. It started earlier this afternoon. I'll be okay."

Timothy nodded and went back to his sandwich.

The front door opened slowly and then was shut, and the three of them watched the doorway. The principal stepped through the door, then paused and looked at each of them. He half-smiled to the boys and walked over to Roger. He leaned over Roger and whispered into his ear.

The sandwich slipped from Roger's fingers and fell apart as it hit the floor.

Roger looked up and asked, "All of them?"

"All who we know in this area...except Tanya. She's the one who told me. I had a bad feeling before I left to go to the meeting, but I couldn't tell if that was just sadness from last night's events or if it was something new."

Roger placed his hands over his face and began to weep.

The principal walked over to the boys and said, "It's no longer safe for any of us. I have just received news that every Caster who was supposed to go the meeting except for Tanya, Roger, and me, have been...attacked."

Brandon started, "By attacked, you mean..."

"Murdered...yes."

Brandon jumped up, "What about my parents?!"

"The only people who were supposed to go to the meeting were on the local council for Casters. Jude used to be a member, so he must have given names and addresses away. Tanya managed to escape. Your parents are safe, Brandon. As are yours, Timothy. For now...and that 'for now' is the problem. You can't go back to them, yet. We have to find a way to keep you safe, so I need both of you to stay here tonight. I will call your parents, Brandon, and convince them to let you stay. Tomorrow, we'll see what we can do. I have a duty to fulfill at school, but Roger can keep an eye on you until I get back."

Timothy grimaced and asked, "So how many Casters are still out there?"

The principal answered, "Well, there are millions all over the world, but locally, there were only a handful to start with. Now, we have no idea who is still here. I heard that some left town after last night's attack. Others have passed on by other means. However many remain is unknown to us. That's one thing we have to figure out tomorrow."

"Why didn't they come after you, Roger, or us?"

The principal thought for a moment, and then said, "I honestly don't know. I have to go make a few calls. I'll bring blankets and pillows for you in a little bit. Then we all have to settle in and try to sleep, as impossible as such a feat seems at this point."

When the principal left the room, Timothy turned to Brandon and said, "I wish we could do something."

Brandon nodded, "Me, too. I know enough Casting to get by, but I don't think I'd be able to take on anyone who can take out that many Casters in one night. I'm actually scared now…and I don't get scared by very much."

Roger turned to them and said, "It's okay to be scared. That's how you know you're not dreaming. In a dream, you can do anything, be anything, and keep coming back to life. In reality, as awesome as the gift is, we're still very limited in what we can do…and we have only one chance at life. Being scared keeps us grounded and keeps us sane. Just don't let the fear control you. If fear controls you instead the other way around, it's all over."

Brandon nodded, then asked, "So what can we do?"

Roger replied, "Wait. Hope."

"Hope." Ralph sat down outside, beneath the principal's living room window and sighed. He was out of breath, exhausted and sweaty. He leaned his head back against the wall and waited.

Timothy was the last one to fall asleep. Roger was supposed to keep watch, but his injuries made him too weak, and he fell asleep soon after Brandon did. Timothy tried to stay up for the sake of the others, but eventually, the silence of the room and the gentle breathing of the other two sent him away into slumber. As his eyes closed, he heard a click.

Probably just the fire.

Then he heard a creaking noise.

Probably just the wind moving a branch outside.

Then he smelled sweat and dirt.

Probably...actually, I don't have an explanation for that.

He slowly opened his eyes, but they shot open the rest of the way when he saw Ralph standing just a few feet away from him. He jumped up and pushed back against the couch and was about to call out to Roger, but Ralph held up both of his hands.

He whispered, "Please! No wake! Talk to you! Talk!"

Timothy whispered back, "You just want to talk? How can I trust you?"

Ralph's eyes seemed to search for the answer as they swept back and forth. He smiled gently as an answer came to him.

"You...alive."

"Well, that's true. You haven't hurt me, yet."

"Me hurt? No. Twisters."

"Uh...*you're* a Twister."

"Not choice. Not no more. Can't out. Need Hope."

"What do you want?"

"Hope."

"You've said this before, but I don't understand!"

Ralph pursed his lips and ground his teeth, searching for a way to tell Timothy.

He pointed to Timothy and said, "You...Hope."

"*I'm* Hope?"

Ralph grinned and nodded.

"How am *I* Hope?"

"You free."

"I free who? I free you?"

Ralph clasped his hands together and grinned wider than before.

"Yes!"

"Free you from what?"

"Contract."

"So…you want me to free you from being a Twister?"

"Yes!"

"Wait, wait! How am I supposed to do that? I don't know how to Cast and I don't have any weapons! I've only read three lines from the book so far…which was stolen by *your* people, by the way!"

"I know…I help you."

"So you'll help me if I help you?"

"No. I help you…SO you help."

"You're going to help us against your people so that I'll help you? Do I understand you?"

Ralph was almost in tears, "Yes!"

Timothy stared at Ralph for several moments, and then asked, "Why?"

"Twisters n- n- not help. Casters kind."

"Why me? Why not ask someone who has actually had experience? What makes me so different that you'd ask me to help you?"

Ralph smiled gently, knowingly, and nodded.

He pointed to Timothy's forehead and said, "Open mind."

Then he pointed to Timothy's chest, tapped it twice and, as he did so, said, "Most important: Clean heart. Curious. Innocent. Does good."

"How is my heart cleaner than any of the other Casters'?"

"New."

"So you need someone who is new to Casting?"

"Yes. Better learning. Better molding. Better Casting."

Timothy shook his head, "Better molding? You intend to mold me?"

"Not me! No! Greater men."

"Roger and my principal are great men."

Ralph shook his head, "Greater."

"When do you need me to go?"

Ralph wrung his hands nervously and shrugged as he said, "Now." It was almost like a question, but Timothy knew it was more of a suggestion—not quite a command, either.

"Ralph, I'm only twelve-years-old! My parents think I'm missing or worse, everyone around me is hurting, and I just watched people *die*! I'm not sure I would be of any use."

"Clean heart. Hope. Please!"

Timothy put his third bag of ice (which had since turned into a plastic bag of cold water) against his face and said, "I'm still not sure I can trust you."

Ralph paused for a moment, and then held out both of his hands, palms facing Timothy, as if saying *Hold on*. He reached out and touched the bag of cold water. Slowly, the water returned to ice and Timothy experienced immediate relief.

Ralph stepped back and said, "I help now. No more hurt."

Timothy sighed and stared at his blanket-covered feet.

So it's important for you to always listen to that little voice and do what is good.

Timothy looked at Ralph's pleading face, looked at Roger, looked at Brandon, and then looked at the floor.

After what seemed like an hour (though it was only a few seconds), Timothy whispered to himself, *Yes, mom.* Then he looked up at Ralph and whispered, "Okay. Let's go."

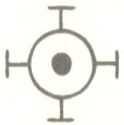

DANGER DANNY'S

"Where are we?" Timothy looked out the window at all of the neon signs and darkened sidewalks as they slowly drove through a part of town several miles beyond where Timothy had ever explored with his parents when they were checking out the area before they moved. In fact, they were advised to *avoid* that part of town. It was nearly two in the morning and only a handful of people were out and about. These weren't the kinds of people you would want to be around for too long, either.

Rough. Scary.

"Danger."

"We're in danger? Great! Thanks! That's helpful. We're off to a great start. I trusted y—"

Ralph shook his head and pointed to a sign hanging above a bar.

Danger Danny's Draughts 'n' Darts

"Oh."

Ralph pulled the car over to the curb and shifted to park.

"In Danger. Two white men. One b-bald. Other has…swords 'n stuff. They help. Must."

"Wait, You're not going in?"

"They…kill me."

"I'm not allowed to go into a *bar*!"

"Eye c-contact. Bar tender. You be fine. M-Me…there." He pointed to a parking spot in front of a clothing store about half of a block down.

"Are you sure about this?"

Ralph nodded.

Timothy inhaled…exhaled. He unbuckled himself, opened the door, and stepped out of the car and then shut the door behind him.

Well, he's had ample opportunity to hurt me by now. He could have killed me at the house if he wanted to.

Ralph pulled away and slowly drove toward the parking spot. Timothy watched him park and turn off the car.

"Psst!"

Timothy spun around, searching frantically for the source of the noise.

"Timothy! Over here by the news vendor."

Timothy squinted as he looked past the metal newspaper stand to find the person talking to him. The voice sounded familiar. Slowly, Brandon stood up and leaned his bike against the stand. Timothy glanced over his shoulders, then walked over to Brandon.

"What are you doing here?"

Brandon scratched his head, "I was wondering the same about you."

"It's a long story. I have to talk to two guys in here. They may be able to help."

"Who is the guy you were with? I heard you leave the house, so I grabbed my bike and followed you two here."

"You followed us here on your bike?!"

"Puh-lease…my grandmother scoots around with her walker faster than that old guy drives!"

Timothy tried to muffle his laughter, but ended up snorting. Out of the corner of his eye, he saw three large men with tattoos, cigarettes and spiked gloves turn the corner. The boys hadn't been seen though…yet.

Timothy nodded and said, "We probably shouldn't be here."

"You think?"

"Let's go in and find those guys before there's trouble."

In a mocking voice, Brandon whispered, "Oh, okay, so let's go walk into a bar! That'll keep us out of trouble for sure!"

Timothy smirked, "If you don't want to come, you don't have to."

"Oh, no! I don't mind! I love a good adventure! I was just messing with you. Let's go. I don't think I can take my bike in, so I'll leave it by the door. I'm sure it'll be gone when we come back out. That would figure!"

Brandon leaned his bike against the wall and they stepped into the bar.

Inside, both boys winced and squinted as the cigarette smoke caused their eyes to burn. Blinking and scanning the room, they saw only about seven people scattered throughout the room. They walked up to speak to the bartender.

"Ah, what've we got here? Sorry, kids, no minors allowed."

Brandon piped up, "Ah, but see we don't work in the mines, so we're okay."

"Funny. Really. My sides—look at them—they're splitting wide open. Seriously, you'll have to leave."

Timothy wanted to make and keep eye contact, but the smoke was stinging his eyes too badly. He felt incredibly awkward, but he forced himself to sit up on the bar stool and look at the bartender.

"What's with the puppy dog eyes? I don't got any more soup for you, either."

Timothy readjusted his seat and tried again.

"Am I supposed to be impressed by something? I told you two that you need to scram. I can't serve youngin's."

Timothy whispered, "Look into my eyes."

Brandon muttered, "This just got real awkward."

Timothy threw his elbow into Brandon's side. Brandon chuckled, grabbed his side, and tried not to fall off the seat he had taken.

"Stop! That tickles." Brandon crossed his arms on the bar and watched.

Timothy shook his head, "Please?"

The bartender was perplexed, but raised his brow, shook his head slightly, and said, "Okaaaay? Are you gonna hypnotize me or somethin'? Some kind of magic trick?"

He leaned over and peered into Timothy's eyes. As he did so, his expression changed. Both Timothy and the bartender saw the golden glittering—in each other's eyes!

The bartender is a Summoned?

The bartender leaned over closer and asked, "In that case, how I can be of assistance?"

Brandon said, "I have no idea. I just followed him."

Timothy rolled his eyes and smiled. "I was sent to find two men who may be able to help us. There's been some trouble."

"Two men, huh? One of 'em is bald? The other throws daggers at my dart board, leaving large holes in my walls that I have to fix every other week?"

"Sounds about right, sir."

"Gotcha. You'll find them in the corner of the bar to your left, around the corner here."

Both boys said their thanks, the bartender winked and went back to work, and the boys walked around the bar. The corner was not as well lit as the other sections, which Timothy assumed was the reason the two men were there. He could see two figures. One was obviously bald. It was hard to tell, but the other appeared to have dreadlocks.

The boys looked at each other, shrugged, and quietly stepped toward the men, listening.

The bald man asked in a deep, smooth voice, "I don't think I've ever even thought to ask you this, but why *do* you have so many bladed weapons?"

The man with the dreadlocks replied, "I don't know. I've just always been fascinated by them."

"I've always been fascinated by stampeding wildebeests…but I don't have a collection of stampeding wildebeests. Do you see me walking around practicing using my stampeding wildebeests, talking about my stampeding wildebeests? No. Do you know why?"

"Uh…'cause you're allergic to hair?"

The bald man growled.

"Come on! You know that was funny! You totally set yourself up for that one."

"I won't deny that, but I don't have to sit here and take it."

"You're standing."

"I don't have to stand here and take it."

"Fine! Stand over there if you want more, 'cause I can do this all day!"

"Yeah, because you never do anything else!"

"Aha! So you're not blind! You would have to see things to know that…"

"Did you just confess to not doing anything?"

"I…Touché!" He reached his hand out in front of the bald man's face and said, "High five!"

"Ha. That's a leg-slapper right there."

"Don't you mean knee—"

"Shut it. Just…don't."

Brandon stepped forward and called, "Excuse me?"

The man with the dreadlocks jumped and spun around, "Whoa! Hi there! Kids in a bar…that's…unethical. How long have you been standing there?"

"Three minutes and thirteen seconds. I saw them when they came in."

The man with the dreadlocks spun back around, "How do you do—nevermind."

Timothy spoke next. "Please! You have to help! The Guild was destroyed, many people were hurt, and some people were killed! They took the Guild Master!"

The older, bald, blind man leaned forward and said, "We heard about the Guild. We're very sorry for the loss. However, you must relax, dear boy! The Guild Master is very skilled. She'll be fine…as long as they didn't take—"

Brandon interrupted. "They took The Text, too."

Both men sat down in a nearby booth to collect their thoughts. Finally, the bald man spoke, saying, "Grab your gear, friend! I hope you brought your hiking shoes, boys."

Brandon tilted his head and asked, "Just like that?"

The men stood up and said together, "Just like that."

The bald man grabbed a brown and black backpack, a black touring cap, and a wooden walking stick with a wolf head carved into the top. The other man grabbed a self-defense baton, a set of four daggers, a leg holster of throwing knives, three pocket knives, and a blue messenger bag. Timothy suspected that there were more knives in the bag. As they stepped toward the door, the three men from the sidewalk appeared in the doorway.

Timothy looked at the two men and said, "Runners! They've been chasing down and murdering Casters all over town!"

The man with the dreadlocks said, "Relax, kid. They're not Runners. They're just thugs. They're not here for you. They're here for me."

The bald man asked, "Again?"

"What can I say? I'm a popular guy!" He grinned and stepped forward.

The first man called out, "Hey! Jackal!"

The man leaned over and told the boys, "My real name is Jeff, but he keeps calling me Jackal. I don't know…I kind of like the nickname. It could be worse!" He stood up again and shouted, "Yo! Fat-head!"

The three men walked around the bar and toward the group.

"It's time for your weekly back-breaking."

"Come on guys! Haven't I broken your backs enough already? When will this game end?"

"Not us! You!"

"Oh, well that's different. I don't really feel like it today, though. Sorry, guys. I've got stuff to do."

"You ain't goin' nowhere!"

Jeff smiled, "Well that's very contradictory and confusing, isn't it? You just gave me permission to leave! Thanks, guys!"

"What?"

"By saying 'You ain't goin' nowhere,' you're saying that I am *not* not going someplace. Therefore, you're actually saying that I'm *going* someplace. How kind!"

"Shut up and prepare to hurt!"

"I didn't realize any preparation was involved! Did you know that, William?"

The bald man chuckled and said, "I was not aware, no."

The angry thug leader started marching toward Jeff.

Jeff shrugged and said, "That's a shame…"

Just before the thug reached him, Jeff tapped a beam above his head. The beam squeezed and swung down, colliding with the thug's forehead. The other two thugs ran over, but with a grab with his left hand, a punch with his right hand, a step with his right foot, and a jab with his right elbow, all three thugs were on the ground.

"A real shame. Tell you what. I'm feeling generous, so I'll give you numbskulls to the count of three," he raised a hand and between his fingers rested three dartboard darts with metal tips, "to get out of here and not come back."

The thugs stood up slowly and scowled at Jeff. The leader called him "a freak!"

"One." He flicked one dart down toward his palm, out of view.

The thugs started backing up.

"Two." He flicked a second dart down.

The thugs bolted toward the door, pushing each other out of the way.

"Three."

As the three thugs threw the door open and rushed out, Jeff flicked his wrist and three darts flew out the door. As the door slammed close, everyone in the bar could hear the three men cry out in pain.

Jeff smiled, "That's a pain in the rump!"

William said, "That wasn't funny," but he was grinning.

As the group left the bar, Jeff called out to the bartender, "This one's for you, Keith! Put it on my tab! Thanks, bud!" His whole body except his left arm was out the door and he flicked his left wrist as he continued to step forward. With a ***thud-d-d***, a dagger stuck in the exact center of the dartboard, which hung on the wall all the way across the room.

As the door bounced closed, the bartender leaned on the bar, smirked, and shook his head.

Outside, the group paused at the bottom of the steps. As Timothy and the two men surveyed the scene, they could hear Brandon talking.

"Yep, I called it! Bike equals gone. Knew that was going to happen. Knew it!"

William asked, "Who sent you to find us?"

"Just great. Birthday present, too."

"The man in the car down there." Timothy pointed to the parked car down the road. The group walked down the sidewalk to the car. It was empty!

Jeff's right hand slowly reached for the baton tucked into his belt.

Timothy shook his head, "I don't understand. He was here in the car. He said he'd wait."

Jeff walked over to the driver's seat. No one was there. He inspected the handle on the outside of the car.

"William, keep your freaky eyes open. There was a struggle."

Brandon rubbed the back of his neck, "I thought he was blind!"

William nodded, "I *am* blind, but that does not mean I can't *see*."

Jeff crawled into the car, but called out a muffled, "Hence, Freaky!"

Brandon looked at Timothy and said, "Okaaayyy. Are you guys, like...*on* something?"

William chuckled, "No, dear boy. Now is not the time to explain, however. I will tell you, when it is necessary to tell you. Jeff, whatever happened, they're gone. Who was it who brought you here?"

Timothy replied, "His name is Ralph, but that's all I know."

The three on the sidewalk heard a thump as Jeff jumped and hit his head on the car ceiling and called out, *"Ralph?!"* He crawled back out and stuck his head over the top of the car, "Creepy old guy who only wears flannel shirts and blue jeans?"

Timothy nodded and said, "Yes, that's him!"

Jeff twisted his lips, furrowed his brow, then ducked back into the car. He dug around in the car and called out a muffled, "Ooh! *Chocolate!*"

William crossed his arms and asked Jeff, "Do you think he really came back?"

Jeff peeked up and through the windshield, shrugged, and said, "I have no idea what that man is capable of. What do you think?"

William shook his head, "I doubt it, but he's too far away for me to be able to tell anything." Jeff's muffled voice came, "Ew. Nevermind...

just an old grape."

William turned toward the boys, "How do you know Ralph?"

"Really old grape. Dat's gross, man."

Timothy answered, "He tried to kill me."

Jeff nodded as he kept searching the car, "Oh, neat. Same with us."

Brandon and Timothy looked at each other, wearing looks of shock and confusion.

Jeff backed out of the car, stood up, and finished, "Except that he was our instructor."

Both boys backed up quickly. Brandon sputtered, "You're Twisters?"

William replied, "No."

Timothy offered, "So you're Casters."

Jeff answered, "Nope."

Brandon asked, "So, what are you?"

"Unique!" Jeff smiled. "No, in all seriousness, that's a long story, but long story *short*, we're on your side."

"How did you know we were Casters?"

William nodded, "We can just tell. Keith the bartender has an even better eye for how a person has aligned themselves, so if he sends someone our way, with a wink, we know it's for a good reason and that we can trust them."

Timothy asked, "How do we know we can trust you?"

Jeff leaned on the car, "You're not dead."

Brandon coughed, "Comforting!"

Jeff smirked, "If *we* were Twisters, you'd already be gone. If *you* were Twisters, you'd already be gone. A-a-a-nd, we haven't even asked for your name or any personal information. That's pretty trusting and trustworthy, no?"

Brandon and Timothy shrugged and nodded.

William said, "Rest assured, boys, you can trust us. We can discuss everything in much more detail, but this is definitely not the place to do it, so we should get moving. We'll get you someplace safe for tonight and set out tomorrow with the daylight."

Jeff closed the car door and the four of them started down the sidewalk.

DEAD END

In the morning, the group sat around the motel room, talking.

Brandon said, "Okay, so the first question that pops into my mind is how you can see if you're blind."

William smirked, "Of all the questions available to you, that was the first you chose? Really? Okay. I died."

Brandon's face contorted into a look of either great confusion or great constipation. He exclaimed, "What?!"

"I died in a battle many years ago, but was given a second chance. Most people don't believe that it's possible, but apparently it is. However, when I was given life again, my eyesight was unable to be restored. I am actually one-hundred-percent blind in the normal sense of the word. However, I was given another gift. Have you ever seen an image through a thermal camera?"

Both boys nodded.

"Well, what I see is a lot like that, but instead of viewing emitted light, I see energy. You see, in a person's body, there are little electric pulses, sending messages and signals to other parts of the body. I see the radiation of these pulses. So the image is not of an entire person's body, but more of their core. It's kind of like what people describe when they see certain types of ghosts."

Brandon's mouth was open. "That's so weird."

"Yes, indeed. However, this means that I can see people before anyone else can. It also means that I can see when an area is Living or Dead. As you may have been told, we can only manipulate things in Living areas. Dead areas have to be Cast into, first. In a Living area, I can see the pulses, but it looks more like a circuit board, electric veins stretching and looping around entire fields and mountains."

Timothy asked, "How can *we* tell if an area is Living or Dead?"

William replied, "It's more difficult without this vision. It takes several years of practicing before you get a *feeling* for areas, but eventually you just kind of *know*. Also, in a Dead area, manipulations won't work...so that's a pretty good indication." He smirked.

Timothy asked the next prompt, "So, if you guys aren't Twisters, and you're not Casters, then what are you?"

Jeff shrugged, "We don't really have a name. We started out as Casters. William started before I did. You two remind me a lot of us when we started. We trained with Ralph at the Guild for a while, but we watched as Ralph changed and turned away from Casting. He kept whispering to us about Twisters and the cool things he heard that they could do. He said there were fewer restrictions and we could have more power than we dreamed was possible. At our young ages, we both found it intriguing. We also trusted him with our lives, so we went with him. We did Twisting for many years. We stayed away from killing anyone, merely defending ourselves as we perfected our skills. Even though we were Twisters, we maintained our good hearts and stuck to missions that didn't involve hurting anyone. We felt like superheroes, really."

William took over, "Then one day, we learned about the greediness of the man we called our leader. The *only* thing he wanted was power. He didn't care how many Twisters had to die to obtain such power. He cared even less about how many Casters had to die. It went against everything we believed in. Then he made a rule that said that any Twister who refused to participate would be either exiled or executed, depending on the severity of their case and their level of resistance."

Jeff finished, "We barely escaped. We could not return to the Casters, either, because they had a rule that said anyone who turns cannot come back. From that point, we continued our trainings ourselves and did what we had to do to stay alive. We have trained on both sides, but we no longer belong to either. The man we called our leader has since passed on, so we are not being hunted, but his daughter took control and she knew of our resistance, so we're still unwelcome there. So we do our own thing, helping those who need help and staying as invisible as possible."

Timothy asked, "Is Ralph a bad man?"

William responded, "He didn't used to be, but his loyalties were always questionable. He fought for himself. He was good to us, but he had no problem with killing someone if he had to."

Jeff chimed in, "He wasn't necessarily *bad*, but he wasn't necessarily *good*. He just did what he thought he had to do in order to achieve his goals. There's definitely good in him, still. He didn't hurt you, and he brought you to us. Everything with life has something good inside of it. You just have to know how to find it."

Timothy and Brandon nodded and smiled. That was quite a reassuring thought.

Brandon finally asked the question that had been bugging him since he woke up, "Are we gonna get to fight anyone?"

William chuckled, "You sound eager to get your hands dirty."

"I am. I've been practicing and I feel like I'm ready."

Timothy shook his head and waved his hands back and forth. "I've only read three lines. I don't know what I'm doing."

William nodded. "We will do everything we can to avoid fighting. Still, something might come up, so here." He reached into his backpack and pulled out a copy of The Text. He handed it to Timothy.

Timothy took the book and looked it over.

"It won't be as *potent* as the original, but it will still allow you to learn the skills. Also, we need a Reader if we enter a Dead area. Would you be okay to take this task? We'll tell you what to read and where to find it."

Timothy smiled, "That's something I can definitely do. Thank you. Why do we need a designated reader?"

"It just makes it easier for us. We haven't memorized the life-casting pieces, yet, as we do more with manipulation and defense."

Jeff cut in, "If we run into trouble, we'll need a reader while we buy said reader time to do said reading. Since you need more practice, you're the perfect candidate!"

Brandon frowned, "So we're not fighting?"

Jeff smiled and said, "Since you two are so young, we're going to do what we can to keep you safe and away from battle, but we probably will run into some Twisters. If they leave us alone, we're good. If they challenge us, we'll try diplomacy. If that doesn't work, we'll bust some faces."

Brandon grinned, "Cool!"

Timothy asked, "So what do we do?"

William started, "Well, from what you've told us, we know a team of Runners-"

Timothy interrupted. "Are they Runners or Twisters?"

William replied, "Both. A Runner is a Twister who is given tasks that require certain aggressive skills. Basically, they're the henchmen who do the dirty work. So, Runners were let into The Guild by a man named Jude. They took The Text and the Guild Master. They used you to destroy the facility and part of the mall. A few lives were lost, but most were just injured. The people who were going to do something were all murdered and now there are only about six of you left who are able to do anything about it."

Brandon nodded, "That about sums it up, yes."

"Right. Okay. Well, the simplest plan is to go get your stuff back. How to do that? I'm not sure. I know where the Twisters are, but I don't know how heavily-guarded the area is. We will need to do some reconnaissance before we can plan any rescue attempt. That's where we start. Neither of us has a car, though, so it'll be a long walk."

The boys nodded and the group stood up, gathered their things, and stepped outside. They walked away from the motel (after paying for their stay, of course) and started down the broken-down sidewalk toward the outskirts of town.

Suddenly, William stopped.

Jeff looked back and asked, "What is it?"

William corrected him, "*Who* is it? And I don't know. I thought I heard something and I have a funny feeling."

Jeff nodded, "That's good enough for me."

The group started walking again, but slowly. Jeff fell back to protect the rear. After a few seconds, Jeff twitched his shoulders, furrowed his brow, and inhaled.

With a **shing** and a **swish**, the blade of one of Jeff's daggers rested less than one centimeter away from a man's neck. Jeff met the man's eyes and slowly lowered the dagger.

"Oh! Eric?"

The principal exhaled slowly as Jeff returned the dagger to its sheath.

"Thank you for not slicing my head off…"

"Sure, no problem. What are you doing here?"

William and the boys walked over. They saw a car a few yards behind the principal on the road. Roger was driving, though it looked like it was difficult for him to do so. The boys looked at their shoes. They knew they were about to be in trouble.

The principal blinked a few times. "I'm looking after the boys."

Jeff chuckled and clapped a hand on the principal's shoulder, "And doing splendidly!"

"They ran away in the middle of the night. How did you find them?"

"Actually, they found us."

The principal scratched his cheek, "How did they do that?"

Jeff crossed his arms and said, "Ralph brought them to us."

"Ralph?!"

Jeff nodded. "Yeah, but he's gone. We don't know if he ran away or if he was kidnapped, but the car he drove was empty."

The principal looked at the boys, "Why did you go with Ralph?"

Timothy shrugged, "He snuck in last night and just wanted to talk to me. He said he needed my help. He said I was his *hope*. He asked

151

me to trust him, so I did. He seemed desperate! He brought me to that bar back there. Brandon had followed us on his bike-"

"Bike?!"

"Yes. And the both of us went in. That's where we met Jeff and William."

Brandon mumbled, "My poor bike."

The principal looked at Jeff, "Well, thank you for looking after them. I'll take them off your hands so you guys can get back to... whatever it is that you do now."

William stepped over and gently grabbed the principal's elbow, "Look. I know there has been a lot of tension between us in the past, but you have a problem you're facing and we can help. You know we can help. We know more about Twisters than you do, so we know The Text cannot stay with them. We want The Text and the Guild Master returned as badly as you do."

The principal thought for a moment, then asked, "What's in it for you?"

Jeff answered, "We won't die as quickly."

"I see."

Brandon asked, "Why don't you and Roger come, too? It'd be nicer if we could ride in a car than have to walk all the way there."

Jeff added, "I'm sure we could use the extra hands, if you don't have any school obligations."

The principal rubbed the nape of his neck, exhaled, then said, "The school is closed until the mall incident has been cleared up. Let me call Tanya."

They needed two vehicles to transport everyone. Roger, the principal, Timothy, and William rode in one vehicle. Tanya brought her car and Jeff, Brandon, and a woman named Anna rode in the other vehicle. Tanya explained that Anna was her sister-in-law from the west coast, and that she was also a Caster. She had told Anna about what happened, and Anna took the next flight to get there. They both reported that other Casters were trying to come and help, but they would not be able to be there until later that night or the next day.

They all hoped that their team of eight would be enough to make a difference. Timothy and Brandon worried that the Guild Master may have been hurt or killed by now. The principal told them that if they had wanted to kill her, they would have done so as soon as they entered The Guild. It didn't mean that she wasn't being hurt or tortured, but it meant that they had more time available to them in order to collect information and make a plan.

They had been driving for about two hours, following William's directions. Finally, they came to a mountain path covered with brush and vines.

William pointed, "Up through there."

The principal opened his door slightly, placed his hand on the ground, and closed his eyes. Everyone watched as the brush and vines coiled and pulled back off the road, opening the path for their vehicles.

They slowed down as they reached the peak of the road. As they drove around the bend, they looked off to the right. Amidst the valleys in the mountain range sat an enormous, though decaying, fortress of stone and vegetation. It didn't look quite like a castle, but it was essentially a castle. It was like a stone, gothic style asylum for the mentally ill from years gone by, embraced by years of healthily-growing vines, shrubs, and ivy.

Jeff nodded, "There it is."

The group parked their cars higher up on the hill and camouflaged them. Then they started a slow, silent walk down the mountain toward the fortress.

As they emerged from the thick brush into a clearing by a road, they could see the walls and front gate of the massive structure off to their right.

William paused and stared, and then said, "It's…"

Jeff finished, "Dead."

The principal moved up next to William, "What?"

Jeff shrugged, "Everything's dead. Granted, there are plants growing here, but this place is void of life, otherwise. This is a Dead area. It has been wiped clean. Just look at the walls."

The walls looked like they had been in the middle of a World War II battle. They were nicked, chipped, and falling apart, and there were gaping holes all along them.

Jeff pointed to the gates and said, "They appear to be sealed shut. Welded, perhaps."

Anna asked, "What's that mean?"

"Maybe nothing. Just keep your eyes open. We're going in."

Jeff walked quickly across the road with William. They knelt by the wall and peered through a gap. After a few seconds, Jeff signaled for the others to cross the road.

William whispered, "The boy to whom I gave the book, what is your name?"

Timothy walked over and knelt beside him, "Timothy, sir."

"Well, Timothy-sir…Just messing. Timothy, now's the perfect time for you to read."

"Why is that?"

"'Cause I can't see a thing. The area is so void of life that as soon as we got to the wall, even Jeff almost left my view."

"Okay. What do I do?"

As the others knelt down beside the wall, William gave Timothy instructions.

Timothy nodded, then took off his shoes and socks. He opened the book to the page William mentioned, found the proper line, and then he inhaled...exhaled.

He ran his pointer finger from left to right across the line, then did the same for the next three lines. His feet tingled, but he kept reading. He pulled his finger off the last symbol and looked around. Nothing looked different, but out of nowhere came a soothing, gentle breeze, like a perfect day at the beach. As the breeze blew past them and over the land, the leaves rustled, the vines twisted, and the grass shivered.

William smiled and said, "Much better. Thank you, Timothy. How do you feel?"

Timothy sighed and said, "I feel wonderful. I feel...peace."

"It's great, isn't it?"

"Yes, sir!"

"Just remember not to let it go to your head. Remember the source of the gift. Remember who wrote the book. None of this would be possible without the work that The Author did."

Timothy nodded.

Jeff and William stood up and crawled through the space in the wall, then helped the others crawl through. The principal and Tanya pulled out binoculars and started searching the area.

William placed his hands one on top of the other on the top of his walking stick, stuck the end of the stick into the ground, and closed his eyelids.

The three of them searched for about two minutes, but none of them found any sign of other visitors or residents...not even any animals.

They still walked slowly and carefully as they pressed forward to the fortress. As they moved forward, they were now completely exposed. Jeff's hand slid to the sheath that held his throwing knives.

Soon, they reached the front doors. These were large, wrought iron doors with large handles but without any specific markings.

When they reached the doors, William placed his hand on the doors and closed his eyes. After a tap of William's hand, the doors slowly swung open toward them, revealing one of the most beautiful renaissance-style interiors any of them had ever seen. Chandeliers, banisters, balconies, large and beautiful portraits of unfamiliar persons, candelabras, shelf after shelf of books and ornamentation, and enormous area rugs full of striking colors and complicated patterns. Large, heavy oak tables and matching chairs were placed in several areas throughout the room.

Timothy's mouth fell open.

And this is just the entrance?!

William and Jeff had, of course, been there before, but seeing it empty and so quiet allowed them to see the structure's true beauty.

Jeff stepped through the portal and said, "My only concern is the apparent lack of dust!"

William said, "Then they were here recently, but cleaned up and left in a hurry. I wonder why they left. Split into teams of two. Search through everything you can find. We're looking for a possible reason why they left. Documents of recent history would be perfect, if they kept any."

The group split up and began searching tables, drawers, shelves, and even behind paintings and tapestries. They lifted rugs, felt for trap doors and secret doors behind walls. They skimmed through every book they could find, leaving disorganized stacks of books in their wake.

Suddenly, William held up his left hand and said, "Ah."

Everyone stopped what they were doing and looked at him.

William smirked and said, "We're not alone."

BENEDICT

Everyone stood still, listening for any indication of other beings inside the building.

William paused between each statement as he said, "Single body. Unmoving, but not dead. One floor down. Appears to be restrained."

Jeff nodded toward a doorway in the left rear corner of the room, drew a dagger, and said, "Let's go."

The group quickly, but silently, ran to the door, and then slowly pushed the door open and walked through. Tanya, Anna, and Roger drew pistols as they turned the corner and entered what appeared to be a large dining room.

The tables were bare, the chairs were tucked in under the table, and the decorations were beginning to collect a thin layer of dust. The group searched this room quickly as they walked through it, but couldn't find anything helpful.

They reached two doors in the far right corner, one door on the wall in front of them, the other on the wall to their right. William pointed to the door on their right and they pushed through it silently.

They began a slow and quiet descent down an old staircase.

As they traveled downwards, it got darker. In fact, they were staring into a void; a black hole of nothingness. Anna pulled out a flashlight, but William used his right hand and gently pushed her hand down, shaking his head. He moved to the front of the group and signaled with a wave of two fingers by his ear to follow him.

They reached the bottom of the staircase and found themselves in a very dark and cold stone-walled basement. From this basement area, several rooms and hallways branched.

William led them left, and down a hallway that ended at a single wooden door. He placed his palm on the door, breathed deeply and slowly, then stepped back and nodded.

Brandon moved closer to Timothy and whispered, "So, what do you think happened to…"

Anna pushed the door open with pistol ready and the view opened up to view a large room filled with what Timothy thought were rather strange looms, weird tables, rusty chains, oddly-shaped fire-pokers, and—

"Ralph?"

Brandon nodded as he turned his head toward the open door, he asked, "Yeah! How did you know what I was gonna…Oh."

On scattered straw, in the corner, arms in shackles above his head, sat Ralph. He was unresponsive, sweaty, and bleeding a little out of the corner of his mouth.

The group walked over slowly as they scanned the room for others. They gathered around Ralph and stared at him.

Anna asked, "Is he with you?"

The principal shook his head, "He used to be. Then he switched sides. He's been a pain in the neck for years. Suddenly he decides to seek help from Casters? We're all a bit confused."

Anna nodded and smirked, "Sounds like my ex."

William reached out with his walking stick and poked Ralph's stomach. Ralph grunted. William poked him again. Ralph's lips bent into a slight smile and he grunted. William poked him a third time. Ralph grunted and then giggled a little. Ralph slowly shook his head, winced, and exhaled slowly.

William called out, "Ralph?"

"Mom?"

"No, Ralph. Billy."

"Billy?" Ralph winced even more and struggled to open his eyes, then shrieked, "Billy!" Ralph tried to kick himself further against the wall, but was already as far back as he could go, so he started curling up.

"Ralph, stop. We're not going to hurt you…yet."

"Yet?"

"If you don't cooperate, we will. If you cooperate, it'll be like old days."

Ralph relaxed slightly, blinked as he stared at empty space, and said, "Old days. Hope."

William knelt down next to him and leaned on his walking stick, slightly, "Yes, Ralph. Now, what happened?"

Ralph licked his lips, then stuck his tongue on the corner of his mouth where there was blood. He seemed to be searching for something in his mind.

"Found me. Found lie."

In very broken English, Ralph explained that when he was at the principal's house, he lied to the Runners who showed up, sending them away. Then he went in to talk to Timothy in order to get his help. They drove to the bar; he parked a block or so down, and waited. While he was waiting, two Runners walked up to the car and asked him to come out and talk. They mentioned something about a new task for him. He slowly stepped out of the car and the two Runners grabbed him, knocked him out, and brought him back here. When he woke up, he was in chains, and four Twisters were standing around him. They started asking him questions about where he had been, what he had done, and why he was parked downtown and not doing anything. They asked about things like who he was waiting for, why he was just sitting there, and why he hadn't returned when he was told to report.

He tried to lie, but they saw right through it. When he didn't give a good enough answer, they hit him. Sometimes they hit him with their fists; sometimes with a metal pole; sometimes with the wall itself, which hurt the most.

"Not tell. Him." He pointed to Timothy as well as he could, considering his arms were chained to the wall.

"You didn't tell them about him?"

"Right."

"What *did* you tell them?"

Ralph bit his lower lip and winced, tears forming in his eyes.

"Ralph! What did you tell them?"

Ralph looked at the principal and his lip started to quiver.

The principal asked, "What is it?"

"Home. Wife."

The principal sighed slowly and closed his eyes, and then said, "You're lucky, Ralph. I had a feeling that something like that might happen, so I made sure my wife went somewhere safe until I tell her to come home.

Ralph sighed and nodded, "Good."

"If I hadn't, you'd be wishing your torturing Twister buddies were here instead of me."

Ralph grimaced, "I'm s- sorry." His eyes pleaded for forgiveness, but the principal looked away.

William probed, "What else?"

"Casters alive. Coming here."

Jeff said, "Well, that explains why the Twisters left in such a hurry."

William shook his head, "Actually, it doesn't. They would outnumber us. There's no reason for them to leave."

Tanya asked, "Why did they leave, Ralph?"

Ralph shrugged, "Didn't tell me. Didn't want me. Left me."

Timothy offered, "Maybe they just didn't need this place anymore. They have The Text and the Guild Master. Maybe they just had to relocate them to some kind of central base or something?"

Jeff nodded, "Good thought. That's possible. Where did they go?"

Ralph scrunched his face as he thought, and then said, "Some...*his* house. Others...to Hollow."

Anna asked, "Hollow?"

Jeff replied, "He's probably referring to Shepherd's Hollow."

Ralph nodded.

Jeff continued, "It's a secret place like this, only much less decorated, and even less known. It's not a good place to be. It's so open that it's like stepping onto a floor completely covered in mouse traps. Trying to reach their bunker there is pretty much a suicide mission."

Brandon asked, "Then what are we waiting for? Let's go kick some Twister butt!" He looked at Ralph and said, "No offense."

Ralph smirked and shrugged.

William asked, "So what do we do with you, then, Ralph?"

Ralph frowned and said, "Leave me."

"Since you're telling the truth and you've done us a favor, we won't just leave you. The Twisters turned on you and left you here to die, so we're going to disappoint them. We'll help you out since you were honest, but on one condition: You stay out of our way. Run away from the Twisters every chance you get and stay away. We'll come find you when it's over. Deal?"

Ralph smiled an awkward and seemingly painful smile and said, "Deal."

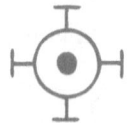

VIVA LAS DESERT

At the airport, Anna handed out tickets to everyone.

Eric accepted the ticket and said, "Thank you, Anna, but we could have afforded our own."

"I have, so I give," Anna smiled.

They boarded their plane without issue, though they had to leave their weapons behind. William was permitted to bring his walking stick along in the cargo hold.

In their seats, Jeff leaned over to Timothy and whispered, "I hate planes."

Timothy frowned, "Why?"

William leaned across the aisle and whispered, "He carries so many daggers that it takes forever to clear the metal detector! He always forgets where he sheathed them all. One time, he was arrested because it took him eleven passes and it still kept going off!"

Jeff nodded, "Yeah, well…I've got it down to a science, now. There will be a large box with my name on it at my cousin's house when we land. I asked him to bring them to the airport to save time."

He noticed a glare from William.

"Don't worry! I won't equip them until we're clear of the parking lot."

"Oh, much better…"

"I thought you'd like that," Jeff grinned.

"Excuse me." A tall, Caucasian, brunette woman walked over to Eric. Walking behind her was a short African-American man with short, curly black hair.

"Melissa! Steve! You made it! We're glad to have you with us. Everyone, these fine people are Melissa and Steve. We were Guild-mates, starting out. Melissa lives in Maine and Steve in Rhode Island, but they've offered to come along and help us."

Everyone hailed a greeting to the newcomers and they all settled in their seats for the long series of flights from New Hampshire to Nevada.

As they were flying over Missouri, Timothy asked Jeff, "What makes this place so special?"

"Shepherd's Hollow? Well, some say that this was the place where The Author first spoke to someone after he died. Some believe he still walks the earth. Some believe his ghost does the walking. Most believe that his death was final and that it's impossible for him to be walking and talking. However, many of these people also believe that memories of The Author could have been fused with various objects and structures. This is one such place.

"Unfortunately, the Twisters won an important battle there, leaving it void of water, and claimed the spot as their own. They can defend that position for weeks before they have to go get more water. Most

Casters just stay away from there."

Timothy nodded, then asked, "Why is it called Shepherd's Hollow?"

"Oh, that's an interesting tale! Apparently, many years ago, a shepherd was moving his flock through when it was green and nice. The area had a lot more caves and hollow areas. There's the Shepherd and the Hollow, but the best part comes next. As he passed one cave entrance, he thought he heard someone call out to him. He entered the cave and looked around, but couldn't find anyone. Then he heard the voice again, but this time, it sounded like it was coming from behind a bush there. He looked around the bush, but couldn't see anyone.

"Confused, he called out for whoever was talking to him. Suddenly, the whole cave filled with this strange voice. The voice told him to sell his sheep and use that money to buy a shovel."

"A shovel?"

"A shovel. He used that shovel to build one of the first official WordCasting facilities in North America. It was nowhere near the size of the Guild, but it served its purpose. That's how the story goes, anyway."

"What's it look like?"

"It's a military bunker with extra fortifications in the middle of a desert?"

Timothy shook his head as he scanned the desert scene before him. He ducked back down behind the boulder and looked at Jeff.

"Told ya. Mister Tech-man, how does it look?"

Steve continued looking through his high-end binoculars as he replied, "If they were to hold the Guild Master anywhere, it would definitely be here. They've got guards on every wall and corner, two small turrets, and I can see the shadows of dozens of people through the windows."

"Meaning?"

"Meaning, there's no way we're getting in during the day."

William shook his head, "Nightfall is almost worse than daytime because they add extra guards and everyone straps on night-vision goggles. At least, they used to when I was here last."

Jeff nodded, "Same when I was here."

Brandon asked, "So, then, what're we doing here? We can't do anything, so let's go somewhere else and wait for them to make the first move!"

"That's exactly what we're going to do," said Eric, "All we can do is watch and wait. Maybe a gap will open up and we'll get a shot at the door. Maybe they'll bring everyone out in the open. We'll wait here tonight and keep watch. If nothing else, we'll work up a plan by morning."

When night had fallen, everyone pulled on a jacket, gloves, and a hat.

William suggested, "Do your best to control your breathing. As the chill covers the desert, we may accidently be sending signals to the watchmen. Choose words wisely, speak gently, and breathe lightly."

Steve watched through his own night-vision goggles; Eric set up radios; and Tanya finished loading the newly-purchased pistols.

Hours passed without incident and a few of the Casters unrolled blankets as they prepared for shifts through the night.

Jeff pulled a blanket around his shoulders and shivered, "It's getting chillier. Anyone else feel that shift?"

William grabbed Jeff's shoulder and whispered, "Everyone be still. That wasn't the weather changing."

Timothy could feel his forehead tingling.

They were being watched.

Jeff drew two knives from his sheaths and silently slid into a nearby bunch of trees. Timothy and Brandon slowly scooted over toward William.

Suddenly, William threw a large blanket over both of the boys and stood up, hands raised.

"Oh, *man*!" A voice came from the other side of the boulder, "I was hoping for a fight!"

Eight Twisters walked over from the desert's edge with guns raised. The rest of the group, except for the boys and Jeff, stood up and raised their hands.

"Alright, everyone move. You two stay here and sort through their things. See if there's anything valuable. Destroy the rest."

Now Timothy and Brandon could only hear footsteps. As one group walked away into the desert, four feet stomped around the area, kicking equipment over, picking tools up and throwing them, and tossing blankets around. Then they heard two soft thuds nearby.

They could hear the sound difference of the air around the blankets when the figure knelt down and grabbed a piece of the blanket.

The boys winced as the blanket was tossed off them.

"I love blanket forts, but I think it's time to get moving."

Timothy grinned, "Jeff!"

Beside Jeff lay two guards, limp as wet noodles.

Brandon pointed, "Are they…"

"Don't ask. About that Twister Butt-Kicking…ready?"

Brandon jumped up and said, "Yeah!"

"Excellent. Now, before we go, I'm going to teach you a few things that may help you live longer."

"Reassuring…"

"Yeah, whatever. Anyway, do what I do."

For the next few minutes, Jeff quietly taught Timothy and Brandon a few self-defense maneuvers. When he thought they were ready enough, he grabbed all the necessary gear and the three were off.

"Identify yourselves."

Jeff grabbed his shirt and looked at the last name printed on the pocket.

"Uh…Adamson and…*Where is it? Where'd it go? Oh, got it…* Svenstinsti…koff…ing…ton."

"Hey!"

Jeff froze and slowly asked, "Uh…What?"

"Just because I can't get your name right, it doesn't mean you can keep making fun of me! I'm sorry, okay?"

Jeff sighed and shrugged it off, saying, "Oh… Okay, okay. I was just messin' around. You know."

"Alright. Come on in."

"*You're lucky that Svenstinstikoff…ing…ton…was so short, kid.*"

Brandon nodded as he exhaled and adjusted his new uniform as they walked past the guard station and into the facility.

The guard asked, "What did you find?"

"Some stuff. Nothing worth mentioning, though."

"*Gee thanks,*" came a whisper from the bag Jeff had slung over his shoulder.

When they were inside and past all of the guards, Jeff gently sat the bag on the ground, opened it, and helped Timothy step out.

Jeff pointed to a hallway that led to the left and said, "Alright, Timothy. You head that way and find the others. That hall looks relatively unused. We'll try to keep everyone else off your back. Good luck!"

Timothy wrapped a dark jacket around his shoulders and started down the hallway.

JAILBREAK

As Timothy walked the halls of the bunker, he could begin to see the unbelievable depth and complexity of this facility. With storage, sleeping, and power-generating rooms around every corner, it was easy for Timothy to see how they could manage to live here for weeks without retrieving supplies. Timothy bet they could even stay here a few months if they reduced the number of people within the facility.

So far, he hadn't run into anybody. Perhaps the reason that this hallway was so empty was that everyone was up and about instead of sleeping. Perhaps it was simply because of the excitement surrounding the arrival of these special guests and such an important relic. Perhaps there really weren't that many people here, after all.

Timothy turned the next corner and stopped in his tracks. He ducked back around the corner and poked his head around to see. Through an observation window at the end of the hall, Timothy could see dozens of people gathering. They were flooding in from all directions to do something.

Never mind.

He jumped back a little when a door nearby opened and two female Twisters walked out of a room.

"Did you hear what the meeting was about?"

"Not really. All I heard was that it was related to the new prisoners."

"I hope we're going to get to see a flogging or something."

"You're sick."

"What? You didn't see the last one? It was truly inspiring!"

As the Twisters turned to the right at the end of the hallway, Timothy slowly walked toward the observation window.

The last one? Who was involved in the last one?

He stood up enough so he could look through the window without allowing too much of his face to be seen. He saw all of the Twisters assembling and standing against the walls, waiting for something. Many were in the dark uniforms, but several were in street clothes.

"*Runners*," Timothy assumed.

He couldn't see any of the Casters, but he suspected that he would, soon. He needed to figure out where they were being held before something happened to them.

Just as he turned to leave, he heard a familiar voice.

"My friends!"

There was a loud applause. As it died down, Timothy looked through the glass and saw the cloaked figure that had attacked The Guild. He was wearing the same clothes except for the lack of a bandana. He could see the man's clean-shaven, pointy jaw, but could not see his nose or eyes, which were hidden in the shadow of his hood. He was standing at the front of the room, on a platform three steps up from the main area's floor. His arms were extended and four robed Twisters stood behind him as he spoke.

"It gives me great joy to see so many of you here! On this day, we celebrate the recovery of The Text. It is in our hands once more! Our Lady is very pleased with all of you for all of your diligence and hard work! To top it all off, we even have several special guests, who we will invite to join us up here later."

Good. There's still time.

"Until then, I offer a traitor for your judgment. What shall we do with our dear friend, Jeff?"

Jeff?!

Timothy watched as two Runners brought Jeff out through a door behind the hooded speaker. He was bent over and it appeared that his hands had been bound. Timothy couldn't tell for sure, but it looked like a small stream of blood was sliding down his chin from the corner of his mouth.

Where's Brandon?

Timothy searched the crowd, but couldn't see Brandon. He needed to get moving, but now he wasn't sure about what to do about Jeff.

Jeff must have known Timothy was watching him because he looked up slightly and carefully met Timothy's eyes. Timothy's eyes grew wide as he heard the crowd yell, "Kill him!"

Jeff's eyes remained unchanged. As cool and steady as ever, Jeff smirked when the crowd shouted for his demise.

Why is he smiling?! They're going to kill him!

"How shall he die?"

"By the blade!"

"So shall it be!"

A Runner carrying a machete walked over and handed the weapon to the leader.

"Traitor, because of your crimes, the people have called for your execution. Any requests?"

Jeff smiled and said, "I ask for one favor."

"Only one? Amusing. What would that be?"

"I ask that my hands be bound in front, not behind, and that the bindings be attached to my belt. Your cuts will be cleaner, then, and I won't flop around like a fish out of water."

The leader raised a brow and thought for a moment, then nodded to one of the Runners. The ropes were undone and his hands were tied to his front, and then the ropes were attached to his belt, as he requested.

"There. Happy?"

"Well, it was more for your sake, but I am quite happy. Thank you."

"Any final thoughts?"

"Yes, actually."

Jeff looked around the room, into every person's eyes, and then he bowed his head slightly so that he could look at Timothy again.

Then he said, "Your men were very thorough and thought that they did a fantastic job…

The leader cocked his head and looked at the Runners, bewildered.

While meeting Timothy's gaze, Jeff winked.

"…but they missed one."

With a kick of his heel, a shift of his leg, a twist of his torso, and a reach with his fingertips, Jeff managed to draw a hunting dagger from a sheath tucked inside of his right boot.

Timothy caught his breath and stared in amazement, but his view was soon blocked as the crowd erupted and raced to the front of the room to try to stop Jeff. Timothy wanted to go and help, but he knew he couldn't. He wanted to stay and watch, but he couldn't do that either.

"Timothy!"

Timothy turned around to face the person who called his name. Brandon was running down the hallway toward him.

"Brandon! There you are! What's happening? Why are you—"

As Timothy tried to ask his last question, two Runners turned the corner behind Brandon and charged toward them.

Brandon yelled, "MOVE!"

After but a moment's hesitation, Timothy took off to the right down an open hallway, Brandon only a few steps behind, leaving the Runners only a few short paces behind them.

One of the Runners shouted, "You're lucky our leader keeps this area Dead, or we would have already killed you both!"

Ah! That explains why the Casters can't get themselves out! That also explains why Jeff was so helpless until he got his knife!

As they flew by different doors, Timothy watched for any sign that would point to where the others would be held. Timothy thought he'd try something.

He yelled back, "I really don't want to be locked up in a basement! I hate the dark!"

The other Runner responded, "Oh, then you'll *really* hate it here, if we even do bother with locking you up down there! Likely, we'll just kill you when we get a hold of you!"

Aha! We need to go down.

As they turned the next corner to the right, Timothy called out, "Why haven't you caught us, yet, anyway? You're taller and stronger, so you should already have us!"

The first Runner replied, "Your legs are shorter, so you're getting more paces in per minute, which increases your speed over our long strides, but we would definitely win in overall distance!"

The other Runner swatted the first Runner's shoulder and said, "Knock it off and run!"

They turned another corner and found themselves entering a large common area with tables and chairs. Timothy and Brandon pulled chairs over as they ran past them. This slowed the Runners a little, but not enough to make them lose the boys.

Brandon pulled a backpack off his shoulders and reached into it as they ran into another hallway and turned left. He pulled out a copy of The Text and threw it to Timothy.

"Do your thing, designated Reader! It won't give life to the whole area since it's just a copy and we're rushed, but it'll give us enough to work with."

As Timothy flipped through the pages, Brandon pulled out what appeared to be a grenade.

"What is that?"

"Never mind. Just read."

Timothy turned the pages until he found the sequence he had read before.

"I can't take off my shoes and socks right now, though!"

"Don't need to. You just have to make contact, skin to target."

"I don't get it."

"Touch your hand to the wall, Timothy!"

"Oh, right. Okay!"

Timothy searched the page until he found the correct line. He slid his finger across the symbols as they turned yet another corner. When his hand glowed, he slammed his hand against the wall as they ran. A sudden breeze filled the hallway.

Brandon was about to place his hand against the wall when they saw three Runners turn into the hallway in front of them.

Everyone stopped. The Runners were all grinning.

The first Runner spoke again, "Thank you for the assistance. Now we will kill you."

Brandon leaned on the wall, out of breath, then said, "We're on a tight schedule. We don't have time to die, today."

He slammed his hand against the wall as the Runners placed their hands on walls near them. Suddenly, sections of each wall—sections between the boys and each group of Runners—slid across the hallway, blocking the Runners completely.

"Now what?" Timothy asked through panting breaths, "It'll only take them a few seconds to alter this."

"I'm thinking."

Before they could do anything, the ground beneath their feet started shaking. Beyond the wall, they could hear a Runner yell, "It's been a treat, really. Enjoy death!"

The boys backed up against the walls closest to either of them and stared at the floor. Suddenly, the shaking stopped. They stared at each other, then sighed with relief.

"I thought for sure the floor was going to—"

Before Brandon could finish, the floor crumbled apart and the boys fell into a black pit.

"Well, that was lucky!" Brandon dusted off his jacket as he stood up.

They were in a dark room, but the ceiling light in the hallway above them illuminated a small portion of the room. They looked around and saw shelves. They were in some kind of storage room, one floor down. They felt around for a door, but could only feel boxes, paint cans, and plastic buckets.

Finally, Timothy located a doorknob and whispered for Brandon to follow him. As he started to turn the knob, however, he could feel the knob being jiggled slightly from the other side. Someone must have heard their fall.

Timothy and Brandon stepped back and tried to find something to hide behind, but nothing was big enough for cover. They stood there and waited to be found. Again.

The door slowly swung open and a bright flashlight shined into their faces.

"Well, well! What do we have here? Looks like I beat you two down here!"

Brandon squinted, "Jeff?"

Jeff turned the flashlight on his own face. "Yep. I'm here."

"You're alive!"

Jeff shined the light on his roughly-bandaged left forearm and said, "Almost not. We need to keep moving. The others are just over here. I did what I could to hold everyone off, but I had to run in the end, so they're probably not far behind."

Okay. This man is my hero.

The three of them left the storage room and approached a door around a corner. Jeff slowly opened the door, but closed it quickly and silently.

"Two guards, but I see the cells where the others are being held. I felt the change from your last Cast, but I don't feel it here, so I don't think it stretched this far. Could you set up a new Cast here?"

Timothy felt around, but couldn't find the copy of The Text, "I must have dropped it upstairs! I'm so sorry!"

"Not to worry. I've always got..." He reached into the backpack Brandon carried and pulled out a metal self-defense club, "...a Plan B."

Jeff swung the door open and stepped out into the room. The guards raised their automatic rifles and stared at Jeff. One appeared to be shaking, slightly.

"Sorry, boys. I don't want to have to hurt you. I'll leave the choice to you. You can walk away and be fine, or you can stay here and get whooped." Jeff flicked his wrist and the self-defense baton extended out.

"We have the guns, Jeff. You should surrender."

"That's a shame," said Jeff as he shook his head and continued to step toward them.

With his left hand, he grabbed the barrel of the gun to his left. With the baton, he deflected the other gun's barrel toward the opposite guard. He stepped over with his right foot and slammed the baton into the first guard's neck, causing the guard to pull the trigger.

The second guard lowered his gun and grabbed his left thigh. He tried to point the gun at Jeff, but Jeff's foot was already stepping on his ankle, causing additional pain, so he couldn't focus. The guard tried once more, but Jeff bent over, grabbed the gun, shook his head, and gently pulled the gun away from the guard. One guard laid there, unconscious, and the other fought back tears and cries of pain while holding his injured leg.

Jeff shook his head again and said, "A real shame."

The boys entered the room and walked over to Jeff. Jeff grabbed keys from the unconscious guard, and the three of them walked through a barred security door and into the cell area.

"Jeff! Boys! That was fast!" Eric called out from one of the four occupied cells.

Tanya called out, "Their leader has The Text somewhere. The Guild Master's in here with me. She's in much better shape than we thought she'd be."

Jeff unlocked all of the cells and accepted the backpack from Brandon. As each Caster left their cell, Jeff handed them a gun from the backpack.

When William limped over, Jeff shrugged and said, "I couldn't fit the walking stick in the backpack for obvious reasons, but there's a spare pool cue in the corner there! We'll do something for your eyes in a minute here, too."

William replied, "A bit unconventional, but I can make it work."

"I know you can. All right, listen up, everyone. Some of us still need to go and get the book, but the rest of you need to get The Guild Master as far away from here as possible."

The Guild Master stood up straight and asked, "And why is that, young man? Because I'm old and can't take care of myself?"

Jeff grimaced and replied, "Actually, I was thinking you could be injured and may need medical attention…"

"I may be aged, but you needn't worry about me. You may find that you will actually need my assistance, so you should never just assume that an old lady needs to be escorted to a *safe* place. Understood, Boy Scout?"

Jeff cracked a smile and said, "Yes, ma'am! All right, so I guess we all go together?"

Everyone nodded.

A REAL SHAME

The eleven Casters worked their way through the lower hallways, guns raised. William laid a hand on Roger's shoulder to be led along. The Guild Master had her cane and limped along. Since the whole group was moving slowly, she was able to keep up.

Brandon whispered, "If there are eleven of us now, why don't we just start Casting? We've got enough people do so some serious damage."

William whispered in return, "Three reasons. First, we don't have any more copies of The Text with us. When Casting into a Dead area for the first time, we need to use The Text, otherwise our own Casting may be tainted. Suppose we don't recall the correct symbol. We could do a lot more harm than good.

"Second, if we Cast, they will find us instantly. Finally, because the power supply was strategically placed in the center of the facility, if we Cast too much and shift too much around, we would basically set off a bomb if that's disrupted. That's the primary reason they actually *try* to keep this area Dead. Regular weapons are our best option until we can clear the facility with The Text."

Brandon nodded as they turned the next corner, which led to a stairway.

Anna whispered, "Do we know where we're actually heading?"

"The roof," replied Jeff.

"Why the roof?"

"They wouldn't expect to find us there; it gives us a good vantage point, and it gives us a wide-open exit."

Three of the Casters walked up the stairs and slowly pushed open the door. When they saw that it was clear, they waved everyone else up. When they were all in the upper hallway, Jeff began leading them. He indicated that they had to go two floors up to find the exit to the roof.

Timothy clutched the backpack with gear against his chest as they walked. With his life more in danger than ever before, he thought of his parents.

"But they're not done clearing the rubble! We don't know that for sure."

"Honey, he's a smart boy. Don't worry."

Mrs. Walker crossed her arms and glared at her husband, screaming, "How can *you* not be worried?!"

Mr. Walker shook his head, "I never said I wasn't! I'm just as worried as you are! I'm just saying that we need to hold on to hope until we know the truth, whichever way it may develop. Timothy is a gifted boy. I'm sure he's just fine."

"You don't know that!"

"I…I *hope* he's just fine."

Mr. Walker sat his wife down on the sofa, sat down next to her, and held her hands.

"My darling, darling beloved. Whatever happens, we will all get through this. Don't lose hope."

Ralph sat in his recliner, staring at a blank TV screen. A bag of chips lay on the side table next to his chair, but it was unopened. Ralph couldn't move. He just stared.

Finally, he found some words, "I'm...s- sorry. Timothy. B- But I needed help. I n- need hope."

He sniffed as he started to cry, and then muttered, "I need y- you to s- see. See hope. Save hope."

Why did I agree to this? How could my parents ever be proud of me after this? How could I ever fix this? I'm sorry, Mom.

Jeff leaned over and whispered, "I'm not your mom."

"Oh. I'm sorry. Did I say all that out loud again?"

"Just the *I'm sorry* part. I didn't hear anything else, though I assume you were thinking about more than that. Typically, people don't rehearse apologizing unless they've done something, first. Unless you're planning to do something that would need an apology. In which case, you might be a psychopath. *Are* you a psychopath?"

"Uh...no."

"Oh, good. Since you asked if you had said it *again*, I was a little concerned. Just a little, mind you. I try not to let too much stuff bother me. Do you like pie?"

"I- Uh...Yes. Wh—"

"Cool. Me, too. Whenever I'm in a stressful situation, I think about pie. Warm apple pie in a bowl with just a little bit of warmed milk. Cherry pie with a thick chocolate drizzle! Have you had Peanut Butter pie? I bet you've never had it with a layer of hazelnut mousse! Oh! How about cold cheesecake with warm raspberry topping? I love that stuff! It's not really a pie, but it's still delicious. You know what else is delicious?"

Timothy could envision everything Jeff described and it made him salivate. Now he was starting to feel hungry, but he didn't mind. He asked, "What else?"

"Caramel-Mocha cappuccinos with homemade butterscotch-flavored whipped topping! That's what. Lasagna, too! But not together! Yuck. That was my favorite as a kid, though. Lasagna. I would even eat it cold, for breakfast. I just loved Lasagna! I wasn't much into pizza, but I'd eat it if it was the only thing available. I also really liked my mother's Strawberry Summer Salad!

"When we were just munchy, mom would sometimes make Hungry Sloppy Joes. We'd scoop it up like a dip with tortilla chips as we watched movies or played games. She called them *Hungry* Sloppy Joes because of the spices she would put in them…because they would *bite back*. Get it? We all thought it was hilarious.

"A strange factoid, though? In many families, it's the mom who sings lullabies, but my dad would always sing for us when we were babies. His bass melodies would always send us right into a *trance*."

"Trance?" Timothy suddenly realized that he had been watching his shoes the whole time he was talking to Jeff. He had no idea where they had been walking or what happened. He looked up and Jeff was looking over his shoulder at him, smiling.

Timothy could smell gunpowder. He started to look around, but Jeff stopped him by saying, "Don't look back. You won't like what you find."

Timothy just turned his head either way slightly to see if everyone else was still there.

They were.

Relieved, Timothy sighed, but he looked over at Eric again. He was holding his left arm with his right hand. Timothy could see blood staining the principal's sleeve.

The principal nodded and said through gritted teeth, "I'll be fine. It could have been a lot worse."

Timothy looked back up at Jeff and asked, "What happened?"

Jeff smirked, "Well, soon after you called me your mom, we walked around the corner and met up with some Twisters, so I used a little mind trick I've been practicing on you and the other boy."

Sarcastically, Brandon asked, "Oh, is *that* all?"

Jeff grinned, "Yep. That's all."

The group turned the next corner, pushed through a door marked *Exit*, and found a staircase that went up or down.

Jeff scanned the area while holding two throwing knives drawn from the backpack.

"Good so far. I don't hear anyone coming from either direction. Head on up! Guns first. Boys, you stay in the back of the group, with me."

Steve and Tanya led the group as they climbed two flights of stairs, guns at the ready. Because of the adrenaline rush that had been driving Timothy all day, he hadn't noticed how sore he had become. Now, as they slowly climbed the stairs, he began to notice. He winced from the pain in his legs as they climbed up to the final landing and faced the roof exit.

Anna shook her head, "That was too easy. Where is everybody?"

Tanya opened the door and Steve led the advance through the exit and onto the roof of the desert facility. It was pitch black, now, but a few distant area lights and search lights lit up a few sections of the now-freezing-cold desert. As Timothy exhaled, he could see his breath.

Deserts are so weird.

Suddenly, four spotlights were switched on and illuminated the roof.

Anna nodded and said, "Ah. Yeah. That explains that."

On the other end of the roof stood several dozen Twisters, one of whom was the cloaked leader. Once again, he wore a bandana, but this one was dark blue and had a white, paisley design on it.

Jeff smirked, "Yeah, I should have seen that coming."

Eric stepped forward, still holding his arm, and called out to the cloaked man, "Give us The Text and let us leave. There are children with us! They need not be in any more danger."

"You're trying to persuade me to just give up? You come here, on my land, in my home, and threaten my position and my team? What if I were to do that to you?"

"You already tried."

"Touche'…Eric."

Eric shook his head, "I'm not surprised that you know my name. You had most of us hunted. I'm sure the coward, Jude, gave you all the information you needed."

"Indeed, he did."

"I'm the principal where these children go to school, so I am responsible for them. They must leave safely."

The leader laughed. "That was very *irresponsible* of you, then. Why should I heed your words when you are the trespassers?"

Tanya replied, "Because you stole what was not yours to steal.

We've simply come to get it back."

"With guns and knives in hand? Dear lady, I'm sure you meant much more than that."

"Simply precautionary," Eric offered, "We know how you people work."

"Nevertheless, I cannot let you take back The Text. The old lady? You can have her. She isn't valuable to us anymore, anyway."

Steve stepped up and asked, "Why do you need The Text, anyway? You have your own copies."

"You think I'm stupid? Copies don't have nearly the same amount of power as the original. Anyway, we don't need the book for the Casting. We need it to find something."

Jeff raised a brow, "Find *what*, exactly?"

"Now, why would I tell you that?"

Jeff shrugged, "'Cause I'm so gosh darn cute?"

The leader stared at Jeff for a few seconds, then shook his head and said, "You people have one chance to leave. I suggest you take it."

Timothy looked over at Brandon, who was smiling from ear to ear.

"Why are you smiling?"

Brandon held out his hand slightly so Timothy could see that he still had the grenade he pulled out earlier.

Timothy shook his head, slowly.

"Don't do it!"

Brandon nodded and winked. He stepped up behind Steve and Jeff and called out, "Hey stupid! Catch!"

He rolled the grenade between Steve's legs and across the rooftop, like bowling.

The leader stretched his hands out in the air and waited, as if he thought it was coming from above.

Jeff muttered, "That's interesting..."

He spun around and forced the others to get down.

Most of the Twisters jumped to the side or jumped down from the roof to a balcony below.

The leader didn't move.

A Twister standing immediately behind the leader reached forward and pulled the leader down, away from the grenade, but as he did so, there was a huge blast of light and bang like a sudden clap of thunder.

The leader and his assistant held their ears and yelled in pain as they tried to stand up.

Brandon stood up and flew across the roof, feet barely touching the ground as he ran. The assistant had been holding The Text before the flashbang detonated.

But he dropped it.

The Text was laying on the ground in front of the leader.

Brandon slid in and kicked The Text soccer-style back toward the group. Timothy raced forward and picked it up, then backed up behind the group. Brandon stood up, but the leader reached out and grabbed his collar before he could run.

"Insolent brat!" He raised his hand and prepared to strike Brandon, but he stopped and yelled out in pain.

The leader held his hand down in front of his face and tried to flex his fingers. Through the center of his palm stuck a knife.

Jeff called out, "Lay another hand on him and the next one finds your skull!"

"Still as accurate as ever. Eh, Jeff?"

"More so."

By this time, most of the Twisters had returned to their places and raised their weapons.

Jeff held up his hands slightly and stepped backwards. Over his shoulder, he whispered, "*Read*, Timothy."

William, who was leaning on the pool cue, called out, "Look! Let's be civil. If you let the boy go, we'll get out of your hair and we'll let you keep your face."

The leader laughed and said, "Oh, no. You're not going anywhere. I gave you a chance and you made your move. Twisters, get their weapons and line them up. We'll have a proper execution today, yet!"

Timothy knelt down and placed his glowing hand on the roof. A cool breeze (made colder by the desert air) blew over all of them. The advancing Twisters stopped and pointed their guns at the Casters again.

William stood up straight and grinned.

Jeff looked at the leader, who also appeared to be grinning.

"What are *you* smiling about?"

The leader responded in a creepy, whispering voice, "I see you."

Jeff leaned toward William slightly and asked, "Are you thinking what I'm thinking?"

William shrugged, "I hope not. If so, this day just got a whole lot worse."

Jeff called out, "How did you get your vision?"

The leader crossed his arms and said, "William can tell you. We both got it the same way, though mine was much more recent."

William shook his head, "Why would such a gift be given to such a cruel man, Mr. Lee?"

Eric blurted out, "Wait…Mr. Lee? You're not Michael, are you?"

The leader lowered his bandana and grinned, "Yes, Eric. And how is my dear sister?"

Timothy's heart jumped into his throat.

Ms. Lee? As in, my teacher? This is Ms. Lee's brother?!

Eric glared, "She's been miserable after your *supposed* death! She misses you terribly! Why did you never tell her?"

Michael shook his head, "She need not know. Let it go. I'm doing what I need to do. She's doing what she wants. We're not in each other's way. That's that. I'm done talking to you people."

Jeff flung a knife straight at Michael's head.

With the speed of a hummingbird, Michael reached up and caught the knife, then sneered.

"Kill them. Bring the book to me."

Brandon continued to try to pull away from the leader, but couldn't get free.

"And where do you think you're going? You were so brave until you were caught!"

Brandon looked at Jeff, who called out, "1-2-3, kid."

Brandon thought for a second, then smiled and nodded.

The Twisters took the safety off their weapons, but as soon as they did, William raised the pool cue like a staff and slammed it into the ground. Ten pillars rose from the ground in front of the Casters and they split up to take cover.

Brandon spun around to his right, slamming his elbow into the inside of Michael's elbow, dislodging the strong lock. He stepped toward Michael and kicked him in the chest, throwing him back slightly. Finally, Brandon slammed his left hand in Michael's wrist, breaking his hold. Brandon turned and raced back toward the group.

Michael bent down and touched the ground. The ground right in front of Brandon flew straight up and created a small wall, into which Brandon slammed. As he tried to stand up, Brandon saw Michael walking toward him. Brandon smirked and slammed his hand on the ground and ducked back down. As he did so, a section of the wall shot out and punched Michael in the chest, throwing him to the ground. Brandon stood up and ran around the wall, but stopped when he saw a rifle barrel pointed at his head.

Quickly, Brandon reached up and touched the gun and jumped to the side. With a loud bang, the shell exploded, breaking the gun apart and firing shrapnel into the wall segment. The gunman dropped the gun and grabbed at his face. Brandon stood up again and ran to join the others behind the pillars.

Gunmen had been riddling the pillars with bullets, spraying ammunition all over the place. As Brandon dove behind the pillar where Timothy was hiding, he heard two bullets fly past his head.

Timothy looked over and smiled at Brandon, then ducked back down, clutching the book to his chest. Eric was still holding his arm. Tanya, Anna, Steve, Roger, and Melissa were firing occasional shots from behind their pillars. Jeff was scanning the area and calling out orders. William stood silently, unmoving, listening to everything transpire. The Guild Master was leaning on her cane and appeared to be deep in thought.

"I need a clip!" Tanya yelled, as one Twister grabbed his chest and fell down.

Steve pulled a spare clip from his pocket and tossed it across to Tanya. As he did so, a bullet grazed his arm. He cried out in pain, but took a handkerchief from another pocket and wrapped it around his arm. Anna leaned out and fired two shots, one of which found its target.

Steve had to drop his gun, but Tanya called out, "Kick it over!"

Steve kicked the gun to Tanya and she picked it up. Standing up, she wrapped her arms around either side of the pillar and began firing at targets, whose positions she had previously memorized. Most of her rounds missed the target, but a few found their mark.

Roger picked off two more that had moved around to attempt to flank them.

"Boys! Are you okay?" Eric called out.

Timothy and Brandon both nodded and stayed down.

Michael shouted from behind the wall segment, "I grow weary of these games!"

Jeff shouted, "Oh, getting tired already? Does someone need to take a nap?" He stuck out his bottom lip and shouted, "Poor baby Michael needs to take whittle nappy-wappy? Awww...poor baby Michael!"

William watched as three Twisters advanced toward the Pillars. He placed a hand against the pillar he was leaning on and bowed his head slightly.

The area right in front of the Twisters appeared to melt and the whole section fell through. So did those Twisters. With shouts of surprise and anger, the Twisters fell into the hole, falling two floors down. Needless to say, they weren't coming back up.

Michael leaned over and placed his hand on the ground and smiled, menacingly.

As Anna leaned out to fire another shot, a spike suddenly grew from the pillar right in front of her face. With a gasp, she jumped back. She watched as many more spikes shot out from the pillar. She ducked as a few bullets shot past her.

Tanya reloaded a pistol, but as she raised it, a spike from her pillar shot out and knocked the pistol out of her hand. Steve was leaning with his back against the pillar, but now he stood up. Just as he did, a spike shot out from where he had been sitting a second before. Each Caster backed up as their pillars filled with spikes. Then the surface beneath them started to shake and split open.

While firing at remaining targets, the Casters had to avoid falling into these opening pits. As the roof split, Anna nearly tripped and fell in, but Melissa reached over and caught her by the arm. Melissa and Anna leapt across the gap and joined Steve and Tanya with their Pistols. Roger helped the Guild Master over to where Eric, Jeff, William, and the boys were gathering. William caused new wall segments to be built up from what remained of the shaking surface.

Jeff called out, "You really should stop moving so much around, Michael! You're going to cause this place to blow up! Your Twisting is going to interfere with the power structures below us!"

Michael was becoming more and more furious and yelled, "Then we'll all go out with a bang! I've already died once. What have I to lose?!"

Eric yelled, "But the children!"

"I don't care about the children! *You* brought them here! It's *your* fault! I only care about the book! My Lady will be very disappointed if I do not hold to my promise. I intend to do what I agreed to do! Give me the book or die!"

As the structure continued to shake, some of the Twisters became too frightened and jumped down to the balcony. Others continued to fight. Tanya, Steve, Melissa, Anna, and Roger continued to pick off open targets.

Melissa grabbed her leg and fell down as a Twister found a place to land. She pulled herself behind an available wall and Steve knelt beside her to cover her and make sure she didn't get worse.

William looked at Jeff and said, "From what I see, one more Cast and we're done. We should kill the area."

Jeff shook his head, "Not yet. This can still be turned around. See what you can do to strengthen the facility."

William nodded and placed his hands on the ground.

By this time, only six Twisters were still fighting. Michael's assistant had long since vanished, and Michael had no intentions of moving from his position.

Michael called out, "I see what you're doing, William! I won't let it happen!"

William began to grimace and said, "Jeff! It's amazing. He's actually stronger than I am. What a gift! What a *wasted* gift! We don't have much time. He's going to see this place destroyed."

Timothy turned to the Guild Master and asked, "Can't you do something to help here?"

The Guild Master smiled and said, "I fight when I am needed."

Brandon remarked, "Uh…I think you're needed!"

She smiled and shook her head, "Not yet."

Then she nodded at Jeff. The boys looked over.

Jeff stared at the ground, grinding his jaw. His hand slid to an inside pocket. He drew the defense baton out, flicked his wrist to extend the baton, and slowly looked up.

Jeff stood up and walked around the barricade. He walked toward Michael.

As bullets flew past Jeff in all directions, he didn't flinch. As if in slow motion, he drew a throwing knife and let it fly as he walked. He did it again. Then again. Then thrice more. Each time, the knife found its mark.

Michael was alone.

Michael stood up as Jeff walked toward him, baton to his side, almost dragging. All of the Casters stood up and watched. Anna, Tanya, Steve, and Roger pointed their guns at Michael, waiting.

"One on one, then?"

Jeff nodded.

Timothy turned to Brandon and asked, "Do you smell that?"

William quietly whispered, "Gas."

Brandon whispered, "Well, it wasn't me!"

William smirked and said, "Wrong kind of gas."

"Oh. What's that mean?"

Timothy stared at The Text and softly said, "That this may be it."

Brandon sighed and said, "I see. I'm gonna miss my bike."

Timothy sighed and said, "I'm going to miss my parents."

"It was a nice bike. It was stolen from me, but it was still nice."

Jeff continued his advance toward Michael, who, to buy himself more time, backed up slowly.

Brandon shook his head. "And Ice Cream. I'm gonna miss Ice Cream."

Jeff paused and said, "All you seek is power, but you know nothing of power or how to use it. You are a selfish fool."

Michael laughed, "*I'm* the fool?! I am working toward greatness! You are babysitting and going on wild goose chases!"

"Let me show you what power is. Children! Friends! It's time for you to go. If this Monkey Turd does one more thing, we're all gone. You need to leave."

Timothy shouted, "You're coming with us!"

Jeff looked over his shoulder and smiled to Timothy, then said, "I know my fate."

Jeff spun around and swung his hands through the air, as if throwing something overboard.

The Casters huddled together as a sudden wind picked up and started tossing them around.

Timothy almost dropped The Text, but at the last second he grabbed it and tucked it under his shirt, and held it there. As he did so, his feet left the ground. With the howling of a thousand wolves, the winds rushed over the group. Like a tornado, the winds enveloped the Casters and swirled them around a central core. Everyone yelled and tried to find something to hang on to.

Michael knew what was coming, yelled, and slammed his hands to the ground.

As large spikes flew up from the surface, the Casters were pulled from their feet by the winds and thrown into the sand far below.

The facility began to tremble and smoke rose from the splits in the surface. Below, remaining Twisters were scrambling to escape the facility. They abandoned their guns and hurried to the exits.

Jeff turned toward Michael and quietly said, "That's a shame."

As Jeff charged toward Michael, baton raised, Michael wore an expression of shock and terror.

As the Casters touched the sand, the winds shifted and pushed them along the ground.

It's like sledding!

Just, you know, without the sled.

And with explosions.

The Casters were set down as they finally entered the edge of the desert and re-entered the forested region. As the last of the winds tousled their hair, the Casters watched fiery plumes of smoke rise above where the facility used to be. After the subtle pressure of a distant shockwave passed, the Casters were faced with a new question.

Mourn…or Run?

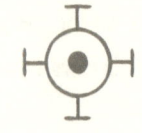

A SHOT IN
THE DARK

The Casters sat around in a circle in the lobby of a hotel in Las Vegas. Roger, Tanya, Anna, and Eric held cups of coffee and stared at the floor. Eric had bandaged his wound and swore to keep going while Steve and Melissa had been admitted to the hospital for their injuries. William sat in the corner, hands folded, staring at his thumbs. He had since left the pool cue behind, seeing as how it would look strange walking around with it in public.

Timothy and Brandon were in the worst shape, emotionally, of the group. They were curled up in their chairs, fighting back tears and sobs of great loss. Timothy's gaze was stuck on the front cover of The Text, which he held in his lap.

The Guild Master limped over to the boys and whispered, "It's okay to mourn a loss. It's okay to cry. Just don't let someone else's end be your own."

The boys nodded and wiped their eyes with their sleeves.

Eric nodded and said, "I had better send word to other Casters. We're going to need help."

Anna asked, "With what? We rescued the Guild Master and The Text. What else is there to do?"

William answered, "As much as I hate to admit it at this point, Eric's right. We're not done. The Lady wants The Text for something, and she won't stop until she has it."

Anna asked, "How do you know?"

"I knew her, once. I thought we would find her at the bunker, but I didn't see her. I don't know where she is, but we need to find her and stop her. She always had more guards than we saw with Michael, so we're going to need extra help."

Anna nodded.

Tanya tipped her head toward the boys, "What about them?"

Eric replied, "I'm going home with them. I've already let them get into too much danger. I didn't think it was going to be *that* risky. Now that we have The Text and freed the Guild Master, we can return them to their parents and fill them in."

Without looking up, Timothy whispered, "Jude's still out there."

"So?" Tanya asked.

Brandon answered, "He'll hunt us, like he led Michael's men to do before."

Eric shook his head and said, "The others will get Jude before he can cause any more problems."

William responded, "How sure about that are you? The boys are right. What if we don't get to him in time? What if we just miss? What if he's already waiting for them?"

"I just don't want to put them in any more danger."

Tanya smirked and said, "It doesn't matter where they go now, there will always be danger. When we stop the Lady, whoever she is, it might be safe enough to take them home."

Roger offered, "With my ribs still hurting so much, I'm not sure how much more I can do, so I could escort them home and find a safe place for The Text."

The Guild Master spoke up now and said, "The Text was never intended for safe-keeping. It was never meant to be kept a secret. It was written so that it could be used. It was written so that whoever reads from it could change the world for the better. What would surprise the Lady the most? Returning The Text to where it started, or bringing it right to her doorstep?"

Eric asked, "What are you suggesting?"

The Guild Master replied, "That we face her together, boys included."

William nodded and then said, "I know someone who may know where we can find her and he only lives a few miles outside Las Vegas. However, my biggest worry is that the Lady is so powerful that the boys may not make it out. They need more training before they can go anywhere near her."

Anna offered, "The Guild Master, Eric, and I can teach them. You, Tanya, and Roger should go talk to your friend."

William nodded.

"So how far back do you go with this guy…Nigel, you said?" Tanya asked.

They had rented a car and were driving out to find William's possible source of information. Tanya drove, William rode shotgun, and Roger sat behind William.

"Nigel, yes. We trained together, though he was much older than me."

"How much older?"

"Let's just say that I hope he's still alive to talk to us."

Tanya nodded.

Roger leaned his forehead against the window and stared out over the buildings and trees. A trace of smoke from the bunker in the distance could still be seen rising up into the sunny sky.

He started, "Do you think it's possible…"

He paused.

William finished, "That Jeff is still alive? Jeff is full of surprises, but when the facility was destroyed, the two energy traces I saw on the roof disappeared. Is it possible? Yes. Is it plausible? No. From everything I could see, Jeff and Michael are both gone."

Roger nodded and said, "I'm sorry for your loss."

William didn't move a muscle, but said, "I'm sorry for the *world's* loss. He was one of the most talented Casters I've ever met."

The Guild Master, Anna, Eric, Timothy, and Brandon gathered in a rented conference room in the hotel, opened The Text on the table and sat around it.

The Guild Master held out a coin for each boy.

"You both understand that when an area is Dead, we must cast into it before it can be manipulated. You've also seen that people can Cast without using The Text. How is this possible? They learned the language of The Text and can *speak* it themselves. Casting from The Text is always going to be more powerful, but it is possible for us to do our own Casting with the language. Twisters are much more skilled in this area since all they rely on is their own ability to manipulate and Cast.

"Again, this is why they're called Twisters. It's not that they're evil. In fact, most are not. Many do exactly what Casters do, and many even work together with Casters. Some Twisters do become evil, though, and this is because they decide to follow their own agenda and they don't care who they have to take out on their way there. Twisters simply choose to use their own methods for Casting instead of relying on The Text. Casters rely on The Text and only use their own methods when it is required."

Timothy asked, "How do Casters Cast from The Text when they don't have The Text or a copy?"

"Memorization. When you've run through certain passages enough times, you just know how The Author would Cast it, so Casting as he did becomes second nature to you. This is what we're going to try to teach you today. We'll help you find key passages that you can easily memorize. You may need to pull from these over the next few days."

Eric stepped away from the table when his cellphone rang. He moved to the side of the room and answered it.

"Hello?"

A frail old man walked from the back room of an antique store and placed an egg-shaped antique on the glass counter. He looked up and asked, "How can I be of assistance?"

"Nigel! Hello! Do you remember me?" William approached the counter while Tanya and Roger looked through shelves and cases of porcelain dolls, tea sets, old farming tools, tin toys, and even an antique sword.

"Billy boy! Of course I remember you! How long has it been? Three years?"

"More like thirty years, Nigel."

"Oh, my. Really? Wow. Well, tell me about what's happened since!"

"I wish I had the time to do so. Unfortunately, we're on a tight schedule. This is Tanya and Roger. They're Casters and we need your help."

"Oh. Hello to you two. I'm sorry, though. I left the Twisting life many years ago. That witch of a woman leads the Twisters and I want no part of it."

"That's actually why we're here. We need to know about that Lady. We hope you know where we can find her."

"You're looking for her? Oh, no. No. I'm not helping with anything that has to do with anyone finding her. If she's lost, then I hope she stays that way. When I expressed my desire to leave and start this business, she harassed me with Runners and threats until I couldn't take it anymore. I had to fake my own death to get away from her!"

"I'm sorry she did those things to you, Nigel. She's been doing the same to the Casters now. We need to find her so we can stop her."

Nigel rubbed his chin with his right hand and thought for a few moments.

"You really think you can stop her?"

William nodded, "At the very least, we intend to try."

"Well…Okay. I'll tell you what I used to know. Now, I don't know anything about her concerning the past few years. I can only tell you what I knew when I was trying to leave."

"That would be fantastic, Nigel. It's a great place to start."

"No, I said 'A great place to *start*.' Dirty. Anyone you can assemble. We need extra hands…No, we don't need *clams*. Hands! Yes, thank you. Okay, good bye."

Timothy stared at the coin in his left palm and ran his right hand across the line the Guild Master was pointing to.

At first, nothing happened, but then the coin began to shake. Suddenly, the coin flew out of Timothy's hand and shot around the room, ricocheting off corners, walls, tables, and chairs. Timothy heard and felt the coin whiz past his face several times. Then the coin returned to his hand.

Timothy looked at the Guild Master with an embarrassed look on his face.

She smiled and said, "That's why we asked for a room without windows."

Timothy smiled, then a look of shock appeared on his face. He shook his hand wildly, dropping the coin onto the table.

"Hot! Wow!"

Everyone laughed, then the Guild Master nodded to Brandon, indicating that it was his turn.

He slid his hand across the passage and watched as the coin shook slightly. Then his coin shot straight up and stuck in the ceiling.

"Oops."

The Guild Master cautioned, "It's about control."

"Control?" Tanya walked over to the counter.

Nigel responded, "Yes. It was always about control for her. She would sit in her so-called throne and just tell everyone what to do. She had them do everything from assassinate a government leader to make her a sandwich. As for me, she kept me for regular seek-and-destroy missions. I got tired of it. As I started contemplating leaving, we all of a sudden had to up and leave. We moved everything to some mountain lodge thing in Colorado. That's the last place I saw her. Really, even though her father was not a nice man, he was much better to serve under than her. In comparison, I really missed him. I didn't serve under her so-called *leadership* for very long, but it was long enough to force me to leave."

Roger asked, "What is her name?"

"Lucille Valentine."

Tanya shook her head, "That figures… The person who bears the name of the patron saint of love is an evil witch."

Roger pulled out his smartphone and activated a map application, "Can you show us where we can find this place?"

"I don't recall the exact location, but it should be somewhere around…here." He traced a circle around an area with his finger and looked up.

William shook Nigel's hand and said, "Thank you so much, old friend! Be well."

"Same to you, Billy."

As the three reached the door, Nigel called out, "Oh, wait! I almost forgot! You'll be needing a few things!"

He held up a backpack of gear and a walking stick with a carved wolf head on it.

"Got everything?" Eric looked over at the boys as they walked through the hotel lobby.

Timothy nodded as he adjusted the straps on his backpack. They had made a quick trip out to the store to buy a few more items for the next leg of the journey.

The Guild Master, Anna, Eric, Brandon, and Timothy walked out of the hotel and stepped into a fifteen-passenger van where William, Roger, and Tanya were waiting.

Timothy asked, "When does the plane leave?"

Eric replied, "Well, since everyone thinks the bunker's explosion was a terrorist attack, all flights are grounded until they sort that out. We're going on a road trip."

Brandon said, "Let's ride in the back of the van! If we hit a big enough bump, we can see if we hit our heads on the roof!"

William, who was holding the new wolf-head walking stick, leaned over to Timothy and whispered, "Ah. That explains some things."

Timothy grinned, but found a seat toward the back and settled in for a long drive.

ROCKY ROAD

Timothy shook his head and sat up in his seat. Brandon was shaking his shoulders gently and calling, "Timothy. Wake up. We're here. Timothy. TIMOTHY! Hey, Timothy! Timmy! Tim-bo! Rin-Tim-Tim! Timbelina! T—"

Timothy turned to Brandon and said, "I'm up! I'm up! Where are we?"

Tanya called back from two seats up, "Colorado. We crossed the state line a few hours ago. We're approaching the area Nigel pointed out. Everyone keep your eyes open. There should be some kind of lodge or complex on the mountain range over there."

They drove around for hours and found houses, lodges, campgrounds, and large facilities, but none of them matched the description Nigel had offered. He recalled a very large facility, but that it was very dark. So far, they had only seen light- to medium-colored facilities, houses, and other structures.

They entered the San Juan Mountain Range area and headed North.

Anna mumbled, "I don't like this area. I hope it's not here."

"Why is that?" Timothy asked.

"This part of the country has a ton of calderas. I don't want to have to do any Casting around those.

Brandon leaned forward and rested his chin on his crossed arms that he placed on the back of the seat in front of him. He said, "Well, of course! It's a mountain range. It had better have cold air. I suppose it would depend on the height of the mountain. I imagine that at lower peaks—"

"Very funny. No. *Calderas*! Magma pockets. Some are insanely massive."

"So?"

"So, if we disrupt it, we could either destroy a city block or the whole world, depending on the size of the caldera."

Eric spoke over his shoulder, "We shouldn't have to disrupt anything. We'll take a small group in and scout everything out. The best strategy is to lead her out into ground that we like."

"And where is that?" Anna asked.

"In the open, on an area not above a caldera. Easy fix. So you need not worry. I'm sure it'll be fine. We just have to make this go as quickly as possible."

The group drove around for quite some time, but they still could not find anything that matched Nigel's description.

"Do you suppose he lied to us?" Tanya asked.

William shook his head, "For as long as I knew Nigel, he never lied…about anything. It's more likely that he just forgot—"

Eric leaned over and asked, "What is it?"

William had stopped speaking and his head was turned to face out the window.

"I thought I saw something. Out there. Can we get there?" He pointed to the San Juan Mountains.

"Well! That's very specific of you!" Tanya smirked and said, "I'll see what I can do. That's in a national park, so I don't know if we'll find anything in there. Wouldn't it already have been explored and exposed by the park rangers?"

Eric nodded, "Or the constant stream of hikers they get?"

"I just want to see," William shrugged.

Tanya drove the van into the mountains and they continued to search for several more hours. Dusk was on its way. Finally, William pointed to the Tower Mountains and said, "There."

Everyone squinted to search the mountainside.

Roger said, "I don't see anything."

William replied, "Me neither. That's just the point. Where you see a mountain, I see a void. That must be it."

Anna shook her head, "Great. I'm sure there's a caldera here. Can we avoid Casting?"

Click.

Roger locked a clip into his gun and said, "That's what I'm thinking."

William, Tanya, Roger, and Anna had to hike up the mountain as the roads did not go that way. The Guild Master, Eric, Timothy, and

Brandon waited in the van. They watched the other group search the side of the mountain. Tanya waved the others over to her position and they pushed a section of rock out of the way. Guns raised, the group entered a cave entrance.

Timothy looked over at Eric and said, "I thought Nigel said it was a lodge-type structure."

Eric shrugged, "Maybe that's what it feels like inside."

Several minutes passed where they just watched through the van windows, waiting to hear something. Anything.

What's going on in there?

Finally, Eric's cellphone buzzed.

"Yep? Okay. We're on our way."

Eric turned to the others as he put his phone away and said, "It's clear. They need us to help look through things."

As Eric helped the Guild Master into the cave entrance, Timothy and Brandon walked down into a cavernous room. Tanya and William were in this room, searching through boxes and papers. Tanya had taken The Text and had already Cast into the area. Three doorways led to rooms adjacent to this room. There was also a staircase carved out of the mountain's stone to their immediate left. This stairway appeared to lead to a section directly below them. Roger and Anna were in an adjacent room to the right.

Tanya tilted her head to indicate that the other four should check out the other rooms. She handed The Text to Timothy as they walked by. Timothy and Brandon walked through the doorway directly in front of them. Eric and the Guild Master entered the room on the left.

Timothy and Brandon found desks, chairs, empty packing boxes, rolled up area rugs, and a few broken coffee mugs in the corner.

Brandon commented, "It looks like they had a full office setup here. I wonder what they were actually up to. Probably nothin' good."

"Well, remember that people have been saying that not all Twisters are bad. It's just that Jude, Michael and Lucille have been working together for some evil scheme, but we still don't know what that is. Also, we don't know that this was just Lucille's base of operations. I'm sure many Twisters could be doing things here, even really good things. Look! See? There's a box over here addressed to the Red Cross."

"You're too nice. You know that? The Twister himself was a self-declared enemy of The Author. Why should we trust any Twisters?"

"It's not their identity that makes them evil. It's what they *do* with it that determines their position."

"Wow! That was very old-person of you. Yeah…I guess I believe that. You've got a really balanced view on this, dude. You're newer than I am and you've already got a very mature view of the situation. How'd that happen?"

"I don't know. I guess I've just always wanted to treat everyone else the same way I would like to be treated."

Brandon nodded as he rummaged through a drawer of papers.

Timothy walked over to another desk and saw a box flipped over on the table. He shifted the box, but there was something large and heavy underneath it. He lifted the box up and tossed it aside. There was a computer underneath!

"Hey guys! In here!"

The others rushed in when they heard Timothy call. Roger and Tanya had their guns raised, but lowered them when they realized there was no threat.

William nodded, "Good find. There might be something valuable on there."

Timothy shrugged, "Its power was cut and I don't see an outlet anywhere."

William smirked, "That was always the neat thing about Twisting." He placed his hand on the computer and looked in Timothy's direction.

"What was?"

"You could bend the rules."

The computer screen blinked and the fan whirred. Timothy and Brandon watched in amazement as the computer came to life. The whirring idled and the screen went black. Then a blinking line appeared on the top left corner of the screen.

William smiled and whispered, "Now watch this."

He walked around to the front of the computer and said, "Where have your masters gone?"

Timothy and Brandon looked at William.

Okay, turning the computer on with Twisting was cool. I'll give him that. Talking to it like it's alive? Please…

The boys' necks nearly snapped when, out of the corner of their eyes, they saw text appear on the monitor and they spun their heads to look at it.

"Timothy, could you please read it to me? I cannot read text unless the text itself is imbued with energy."

"They were never my masters. They disowned me. They took my brethren and left me alone to rust and rot beneath that corrugated container."

"Whoever they were, where did they go?"

"… Retrieving Recently Accessed Files …"

The screen flickered and a handful of webpages and documents expanded onto the screen. Roger walked over and looked at the screen, then asked, "Can you pull up the last three pages they viewed?"

A textbox appeared on screen. "Yes. I can."

Nothing happened for several seconds. Roger laughed, "Oh, okay! I get it! Please pull up the last three pages they viewed."

Roger looked them over. There was a page about good names for pet birds, a document with a love letter being written, and a page with a weblog about the battles between coffee bean growers and their distribution centers' security officers concerning the need for the officers to receive free coffee samples in order to maintain their current contracts.

"Okay. *That* didn't help. Pull up all webpages used in the last two days concerning geographic locations and travel."

Tanya asked, "Two days?"

"None of the papers I looked through were dated any more recently than two days ago. I assume they left very recently, after finishing with those papers."

"I saw the same," said Anna.

Seven webpages expanded onto the screen. Five pages mentioned New York. Two of those mentioned the Finger Lakes.

Eric nodded, "The Finger Lakes? What would they want there?"

The Guild Master exhaled, "Ahhh... An ancient legend. A home long forgotten."

The group looked at her and waited.

And waited.

"What? Oh! You want to hear about it?"

Brandon whispered to Timothy, "Sheesh! Why did we bring her, again?"

Timothy whispered, "She was going to be helpful."

Brandon nodded, "Riiiight. Right. Got it. So…Why did we bring her, again?"

The Guild Master began, "It was once said that The Twister could be brought back to our realm through the use of seven relics. They can be used to split the dimensional rift and thus create a door for him to simply walk through. The passageway is said to recreate the person's body and last-remembered state of existence. If I'm correct, Lucille is looking for those Relics."

Anna said, "Well, there are lots of places to hide relics there. Even if you toss one into each lake, there are eleven lakes, so it's hit or miss when searching. It'll take them quite a while."

The Guild Master shook her head, "If the legend is true, then the relics are all together in the same room."

"Room?"

"An underground lair of sorts."

Brandon threw his hands up and exclaimed, "Why is it *always* underground? Everything's underground! My *bicycle* is probably underground!"

The Guild Master smiled and replied, "The best places to hide something are right in front of someone or right below their feet."

Anna prompted, "So, do we know *where* in the Finger Lakes they'll be?"

Roger turned back to the computer and said, "Pull up anything recently searched for about specific locations near the Finger Lakes."

A textbox appeared which read, "No such searches have been conducted."

Eric crossed his arms, "Well, that's all we have to go on, then."

"That will be enough," William nodded.

Tanya waved, "Let's get going, then. We can't let them get those relics."

As they were leaving the room, they did not notice a new textbox appear, reading, "`Good luck.`"

When they entered the main room, William suddenly pushed those nearest to him toward the stairway, whispering, "Someone's coming. Get downstairs. Quickly."

As they all settled onto the stairs, William and Timothy watched two park rangers enter the cave.

The closest ranger commented, "Well, I'll be! This has been here all this time and no one's noticed? It's fantastic! Man-made, it seems. It looks like someone's been using it for some sort of office. Call for backup. I'm going to check down these stairs."

William and Timothy leaned back out of sight. The stairwell was very dark, so they assumed they were hidden well enough. The ranger approached and pulled a flashlight from his belt. He turned it on and pointed it down the stairs. Since the stairway was curved, William and Timothy were just out of sight.

William placed his hand on the wall and caused a large rock to dislodge from the ceiling and collide with the head of the ranger's flashlight, shattering it.

"Whoa! That was weird! Hey, Ed, I need to borrow your flashlight. He walked back over to the other ranger.

William and Timothy peered around the wall to watch the rangers. They heard two loud popping noises, saw four strings shoot across and attach themselves to the rangers, and then they watched as the rangers convulsed and fell to the ground.

Two robed figures entered the cave and looked around. One turned to the other and said, "They're here. You check the rooms. I'll check downstairs."

The closer robed figure walked toward the stairway and took a step down. William pushed Timothy back, slightly, then stepped out and swung his walking stick. The back of the wolf's head collided with the nose of the robed figure.

As the robed figure bent over and grabbed at his nose, William touched the staff to the wall. A pillar of stone shot down from the ceiling, slamming into the back of the robed figure's head.

The second figure heard the falling rock and ran in from the room across the way.

"William, old friend! Long time, no see! Shall we so end our previous grudge toward one another?"

William didn't respond. He just glared. He tapped the bottom of the staff to the ground. The floor shook slightly and the Twister steadied himself. Suddenly, rows of spikes shot out from the ground. The Twister threw himself backwards, out of the way.

"Sneaky! Very sneaky! Yet, not good enough. Typical."

William sneered and tapped the ground again.

As the ground beneath the Twister split open, he shifted his weight and stood up on the right side and peered down into the black pit.

"You're so predictable!"

William asked, "Am I?" He nodded his head toward the opening.

The Twister peered over the edge again and watched as a large stone fist rose from the pit. The Twister touched the fist, causing it to break up into small pieces, and called, "That's it?"

William answered, "No."

A stone fist formed from the wall behind the Twister and slammed into his back. This threw the Twister across the pit opening and onto his chest. Gasping for breath, the Twister started to stand up. Another fist rose up from the pit and grabbed the Twister's ankle. The Twister tried to reach out with his right hand, but found that his arm had been broken.

William called out, "Let us go, and I'll do the same for you."

"No!"

"So be it."

The fist pulled the Twister, sliding him across the floor and into the opening. Before he was dragged into the abyss, the Twister slammed his left hand on the ground. The fist, Twister, and opening vanished, leaving the scene very quiet.

The Casters started to move out of the stairway, but the stairs suddenly started moving. Backwards and downwards! As the stairs would move, new steps were created at the top, creating a stairway much like the one Timothy traversed only a few days earlier. Just... you know...scarier. They heard a loud noise from the bottom of the stairway—it was like two grind wheels in a water mill.

William leapt from the stairs and into the main cave. He stood up and reached out his hand for Timothy. He pulled Timothy into the room and reached out for Brandon. The others were further away, so he reached the staff down the stairway as they hurriedly climbed the descending escalator. He helped Tanya into the room, followed by Roger. He then helped the Guild Master exit the stair trap. Eric was soon to follow. As Anna worked her way up the Impossible Exercise Stairway of Death, everyone could begin to see where the grinding noise was coming from.

Like rows of shark teeth, rings of stone spikes were eating away at the descending stairs and climbing to the top. As the stone-spiked mining-machine-wall-thing came closer, Anna started to lose her footing. William was holding the staff out for her, but she couldn't reach it.

William turned and slammed the end of the staff into the wall. He held it there, a look of intense pain emerging on his face. As he held his position, the grinding rings started to slow down. Suddenly, Anna slipped. With a shriek, she fell onto her back and watched her feet enter the stone grinder. Though it was slowing down, the spikes still cut into Anna's legs.

Suddenly, the rings stopped and the spikes shattered.

William stepped back from the wall, leaned over, and breathed heavily. Anna began bawling as she realized how close she came to death. Still, her legs were now trapped in stone and she could no longer feel anything in them.

Eric ran over and was about to place his hands on the wall, but was stopped by the Guild Master.

"Wait! This is a very delicate thing. One wrong step and it could crush her legs permanently. Allow me. The rest of you should get those rangers and the Twister out of here."

She slowly knelt down and placed her hands on the wall. She closed her eyes and began Casting as if she was breaking into a vault.

William leaned on the walking stick and commented, "He was stronger than the last time I fought with him. That was difficult to counter. I am sorry I could not have done better."

Through deep breaths and streams of tears, Anna shook her head and said, "This was sufficient. Thank you!"

William turned to the others and said, "Everyone who does not need to be in here needs to get out of here. It's very unstable. Tanya, you and I need to work at cleanup while the Guild Master gets her out of this."

Tanya and William stood at opposite ends of the room and placed their hands on the walls. Timothy and Brandon watched with Eric and Roger from outside the entrance.

The ground beneath them shook slightly and they could hear stone grinding against stone. What had broken off was reabsorbed and returned to its place. Everything seemed to be re-aligning properly.

Finally, segments of wall slid away and Anna's legs were free. Roger ran in and picked her up to carry her back outside. The Guild Master limped behind him and exited the cave. The wall segment fell apart, and a staircase reappeared. Tanya and William removed their hands from the wall and began to walk toward the exit.

Then the ground shook again.

Tanya and William turned around and watched as the ground began to split open again. A charred hand reached up and grabbed the edge. A second hand appeared. The Twister pulled himself up and began pulling himself out of the opened floor.

The Twister's body was blackened, smoking, and blistered. His eyes were sealed shut and his mouth was hanging open as he gasped for air.

William turned to the others and yelled, "Get out of here! We'll meet you by the van! Go!"

Timothy backed up and watched as the Twister slammed his hand against the ground again. The cave entrance groaned and closed, like a whale gathering krill.

In shock, Timothy could not move. He could only stare.

Now what?

"Timothy! Come on!" Brandon called.

Timothy looked around. The rangers were finally standing up; Eric was explaining things to them, and Roger was already moving down the mountain with Anna and the Guild Master. The rangers helped Eric carry the Twister and they all moved down the mountainside as quickly as they could.

As they ran, they could feel the ground shaking. Timothy looked over his shoulder and saw the peak of the mountain begin to break apart and fall into itself.

When they reached the van, everyone climbed in. Roger started the vehicle and they all watched.

Like an ice-crusted pile of snow in spring, the mountain's peak folded into itself. In its place, smoke rose to the sky. A thick red substance began flowing down the hill.

Roger shook his head and said, "We've got to go."

As they pulled away, everyone watched, expecting William and Tanya to bust out and run down the hill.

No one came running down the hill.

A ranger said, "A volcano in this region? I know there's Dotsero, but that's miles away. This is really fascinating!"

No one else spoke.

No one else even wanted to breathe.

They just listened.

And cried.

After they dropped Anna, the rangers, and the Twister off at the nearest hospital, the remaining five Casters drove to the airport.

On their way there, as Timothy leaned his head against the window, he asked Eric, "Why does everything have to blow up? So far, that's all that's happened! What about the cleanup stuff?"

Eric replied, "It doesn't always blow up. Sometimes it just collapses, sometimes it disintegrates, sometimes it simply burns, and sometimes it slides into a fault. We just happen to be having all the bad luck of going to places with power supplies and magma. Cleanup is crucial, if it can be done."

Roger had the radio on, playing music, but a news broadcast interrupted the music.

"A new volcano has been identified in southwest Colorado today. Scientists are…confused. Residents in or around the San Juan Mountains are cautioned to evacuate the area until further notice."

Eric finished, "Otherwise, we get *that*."

Nothing more was said by anyone until they reached the airport. They parked their van, grabbed their bags, and walked into the airport.

They approached the ticket counter and were about to speak, but the cashier asked, "Seven flying today?"

Eric shook his head angrily and said, "No. You can clearly see that there are five of us here. There will be five flying."

The cashier smiled and asked, "Are you sure?"

Roger nearly shouted, "Yes, he's sure!"

The cashier pointed toward the waiting area and said, "I was told seven."

Everyone looked over.

Standing in the waiting area with weary grins on their faces were Tanya and William.

REVELATIONS

After a series of flights, the team finally landed in New York. They walked to a café, purchased food and beverages, and sat down around a large table. Timothy laid The Text down on the table beside his plate.

Brandon asked, "So what's next? How do we find these guys at the Finger Lakes?"

William answered, "I believe the best bet is to have a few of us use a helicopter to fly over each lake, looking for a sign of their presence. The others will retrieve supplies and food, and will secure a vehicle. That's the easiest route, anyway."

"Won't they figure out who is flying past?"

"Probably not…unless they have someone else like Michael. My bet would be that they don't. Besides, if the area is Living, I will be able to tell without getting too close."

Eric was on the phone with his wife; Tanya was stirring her coffee; Roger was nibbling at his salad; the Guild Master was staring at her Danish pastry; William was twiddling his thumbs; and Timothy was poking his sandwich with his straw. Brandon, on the other hand, was diving into his sandwich.

A busser walked by and asked, "How is everything?"

Everyone nodded and said, "It's good," then continued doing what they had been doing.

"Enough of the pity party. Open the book."

Timothy looked over at Brandon and asked, "What?"

Brandon, who had just taken a massive bite, wiped a little mayonnaise off his face and mumbled through his food, "I didn't say anything."

Timothy turned to William.

"Nor did I."

That was weird.

"Open the book."

Timothy looked around, but no one was talking to him.

What's going on?

Suddenly, Timothy's glass of water tipped and dumped all over the table, running onto his lap and splashing The Text.

"Whoa!"

Everyone looked up, but no one's expression changed.

William grabbed a handful of napkins and passed them to Timothy.

"I'm sorry," said Timothy as he wiped up the spill with the napkins. He reached over to The Text, picked it up, and wiped off the cover and spine, which were the only areas that got wet.

Timothy placed The Text on a drier spot of the table and opened it up to see if the pages were okay. He flipped through the book until he was almost all the way through it. Then he stopped. There was a symbol there that looked quite different from all the others he had since seen.

Timothy looked around the table. Everyone was busy doing something else (or busy doing nothing), so he went ahead and ran his finger over the symbol.

Nothing happened.

Then something did.

The world around him seemed to glow, and he couldn't hear anything in the café. Instead, he heard gentle music and a calm, soft, male voice. As he listened, Timothy's pupils dilated, his forehead started sweating, his right hand started twitching, and his mouth hung open. It felt like an eternity, sitting there listening to the man's voice. Yet, it was a comfortable eternity. He was in awe, but at peace. It was the most wonderful sensation he had ever experienced.

Brandon took a sip of his soda and glanced over at Timothy. He spat out his drink and laughed.

"What's wrong with your face?"

Timothy's vision ended and he turned to face Brandon, "What? Nothing. I'm fine. Tired, I guess."

"Okay…You looked ridiculous, though! Here! You looked like this." Brandon contorted his face to mimic Timothy's, though it was much more exaggerated. He opened his eyes as wide as he could, pulled on his right cheek, and raised the left side of his upper lip. Then he stuck his tongue out for good measure.

Timothy didn't respond, but closed The Text and began eating his sandwich, instead.

"Finally! You found me. Now, let's really get this party started."

William noted as he finished wiping Brandon's spit off his face, "My face is sticky. Thanks, Brandon."

William and Roger managed to secure a helicopter ride over the Finger Lakes later that afternoon. Meanwhile, the Guild Master, Tanya, Eric, Brandon, and Timothy went out to various stores and purchased things they were not permitted to take on the flights. They also purchased food, water bottles, and new socks for everyone.

Someone's feet were starting to smell like old macaroni and cheese, but no one would 'fess up, so they figured on new socks for everybody.

William and Roger met up with the others at a nearby park and Roger shared, "We've got them. We're gonna need extra hands, though."

Eric nodded, "Like that?"

William and Roger turned around to see ten Casters walking toward them, all carrying concealed weapons or walking sticks. One even wore a spiked collar and spiked gloves. Another wore a flak vest, a tactical helmet, and carried a large metal bat.

Roger smiled, "That'll do."

Seventeen Casters walked south, toward the northern edge of the Y-shaped intersection of Keuka Lake. A tanned, male Caster with a buzz-cut drew a machete from inside his full-length coat. A female Caster with curly, black hair checked the safety and clips of two automatic pistols and tucked them into shoulder holsters. A large, muscular, Asian, male Caster cracked his knuckles, made fists, and cracked his neck. A short, middle-eastern female Caster finished connecting pieces of a custom, concealable assault rifle. They came in all shapes and sizes, wielding various weapons. They crept along, through the trees and bushes, making their way to the point of the intersection.

A resident who saw the Casters sneaking around called the police, but the policeman who answered the call happened to be a Caster and knew of the effort, so reassured the resident that she was in no danger. He convinced her that they were rehearsing for a movie that will be filmed a few months later, but cautioned that they were not to be interrupted or watched—so it didn't ruin the surprise.

When they reached the top of the hill, William motioned for everyone to find cover and stay low. Timothy peered through the foliage and saw tents, tables, and dig sites. William motioned to Timothy that the area was Dead and that he couldn't see past the tree against which he was leaning. Timothy removed his socks and shoes, then waited for the order.

Brandon reached into his backpack and pulled out a small parabolic dish (used for enhancing sounds at long distances from the listeners) and handed it to Timothy. He pulled out a second one for himself. They both pointed the dishes at the site and waited. They heard shovels digging, people grunting, speedboats passing, and birds chirping.

Timothy pointed his dish toward a tent in the center of the area and listened.

"What do you mean he still hasn't sent word? He should have already been here, himself!"

"Yes, my lady. I'm doing everything I can to reach him. There was that accident there a few days ago. Perhaps something—"

"Michael doesn't let accidents happen! It was an *intentional* explosion. The Casters probably got too close and he cleaned everything up. The question is why he isn't *here*, yet."

Timothy turned to Eric and nodded, who nodded in response. Eric turned to everyone behind him, gave a thumbs up, then signaled for them to watch closely and be ready.

Brandon tapped Timothy's shoulder and pointed to the dish. Timothy listened again.

"…n't care about old vases or bones. I don't care if this was a burial ground or whatever. I need that entrance. I need what's in there. With those relics, we can start a new era for the Twisters and finally have supreme power. Why don't you see the importance of this?! Get back out there and only report when you've found the entrance. Scrap anything else you find."

There was a pause while the person left the tent, then the lady continued, "As soon as Michael gets here, we won't need to dig anymore. He'll find it as soon as he looks around."

"So, why are we digging *now*?"

"Because he's not here, idiot. When he gets here with The Text, we'll bring this area to Life and find the way in."

Timothy placed his dish on the ground and slowly crept back to Eric to report what he heard.

Several hours went by. The Casters all continued to hold their positions, though some had to rest or eat. There weren't any more important conversations heard through the parabolic dishes, and activity was minimal.

Suddenly, a loud cheer rose up through the Twister camp. Timothy and Brandon threw on their headsets and listened.

"They found it? That was faster than I thought it would be! Give the finders a bonus of some sort, after they get it opened. If Michael arrives, either shoot him or send him away. We don't need him, anymore."

As Lucille exited her tent, she enthusiastically waved her hands in the air and shouted, "The founder's lair! At last!"

The founder's lair? The Twister's *lair? That's one reason this is so important to her.*

Timothy watched as Lucille's crazy, black, curly hair bounced in the breeze. She wore a black robe over her black attire, her hair tied in a very loose bun, and wore very black, very gothic, makeup.

When the coast seemed clear, Timothy gave Eric a thumbs-up. The Casters all moved forward to the edge of the tree line and toward the clearing where the Twister camp was set up. William stayed back because he still couldn't see. There were two guards by the central tent. Two Casters with blowguns fired tranquilizers at the guards. As the guards fell, the Casters ran up, caught them, and dragged them back to the foliage to bind them up.

Eric, Timothy, Brandon, and two other Casters Timothy never met moved up behind the tents so they could watch the Twisters. As they peered around the tents, they saw Lucille lead the Twisters down into a dig site a few yards from the water's edge. As the Twisters disappeared, the Casters prepared to move in.

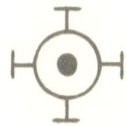

THE GAME IS AFOOT

Four Twister guards remained outside the entrance to the underground lair of The Twister. Each Twister guard was facing in a different direction so they could make sure every angle was covered. The Casters watched and saw three scuba divers surface and dive in the lake, beyond the guards.

Why are they still diving if they found the entrance?

Eric whispered, "I'm not sure why there are still divers, but I suspect they're just extra guards."

That answers that.

Eric waved his hand and two of the four guards grabbed at their necks, pulling tranquilizer darts out and subsequently passing out. The other two turned to see what happened, only to reach for their necks as well. Six Casters rushed out and grabbed the fallen guards.

Suddenly, the three divers surfaced and raised automatic, waterproof submachine guns.

One of the Casters shook his head and pointed to the tree line.

The divers looked over and watched as Casters with assault rifles, blowguns, and pistols stepped out of the trees and raised their weapons.

Slowly, the divers raised their hands and dropped their guns into the water.

With all of the guards bound and gagged, and some still knocked out, the Casters approached the entrance to the lair. The dig site dropped about six feet and a small entrance was visible. The original door appeared to have been wooden, but had long since rotted away. William joined the group with his hand on Timothy's shoulder. Brandon stood beside them as everyone peered into the hole.

Timothy whispered, "What if they're right there?"

The middle-eastern Caster named Rachel, the one with the custom assault rifle, held up her hand, tucked the rifle butt under her arm, and leapt into the dig site. Landing as gently and as quietly as a deer on the meadow, she looked down the iron sights into the opening. She flicked on a flashlight and stared into the entrance. After a few seconds, she waved her hand to signal that it was clear.

One by one, the Casters jumped into, or climbed down into (since a basic ladder was leaned against the dirt walls), the hole and stepped through the entrance. Timothy and Brandon helped William step down the ladder to the ground. Six Casters with rifles stayed behind to watch for other Twisters and keep an eye on the captured guards.

Timothy and Brandon escorted William through the entrance and down the first hallway. The other Casters were standing still in a large room. From this room stemmed six hallways.

William asked Timothy to describe the room to him.

William grinned, "It's a labyrinth."

Brandon shook his head, "Just like the movies! Why does it have to be just like the movies?"

Eric nodded, "Which means that we need to watch out for booby-traps."

Brandon's frown cracked into a smirk and he started snickering. He bumped Timothy with his elbow and said, "He said—"

Timothy quickly jabbed Brandon in the side with his elbow and shook his head, even though he was struggling to hold back his own snickering.

William said, "As much as I hate to do this, if we make the area Live, I can guide us through."

Eric cautioned, "I'm not sure we should do that. They'll know we're here, instantly."

The Asian Caster, Jon, crossed his massive arms and said, "That's why we're here."

Rachel turned and said, "I didn't come all this way with my baby," she patted the gun, "to avoid combat. Light it up!"

Brandon leaned over to Timothy and whispered, "I like them."

Timothy nodded in agreement.

William smiled and said, "Alright, Timothy. You heard the lady."

Timothy, still barefoot, slid his hand across the now-familiar series of symbols and felt a chill through his shoulders as a cool breeze flowed in through the entrance.

William stood up straight and looked around. He pointed to the second doorway to their left. Two Casters stayed behind to guard the other doorways. The remaining nine Casters walked through the doorway and began their journey through The Twister's labyrinth.

William led through the maze with ease, as he could see the twists, turns, and dead ends before they came to them. Through his eyes, the walls appeared to be made of wire and practically see-through, and the floors were all illuminated. To be safe, Roger used a permanent marker to leave marks on the walls, like leaving a bread-trail.

As they walked along, everyone watched for traps, but found nothing.

They exited the enormous maze and entered another large room. They realized that there was a slope to the ground, so as they walked the maze, they actually walked downward. They were now below sea-level, not just at wading-level like before.

Six large, wooden doors were before them, all exactly alike.

Timothy asked William, "Now what?"

Brandon interrupted, "What's the Elfish word for *What The Heck?!*"

Timothy replied in a guttural impersonation, "Hunka-Hunka-Burnin' *Mercy?*"

Brandon laughed and said, "*Elfish*, not Elvis!"

William shrugged, "I guess we pick a door?"

The Caster wearing the flak vest and tactical helmet, Lucas, walked up to the second door from the left, pointed at it, and looked to Eric and William with an expression that asked, *'This one?'*

Eric shrugged and nodded.

Lucas placed his hand on the doorknob, paused, and looked at the handle. Quickly, he released the handle and shouted in pain. There was a large burn mark on his palm.

He shook his hand around and said, "I guess that wasn't it."

Rachel walked over and twisted the handle of the door on the far right. It was fortunate that she was slightly off-center with the door because as she twisted the handle, a large spike shot through the door and the point rested less than an inch from her left ear. She exhaled, tried to pull the door open, then stepped back, shaking her head.

Eric muttered, "Only three death-traps to go…"

William shook his head and said, "Everyone down."

As everyone ducked, William slammed his walking stick into the ground. With a concussive blast, all six doors were splintered and thrown back into their hallways. Only one doorway, the third door in from the right, had a hallway that continued past six feet.

William pointed to that doorway and said, "That one."

Lucas, the Caster with the burned hand, asked, "Why didn't you do that *before?*"

William shrugged and said, "I didn't think of it until just now."

The Casters walked down this hallway until they came to a third room. In this room were five medieval-looking levers located around the circular room at near-even distances. Lucas walked over to a lever and pulled.

Eric said, "We probably should have done some research, first!"

Everyone heard a sliding or grinding noise. Lucas turned to face the wall and saw a medium-sized square hole there. The sound seemed to be coming from that hole.

Before he could move, a large wooden beam flew out from the hole and square into the Lucas' chest. He flew backwards from the impact and slid across the cobble-stoned floor on his back. Everyone ran over to check on him. His helmet fell off and his metal bat rolled a few feet away, but he stood up slowly.

Brandon asked, "Are you okay?"

Lucas nodded and said, "This vest can stop things…but it still hurts. I think I have a broken rib…or four…"

Eric said, "Okay, fan out and look for indications of traps before we pull any more levers."

Everyone searched the other levers and areas near them.

Suddenly, Timothy turned around and asked Brandon, "Where's the sixth lever?"

Brandon's mouth hung open slightly as he stared at Timothy. Then he said, "There are only five."

"Yeah. Why?"

"What do you mean, *Why*? The Twister probably wanted to have five levers, so he put in five levers."

"Six hallways and six doors so far. How many paintings do you see?"

"What? Oh! I didn't see those before."

Around the room hung various paintings.

Brandon nodded and said, "Six."

"So, why five levers?"

The Guild Master smiled and pointed at the beam lying on the floor. She whispered, "Six."

Eric and Roger ran over and lifted the beam. They placed a section of it back inside the hole and pulled up. Like a giant light switch, the beam raised, and shifted something behind the stone walls.

Everyone turned as a section of the center of the floor slid away. They heard chains rattling and pulling somewhere beneath their feet. With a loud slam, the moving floor piece halted.

Brandon shook his head, "I knew it! We're in a movie!"

William held his pointer finger to his lips, signaling Brandon to be quiet. He pointed to his ear. Everyone listened intently. From down the hole and a few hundred feet away, muffled voices could be heard.

Rachel, Eric, and Roger raised their weapons and were the first to enter the exposed passageway. Lucas, the Guild Master, William, Timothy, Brandon, and Tanya followed.

They silently walked down the pitch black hallway, listening. The hallway did not get any brighter, but the voices got louder.

William whispered, "There's a door ahead."

Rachel stuck her hand out as they walked, until she found the door. Everyone moved in close to the door and listened. A female voice could be heard.

"Well, search it again! Search harder! They have to be here!"

A male voice responded, "I promise you, we've searched everything! It's completely empty. Someone could have gotten here before us. Perhaps it was just a legend and nothing more?"

The male voice gagged and the female voice yelled, "I did not spend half of my adult life looking for a nonexistent *legend*. We *will* find the relics. We *must* find the relics. Do you understand?"

The male person breathed deeply and said, "Yes, my lady. Keep searching, everyone!"

"Now, assuming that someone did get here before us, where would they take the relics?"

"I don't know, my lady. If it was a Twister, they could have taken it anywhere, but surely we all would have known about it. If it was a Caster, they probably have them stored in some super-secret place or perhaps could have even destroyed them."

"I already have someone searching other known Caster locations for them. If they *have* destroyed them, then I will hunt down every known Caster as punishment for their crime against us."

Lucas whispered as he shook his head, "Crime against *them*? Who *started* this fight?"

"When Michael gets here with that book, we'll do an extra-thorough search. I didn't think it was going to be this difficult to find a couple of *antiques*! You! Go check with the guards outside and see if Michael has arrived."

William huddled everyone close together and quickly whispered a new plan.

The Twister opened the door and nearly jumped backwards when he saw William walking with his hand on the Guild Master's shoulder and The Text under his other arm. The Guild Master carried the walking stick.

"Oh! My lady, it appears that Michael just arrived!"

Lucille spun around with a look of excitement and great expectation on her face. Her expression swiftly changed to one of confusion.

She pointed to each thing as she slowly said, "I know the *old hag*. I know that *book*. You? I don't know *you*. You're not Michael!"

Nobody moved.

She crossed her arms and said, "Kill them both."

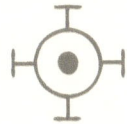

FACING THE LADY

William smirked and leaned over the Guild Master's shoulder, and then whispered, "Show them what you can do."

In the blink of an eye, William threw The Text backwards to Timothy, caught the walking stick that the Guild Master tossed to him, and sent four pillars to the ceiling for cover.

The Guild Master didn't move, but instead seemed to grow. She stood up to her full height, straightened her back, stretched out her arms, and stared into Lucille's eyes.

Watching from behind the half-closed door, Brandon's mouth fell open and he nudged Timothy, yelling, "Dude! She's like seven feet tall!"

Timothy was in awe.

How did she do that?

She wasn't really seven feet tall, but compared to her four-foot tall, hunched figure, she now seemed giant. She was almost William's height.

All of the Casters stared, except William.

Eric shook his head and started to smile. He said, "I've got a funny feeling."

Timothy looked at him, "A *bad* funny feeling?"

"A good funny feeling."

The Twisters began firing at the Guild Master. Everyone in the tunnel ducked to avoid stray bullets, but none came.

They looked at the Guild Master and she wasn't moving. Except for her hands. She stood quite still, but her hands were twitching. Pieces of stone flew off the wall behind her and bullets fell harmlessly to the floor.

This went on for about forty seconds, Twisters unloading two to three clips, each. The Twisters stopped and stared. Lucille even backed up a few steps, clearly intimidated.

On the wall, behind the Guild Master, spelled out in bullet marks, were the words **YOU MISSED**.

The Guild Master lowered her hands and declared, "My name is Vera Pados, and I fight in the name of The Author!"

Swiftly, she faced her palms toward the Twisters and pushed her hands up and out in front of her. As she did so, a strong wind funneled through the doorway, opening the door all the way as it passed, and slammed into the Twisters. All of the Twisters, including Lucille, were thrown backwards and slammed into walls behind them.

All but one of the Twisters stood back up.

Lucille angrily yelled, "Fire again!"

Vera raised her hands and Tanya, Rachel, Eric, and Roger entered the room, guns raised. As they raced to cover, the Twisters opened fire.

Into the ceiling.

As bullets flew toward the Casters, an invisible current lifted them and threw them straight up into the ceiling.

The Casters returned fire.

Lucille touched the wall behind her and several wall segments burst from the floor. The Twisters found cover, but not before three of their large number were hit. Lucille ducked into a nearby room. There were three adjoining rooms, but they were vacant before the first rounds were fired.

Timothy, Brandon, and Lucas stayed low in the hallway as they did not have firearms. Timothy wondered what he could do, but it looked like everything was already being done.

William tapped the ground with his walking stick and several more wall segments rose up. The Casters moved around between segments to find better angles. No matter how they fired, the Twisters' rounds always found the ceiling, so they stayed down and waited until something changed.

Lucille stepped out from behind the wall and was about to place her hand on the ground, but Tanya fired a round at her.

With a smooth motion, Lucille spun around and just barely touched the bullet with her hand. The bullet melted and splattered a small pool of lead against the wall.

Brandon stared, "Okay. That *was* kinda cool."

Lucille slammed her hand on the ground, sending a wave of stone directly at Vera. Vera merely touched the wave and it broke into millions of fragments. Yet, this made her drop her arms.

"Fire!"

Twisters got up and unloaded at the Casters. Vera was right in the center of the room now and was completely exposed. Three rounds were inches from her torso.

William spun around and swung the wolf head into the path of the bullets. With three popping sounds, the rounds were fired back in the other direction. As William pushed Vera behind cover, one of the bullets found a Twister's right shoulder, his favored side. The Twister dropped his rifle and drew a pistol with his left hand.

Bullets flew across the room in both directions, but few found their mark.

Suddenly, the Twisters stopped firing.

The Casters stopped and watched.

Click. Click, click, click. Click.

Lucille screamed, "You're Twisters, for crying out loud! Go get them!"

Dozens of Twisters vaulted over their barricades and ran toward the Casters. Rachel switched to burst and began firing into the line of advancing Twisters. Eric fired until he ran out of bullets, and then drew a knife from his pocket. Roger dropped his gun, made fists, and took a defensive position. Tanya drew a second pistol and kept firing. William and Vera remained behind cover until this moment. They both stepped out and prepared for hand-to-hand combat.

Lucas stood up and grinned, "That's my cue!" He rushed out the door and got a grip on the metal bat. With a loud yell, he jumped over the crouching Casters, over the barricades, and into the first of the advancing Twisters, bat swinging.

Brandon grinned, "That dude is *insane!*"

Timothy exclaimed, "No kidding!"

The boys turned and faced each other, then said in unison, "I like him!"

As the Twisters advanced, many fell, but many filled their spots.

Lucille had many followers with her for this endeavor.

William ran out to meet the Twisters, but stopped short and planted the staff into the stone wall beside him. A large stone fist shot out from the wall and slammed into the chest of the closest Twister, throwing him backwards. He didn't get back up. The fist rose up and slammed down on top of the next Twister. He didn't get back up, either.

As the fist returned to the wall, William stepped forward and swung the staff hard. The back of the wolf head collided with the chin of the next Twister. The Twister fell to the ground and grabbed at his jaw. William thrust the other end of the walking stick into the stomach of another, and planted his own fist into the face of yet another.

Lucas wasn't visible in the crowd of Twisters, but every now and then, the others would hear a metal twang and loud thud, so they knew he was okay. Tanya and Rachel were still picking people off, but paused when Lucas was thrown into a pillar between them, slamming into it with his chest.

Peeling himself off the pillar, he grinned at the women and said, "That's why I wear the vest! Heeeee-yah!" He swung around and found a Twister's helmet with the end of the bat. Laughing, he charged the lines again.

Roger was grappling with three Twisters, shifting, stepping, and binding. Breaking the arm of one Twister, he kicked into the ribs of the second, then forced his right elbow into the nose of the third.

Eric was also grappling, and seemed to be having some difficulty now, but the growing pile of injured, groaning Twisters behind him indicated to the boys that he was quite proficient with a knife.

Brandon commented, "I always knew our principal was a good fighter."

Timothy looked over at Brandon, "Really?"

"Nope. Actually, I always assumed he was a tea-sipping, antique-collecting, classical-music-loving academic who basically stayed to himself and hates social engagements."

"Umm…He is."

Brandon looked shocked, "Really?"

"Yes."

"Oh…"

The boys turned back to look at Eric, who now had one Twister in a headlock while he sent a stone fist into the stomach of another.

"Sweet…" Brandon and Timothy whispered at the same time.

Vera fought like a martial arts expert, even throwing Twisters into pillars and walls. Occasionally, she would cause a wall to move or grow, slamming Twisters or tripping them. At one point, a Twister leapt into the air toward her and she caused a pillar to rise and collide with his chest, then pin him to the ceiling.

After ten minutes of fighting, only a handful of Twisters were still fighting. Only a small number of the fallen would never be able to fight again even though the Casters did everything they could to avoid total loss of life, preferring to only injure and disarm.

The Casters were taking quite a beating, too, though. Roger kept favoring his right leg and held his left hand like it was broken. Eric's left eye had swollen shut and his left ear was bleeding. Tanya had a few knife cuts on her arms. Rachel's nose and mouth were bleeding. Vera was breathing heavily and holding her side. William's bald head had a few bloody spots and he was now limping, using the walking stick more for walking than for Casting.

Lucille saw the dwindling numbers, so decided that it was time for her to step in. She took three steps forward and slammed both of her hands on the ground. Spikes shot up from the ground all around. One barely got to Tanya, cutting the outside of her right leg.

Vera looked over and asked, "William, what is directly above us?"

William stepped backwards, away from a spike, and said, "The forest area."

Vera nodded and leaned against the wall behind her.

Lucille laughed, "Getting tired, old lady?"

Vera grimaced and said, "You should really respect your elders!"

The ceiling above Lucille shook and a large chunk of the ceiling fell. Lucille stepped aside and laughed again, "Is that it?"

A tiny hole had been created at that spot in the ceiling, but Lucille didn't notice it. Suddenly, vines stretched through the hole and began wrapping themselves around Lucille's arms and legs.

Lucille shrieked and struggled as the vines lifted her into the air. The vines started shaking—vibrating, really. Small plumes of smoke could be seen coming from the vines. Instantaneously, the whole vine burst into flames, releasing her and Lucille fell three feet to the ground. Standing up, she placed her hand on the wall behind her.

Lucas shouted, "My turn!" Leaping forward, he threw the bat like a boomerang, straight at Lucille's head.

She ducked and looked behind her as the bat clanged off the back wall in the next room.

As she turned her head back around, she said, "Ha! You mi—Oh!"

Lucas, silent as a ninja somehow, was standing three inches away from Lucille.

He smiled politely and said, "Hi!" Then his rock-solid fist struck Lucille across the cheek.

She fell to the ground and grabbed her face. Through her numbing lips, she muttered, "You hit a lady!"

Lucas put his hands on his hips and laughed, "You're nothing like a *lady*!"

Lucille slammed her hand on the ground next to her and a large chunk of rock flew from the wall and collided with Lucas' chest. Holding the rock like a medicine ball while on his back, he stuck his pointer finger in the air and yelled, "See, that's exactly what I'm talking about!"

Realizing that the last of the Twister underlings had been subdued, Lucille stood in the door and placed a hand on either side. She yelled, "I'm done with you!"

Timothy clutched The Text to his chest and steadied himself as the entire cavern started shaking.

"*Timothy. Let me show you something. I need you to be brave. I need you to lead them. I need you to show them.*"

Timothy shook his head and looked around.

Brandon shook Timothy's shoulder and asked, "What's wrong? You've got that look on your face again."

"*You wanted to help people? You will. Trust me and follow my next instructions.*"

So it's important for you to always listen to that little voice and do what is good.

Timothy looked back at Brandon with a look of terror on his face and said, "Yes, mom."

"Mom? What?! Have you snapped? I mean, I know there's a lot of pressure, but come on! Come back to the *liiiight*. Timothy? Timothy!"

Brandon tried to stop Timothy, but wasn't fast enough. Timothy ran into the cavern and yelled, "Stop! Look!"

Everyone looked at where he was pointing. A small pool of water was in the middle of the floor. A split in the side of the cavern was allowing water to leak in.

"If you keep going, we'll all drown! You're letting water in! All it takes is one more split and that pool becomes a lake, and there's no way any of us will get out on time. Then you'll *never* complete your mission!"

Lucille didn't care now.

Timothy stared at her, then at The Text. He stood there for a moment, then his eyes softened and he whispered, "I challenge you."

Lucille shouted, "What?"

Timothy walked past the pool of water and dropped The Text on the ground.

"I challenge you to a duel! Hand to hand! You and me! No Casting!"

Lucille dropped her hands and laughed, "You? The smallest of your group? You're gonna challenge m—Okay. Sure. This won't take long. Then I'll finish the rest of you. Bring it, Shrimp!"

When she lowered her hands, the trembling stopped. Timothy stepped forward and raised his hands up like he was preparing to box.

I bet I look ridiculous. I have no idea what I'm doing! I bet it shows. I can see it in her eyes. She knows I can't do this.

Lucille raised her hands in the same way, but she looked like she had thrown a punch or two before.

Eric shouted, "No, Timothy! Walk away! We can handle this."

Timothy looked back at Eric with sorrowful eyes and said, "That's not what The Author said."

No one moved, not even Lucille.

Brandon asked, "You heard The Author?"

Timothy smiled and said, "No. He made me listen."

Brandon's face fell and he looked at Tanya beside him, then asked, "What's that mean?"

Tanya shrugged.

Timothy turned back toward Lucille and said, "Do what you must."

Lucille sneered and threw the first punch. Timothy tried to block, but his hand bounced off of Lucille's hand and served no purpose. With a shout of pain, Timothy fell down to his right and blinked continuously.

"Get up, Timothy!" Brandon yelled. "Why aren't we helping him?"

William answered, "First, when you challenge someone to a duel like this, no one else is supposed to step in. Second, if The Author told that boy to do something, he'd better do it."

Brandon shook his head and said, "I thought The Author was dead!"

William nodded, "So did the rest of us."

"Well, what if he's lying and he *thought* he heard The Author, but really didn't?"

Eric placed a hand on Brandon's shoulder and said, "Timothy… doesn't lie."

"What if he's mistaken?"

Vera looked at Brandon while wearing a pained expression. She shook her head.

Brandon, horrified, shouted again, "Get up, Timothy!"

Timothy rubbed his cheek and forced himself to stand up again.

Wee! The spin is rooming! I mean, the rim is spoon—Wait, no. Oh, whatever. It's pretty, though!

Timothy looked over at Lucille, winced, and held up his hands again.

Lucille's fist found Timothy's stomach. Doubled over, Timothy stepped backwards twice. Lucille stepped forward and kicked her knee into his forehead.

Timothy shook it off and raised his fists again.

Lucille mocked him, saying, "You like to take a beating! You get a lot of practice in that at school? Come on! Try to hit me!"

What do you think I've been doing?

Timothy took a swing, but missed. Lucille caught his arm with her left hand and swung in with her right. Timothy spun around while holding his right eye and fell over.

He tried to stand up one more time, but Lucille walked over, shouted, "Stay down," and kicked him in the side of the head.

There's that sweet music again. Ooh, it's bright in here! Now it's dark. Now it's bright. Now it's dark again! Quit flipping the switch, I'm trying to sleep! What am I touching?! Oh, it's a book.

"Timothy Walker."

"Present!"

"Timothy Walker."

"I said I'm present! I'm right here! Who's there? What do you need? I'm busy!"

"Look at me!"

"Right now, all I can see is a bear. *Bear?!* Oh, never mind! That's facial hair. Well, hello! I see you."

Timothy squinted as he looked up toward the ceiling. Standing over him was a shaggy-haired man with golden-tinted eyes. It was the man from the dream.

"Oh! It's you again! I found you! *I found you!* Whatever that means.

You're it!"

"We're not playing Hide-And-Seek, Timothy, although that's not too far off. You did find me, and I'm proud of you for that. I needed you to find me so that I could use you."

"*Use* me? For what?" Timothy was still really groggy, but his thinking was getting clearer.

"Take my hand, stand up, and I'll show you."

Timothy reached up and tried to grab the man's hand, but kept missing.

"I'm sorry! My numb is a little mind. I mean…whatever."

"I understand. Let me help you."

The man grabbed Timothy's hand and started to pull him up. Timothy realized his hand was glowing.

"Pretty…"

"Timothy, snap out of it."

Timothy shook his head and became aware of what was happening.

"Whoa! It's you! What are you doing here?"

"I'm not really here, but I am. It's confusing, but you'll understand some day. In the meantime, I need you to trust me."

"Yeah, this isn't the best time to confuse me."

Brandon shouted, "He's standing up again! It's not over! Go Timothy!"

The man placed his left hand in the center of Timothy's back and grabbed Timothy's right wrist with his right hand. He led Timothy forward.

"We're going to her again? I don't like that. I'd really prefer to not get hit again!"

"You won't. Just say what I say."

Timothy walked toward Lucille and raised his hand, which was no longer glowing.

Lucille laughed, then glared, and asked, "What are you doing?"

Timothy walked closer. He was two steps away from her. Lucille put up her fists and prepared to throw another punch.

Timothy placed his hand on her forehead.

She paused, stared at Timothy, and asked, "Is this some kind of game?"

Timothy's eyes twinkled slightly and his expression went from confusion and near-death to sorrow, pity, and compassion.

Timothy whispered, "I'm sorry for your pain. I'm sorry for your loss. I'm sorry things went badly for you. …I'm sorry."

Lucille sneered, but Timothy could see a sparkle of a tear forming.

Lucille shouted, "Stop doin—"She tried to move, but found it impossible to do so.

Timothy nodded, then interrupted her and loudly declared, "I cast light into the darkness! I cast day into the night! I cast joy into the pain! I cast love into the hatred! I cast *life* into the *void!*"

Lucille's expression transformed into a look of absolute terror. She lowered her arms, clenched her fists, and tried to catch her breath. She grabbed at her stomach and throat, becoming increasingly pained as time went on. As she hyperventilated, she slowly sank to the floor. She closed her eyes and stopped moving.

Timothy leaned on his knees as he bent over and gasped for air. He spun his head around to look at the other Casters as they hurriedly approached him. The man from the dream—The Author—was gone.

As Timothy recovered, footsteps were heard walking down the hallway behind them. The Casters who were standing guard entered with hands behind their heads. A new flood of Twisters entered the room behind them, guns raised.

"Well, well! What have we here?"

Jude stepped through the doorway, gun in hand, and sneered.

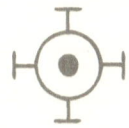

THE ESCAPE

All of the Casters turned to look at Jude. Tanya almost raised a gun, but realized it wouldn't be worth the risk. All of the Casters were too close together, and Jude was too far away.

Jude pointed at The Text and said, "Give me the book and I'm gone."

Brandon crossed his arms and asked, "This again? What is your problem, dude? Why do you want the book so badly?"

"I don't have a problem! You have the problem. Wait, why am I fighting with a five-year-old?"

"I'm thirteen!"

"Whatever. I need the book to find the relics."

"You're after the relics, too?"

"Of course! With Lucille now out of commission, the Twisters need a leader. I was promised that position if the others fell. The others fell.

Ergo, I'm the new leader."

Eric spat, "You're the worst person to lead *anything!*"

Jude smirked and shrugged, saying, "Hey! I didn't say I was perfect. I said that I'm now in charge. Those relics will help me secure my place and achieve greater power than I have ever known. Now, I really don't have time for games or drawn-out battles, so I'm going to say this once."

He raised a gun to the head of the Caster wearing the spike collar and gloves. He said, "Give me the book or one more Caster falls."

The Caster pursed his lips and shook his head while staring at the other Casters. He said, "I'm willing to die. Hang on to The Text for as long as you can."

Jude grinned a wicked grin and said, "Aww. Someone's playing martyr. I *hate* martyrs! For that reason, I won't kill you. Yet."

BANG

The Caster grabbed his left thigh and fell to the floor.

Jude looked at the Casters and said, "Fine. We'll have to do this the hard way." Jude stepped close to the wall and was about to place his hand against it.

All of the Casters started yelling, and pointed at the small pool of water in the center of the room.

He didn't listen to them.

He placed his hand on the wall, and large pillars grew up from the ground around the Casters, trapping them in a cage of stone columns.

Jude walked over toward the cage and said, "If you try to Cast anything, my followers will shoot you. Hand me the book."

Lucas called out, "Hey, genius! Look down!"

Jude glanced down and saw that his feet were slowly being

submerged in water. He looked up with a shocked look on his face.

"I- I didn't realize! Give me the book! Give me the book! I've got to get out of here!"

Brandon shouted, "Umm...So do we!"

Jude reached into the stone cage toward Timothy, who was now standing up and holding The Text tightly.

Tanya grabbed Jude's hand and pulled it back against a column.

Shouting in pain, Jude wrestled his arm free and backed up.

He glared at the Casters and raised his gun.

His hand was empty.

He looked around and searched his larger pockets in his jacket.

Tanya smirked and briefly waved the gun in the air, then handed it over to Lucas.

Jude snarled and turned around. The water was now half-way up his calves. The Casters were on slightly higher elevation in the room, so the water was still only up to their ankles, but it seemed to be flowing in more rapidly.

Jude rushed through the water toward the door. He hurried past the Caster with the leg wound, but as he did, the Caster slammed the back of his hand into the back of Jude's knee, tripping him and causing small puncture wounds with the spiked gloves. Jude waved him off, stood up, and limped away. His followers soon turned to leave with him, but as they did, the muscular Caster from earlier spun around and grabbed two Twisters by their throats. He held them up in the air against the wall until they dropped their guns. Another Caster turned and slammed his elbow into a Twister's chest and pushed him to the ground. The other Twisters didn't turn and help; they just ran.

Vera calmly said, "We should go."

Timothy just now realized that she had returned to her limping, hunched-over frame. As the water reached their knees, Vera placed her hands on one of the pillars. Instantly, the structure shattered as if it were glass. The Casters quickly stepped out of the circle of columns and headed toward the door.

As they walked, Timothy saw many Twisters who were struggling to keep their heads above water. He also saw that some may have been drowning or already had.

"What about them?"

Everyone looked around at the Twisters. A few were now standing up and looking at them with despair in their eyes. Roger walked over to one and stared at him for a few seconds. The Twister looked away and cradled his broken arm.

Roger placed a hand on the Twister's unaffected arm and said, "As brothers and sisters were we all created. As enemies, we fought. As brothers and sisters shall we die. Come."

Eric picked up Lucille's limp form and waded over toward the door. Jon picked up two Casters around their waists and marched toward the door. Rachel and Tanya chair-carried a Twister who had blood all over his face and two broken legs. Lucas tucked the pistol into his belt and hoisted a Twister over his shoulder. Timothy and Brandon supported the Caster with the leg-wound. A female Twister with a few broken ribs walked over and helped support William as they walked.

Vera smiled and said, "I'll take care of the rest. Go. Go! Through the door. The water is rising and will rise even faster when I do this. I'll give you all a head start, but if you see me running, you had better be running faster."

It was uncomfortable for everyone, being so close to the people they had just fought, but they all knew it was the right thing to do.

Hobbling as quickly as they could, they finally reached the labyrinth. Vera was still not behind them, but they pressed forward.

Roger mentioned, "We don't have time to work our way through, do we? I mean, I marked the trail, but it's still going to take too long with all the twists and turns.

William and the Twister stepped forward. William tapped the walking stick on the ground. The walls of the labyrinth shook and a central divide appeared. Rock walls slid aside, creating a passage way that was simply a straight run across. It was still a good distance, but this certainly would save time.

The Twister with William smiled and said, "I have *got* to get me one of those!"

Lucas shook his head, "Again. Why didn't you do that earlier?"

"I didn't think about it, earlier!"

They continued their fast-paced hobbling toward the exit as water started flowing into the room behind them.

Timothy looked back and asked, "Do you think she's okay? She should be here by now."

They all started hearing loud thuds and splashes coming from the hallway behind them.

Brandon smiled and said, "You always seem to have perfect timin— Whoa! What is that?"

Thundering around the bend in the hallway was a stone golem of some sort, carrying a very wet Guild Master.

She called out, "Why aren't you running? Get a move on!"

Suddenly, everyone could see a whole line of stone soldiers rushing down the flooded hallway. Each stone soldier was carrying at least two Twisters. Standing at about eight feet tall, their frames filled the hallway. As they neared the exit, Timothy recalled the large wooden doors from the Guild. These were not quite as large, but there was definitely more mass to these.

Everyone turned back around and moved as quickly as they could toward the exit. The water level was now reaching their ankles, but the run was a slight uphill climb, so as long as they could stay ahead of it, they would be fine.

However, most of them were limping or carrying someone, so moving quickly was not possible. As they walked, the water rose to their calves, then to their knees.

Timothy looked over to his left and saw a stone soldier moving ahead of him, carrying four Twisters. Then, the one carrying the Guild Master passed him.

They were only halfway and the water was up to his navel. Lucas walked up beside the boys and said, "I've got him. You two run ahead."

Brandon asked, "Why?"

"'Cause you're short. That's why! Get up there where you won't drown!" Lucas carried a Twister over his shoulders and supported the Caster as he walked.

Timothy looked behind him and saw a row of stone soldiers wading through the rising water. One looked at him as it passed. It had eyes like onyx, teeth like pearls, and eyebrows like really beat-up car bumpers. Timothy glanced at its massive arms. A glint of gold caught his eye. He looked more closely at the creature's shoulder.

Is that part of an urn?

Timothy called out, "Hey! Is that a…"

So the relics were here! They were literally in the lair! No one could find them because they were actually built into the lair! Now to be guarded by stone soldiers for all time! This is so epic!

Another stone soldier walked beside Timothy and when their eyes met, Timothy saw another golden glint, but it wasn't a relic. It was in the stone soldier's eyes! The creature looked back at Timothy as it walked on, and winked!

As they waded through chest-deep water, they finally reached the exit. Everyone filtered out as quickly as they could. Those who were the first ones out helped lift people out of the pit and onto dry land. As water began filling the pit, the final people exited the underground lair.

As Timothy prepared to step out, he looked back. The soldiers, now empty-handed, were slowly marching back down into the water.

Eric was the last one out, carrying Lucille. As he entered the pit, the water reached the top of the chamber. Eric floated as he handed Lucille up to two other Casters.

"Wow! That was fantastic!"

Everyone looked up. A woman was standing by the water's edge, watching.

"That'll be great in the movie! Good job, everyone!"

With that, she walked away, smiling. No one said anything for a few seconds. Finally, Rachel pointed.

Jude could be seen through the trees, limping away. A few of his followers were right behind him.

Timothy asked, "What do we do?"

William shook his head and said, "Nothing. He represents chaos and nature has a way of balancing or eliminating chaos. We'll let nature take care of itself." He limped over and tapped a tree with the end of his walking stick.

A breeze blew through the trees and they started swaying and twisting.

Suddenly, in the distance, several loud screams could be heard.

After ten minutes of silence, Timothy spoke as he shivered.

"I want to go home."

HOPE

"Ralph!"

Ralph spun around on the park bench and saw three people walking toward him. He scrambled and hid behind a large tree nearby. Roger, Steve, and Lucas walked up to the park bench and stopped.

Roger chuckled and said, "It's okay, Ralph. We've come with good news."

The men discussed what had transpired in the past few weeks. As they shared the account, Ralph's expressions changed to follow the story. He smiled at the success stories, he frowned at the sad news, and he cheered when he heard the summary.

With new confidence from this news, Ralph's speech was clearer and more complete. "I c- c- can't tell y- you how h- happy! With her b-b-beaten, my c- contract is obsol- obsolete. I am f- free! Th- Thank you!"

Timothy looked up from his magazine. He was in a hospital bed, being treated for his bruises, broken ribs, nearly-broken jaw, and concussion. He looked up when he heard a knock on the doorway.

His face lit up as his parents rushed into the room and embraced him. Their eyes were bloodshot, their cheeks were red, and tears kept streaming down their faces. Laughing and crying at the same time, his parents simply couldn't find words. As he hugged his mom and dad, he looked up and saw Eric in the doorway. He had ice packs wrapped against his eye and face, and was leaning against the doorway. He grinned as well as his swollen face would allow, gave Timothy a thumbs up, and turned to leave.

Eric had filled Timothy's parents in on everything while Timothy was being treated. It took plenty of time for them to comprehend what they were hearing, but they were just glad that he was okay. They promised to sort out the details of what happened with Timothy later.

As Timothy was sharing stories with his parents, a couple ran into the room and said, "Honey! We love you!"

Timothy stared at them, thinking, *I don't know you...*

He sighed with relief when he realized they were talking to the other patient in the room.

He heard Brandon reply, "I love you, too."

"Excuse me?" A nurse stepped into the doorway with a young, black-haired girl.

Everyone looked up.

"This young lady wanted to say something to the boys."

Mindy!

It was the girl from the Guild who had gone into a coma. The girl crossed her arms in front of her at the wrists and twisted back and forth slightly as she spoke.

"I heard about what you two did. Actually, I also dreamed about it. It was kind of strange, but very cool. You were both very heroic. I wanted to say thanks on behalf of…well…everyone."

Brandon grinned and said, "You hear that, Timothy? I'm a hero, too!"

Timothy tried to laugh, but it hurt too much. He laughed on the inside.

Eric patted Ms. Lee on the shoulder and left her classroom, silently. Ms. Lee exhaled slowly and fought back tears. She placed her hand on the picture frame that held the photo of Michael. She stared at it for several moments, then slammed it face-down on the desk. Burying her face in her hands, she sobbed uncontrollably.

A man tapped on the door and slowly asked, "You okay, babe?"

Ms. Lee breathed slowly and regained her composure, then said, "Don't call me 'babe,' and yes, I'm okay now that you're here. Are you ready to go?"

The man's face showed intense compassion and said, "I will be ready whenever you are ready. I want to be here for you, b—I mean, Jen."

Ms. Lee nodded and said, "Thank you. I'm ready. Let's go."

Ms. Lee's boyfriend walked her outside, holding her hand. As they exited the building, she stopped, turned to him, and cried into his chest. Taken off guard, he slowly wrapped his arms around her and leaned his head on hers.

William leaned on the wolf-head walking stick and stared at the headstone. A memorial marker had been set up to honor Jeff, his fallen friend. William simply stood there and stared, reading the monument over and over. His favorite line was the last one, which read, *To lose such a man is a shame…a real shame.*

Tanya walked over and stood next to William, then looked at the memorial. She crossed her hands at her waist and looked over at William. She whispered, "I'm so sorry. I so wish Jeff's story had a happy ending."

William softly whispered, "Not every ending is a happy one. Nor should it be so. But it does not mean it wasn't worth the journey."

William continued to stare at the memorial, then smiled, nodded, and walked away.

Lucas sat in a chair beside Lucille's hospital bed. She was in a coma, but was otherwise stable. Lucas rested his helmet on his knee and stared at the young woman covered in tubes and wires.

He took Lucille's hand and spoke softly, "I'm sorry I had to hit you like that. I hope you know I really didn't have another choice, though. What did you do to yourself? How did you get this way? Why did you leave? Mom and Dad are gone and no one's left but you and me. I miss the real you. I miss my sister."

He couldn't be sure, but Lucas thought he felt Lucille gently squeeze his hand.

Ralph adjusted a new maroon-colored tie and tugged on the sleeves of his flannel shirt. He looked down past his blue jeans and inspected his black dress shoes.

He was standing at the bottom of the steps for house #316. He swallowed hard, shook off the nervousness (or, at least, he tried to do so), and walked up to the door.

He raised his right hand and hovered his knuckles near the door. Sighing, he dropped his arm, turned around and ran his fingers through his hair in frustration. He regained his composure, steadied himself, and turned around. This time, he did it without thinking about it. He just walked up and knocked on the door.

"Whose house is that?" Timothy looked over at Eric.

They were standing on the sidewalk a few houses down. Ralph didn't know they were watching him. Eric had one of those hunches and wanted Timothy to be there so things could make sense, finally.

Eric replied, "It's been many years since he's knocked on that door. When things changed for the Twisters and Ralph became a Runner, he promised to not return to this house until he was free. You were the key he needed to be able to be free from his obligations and be able to come back here."

"So who lives there?"

"He used to, but someone else moved in after he moved out."

Ralph waited impatiently for a few moments, bobbing up and down, breathing quickly, but straightened up when he heard the clicking of a bolt lock and a standard doorknob lock. Slowly, the door opened and the young woman with the daughter stood in the doorway.

"Hello…H- H- Hope."

The lady stared at Ralph for several seconds, and then took a step backwards.

"…Dad?"

Timothy slowly walked back into his bedroom and slumped down on his bed. He was still sore, but already feeling quite a bit better.

"Finally home! It'll actually be nice to get back to school when everything reopens next week!"

As he sat, he listened to the silence and just breathed. Inhale... exhale. Then he felt something bump one of the legs of the bed. Slowly and carefully, Timothy leaned over and examined the scene. He reached under the bed and slowly pulled out a T-Rex figure. Its left leg was twitching and it appeared to be panting heavily. It tried to whinny, but didn't have the energy to do so.

"I'm so sorry, pal!"

Timothy gently placed the T-Rex on his desk and reached for his copy of The Text (the original was given to the Guild Master for safe keeping while a new location for the Guild was determined).

"Let's see..." He scanned the pages, looking for a certain sequence he had seen just the other day. When he found it, he ran his finger across it and gently placed his hand on the T-Rex. Suddenly, the T-Rex stopped moving, exhaled, and returned to its original form. No more running in circles. No more whinnying. It was back to just being a regular T-Rex figure.

Peace I leave with you; My peace I give you.

Timothy smiled as he read the lines one more time and gently closed the book.